Craving Beauty
by Nalini Singh

A Bridal Promise

When brooding entrepreneur Marc Bordeaux offered Hira his hand in marriage, it was as if he had stepped out of some fable. The scars he bore suggested a troubled past, yet the sheltered beauty was not afraid. Something in his ghost-grey eyes promised more than just escape from her stifling existence.

Passion With A Price

Whisked from the privilege of her desert home to the rough Louisiana bayou, innocent Hira started to lose her nerve. Suddenly the marriage bed had awakened her soul, but she feared Marc's shadowy secrets now sentenced her to a life of unrequited love. Could this beauty reach the beast?

His Wedding-Night Wager
by Katherine Garbera

ᗡᕁᕹᕕ

"I came back because of you, Hayden."

Because she'd never really forgotten him. "I can't move on. Not until I work out what went wrong between us."

He looked at her with that electric gaze of his. "Hell, Shelby, that's an easy one."

"Please don't say it again. I wish I had the money to pay your father back."

He narrowed his eyes and walked towards her. "So what do you say to some sort of reparation? You give me what I paid for."

"What your father paid for," she said.

"I paid for it in ways you can never understand."

But she did and it made her ache to realise it. "A night of sex? Is that what you want? I don't think I'm worth a million dollars."

He stood within an inch of her now. "Not a night," he whispered. "How about a week?"

Available in January 2007 from Silhouette Desire

Craving Beauty
NALINI SINGH

His Wedding-Night Wager
KATHERINE GARBERA

*Silhouette, Silhouette Desire and Colophon are registered
trademarks of Harlequin Books S.A., used under licence.*

*First published in Great Britain 2007
Silhouette Books, Eton House, 18-24 Paradise Road,
Richmond, Surrey TW9 1SR*

The publisher acknowledges the copyright holders of the
individual works as follows:

Craving Beauty ©Nalini Singh 2005
His Wedding-Night Wager © Katherine Garbera 2006

*ISBN-13: 978 0 373 40225 0
ISBN-10: 0 373 40225 2*

51-0107

*Printed and bound in Spain
by Litografia Rosés S.A., Barcelona*

CRAVING BEAUTY

by
Nalini Singh

NALINI SINGH

has always wanted to be a writer. Along the way to her dream, she obtained degrees in both the arts and law (because being a starving writer didn't appeal). After a short stint as a lawyer, she sold her first book and from that point, there was no going back. Now an escapee from the corporate world, she is looking forward to a lifetime of writing, interspersed with as much travel as possible. Currently residing in Japan, Nalini loves to hear from readers. You can contact her via the following e-mail address: nalini@nalinisingh.com; or by writing to her c/o Silhouette Books, 233 Broadway, Suite 1001, New York, NY, 10279, USA.

The Clendon readers are the first-round judges for the Clendon Award, founded by Barbara and Peter Clendon. Though their identities are fiercely guarded, I've met many of them through the score sheets they filled out for my entries for the award.

Their comments and encouragement were invaluable to a writer walking the rocky road to publication. I'd like to take this chance to thank those anonymous judges for the work that they do, and the Clendons, for creating the award.
Merci beaucoup.

One

"**W**ith this bond, I take my life and put it in the keeping of Marc Pierre Bordeaux. Forever and eternity." Hira's heart shattered into a thousand pieces as she repeated the ritual words.

Smiling, the elder lifted the trailing edge of the silken red ribbon tied around Hira's wrist and fed it through the lacy aperture atop the wall dividing the men from the women. The marriage ceremony was almost complete— soon she'd be wife to a man with ghost-gray eyes.

What should've been the most wonderful day of her life was instead marking the destruction of her dreams. Dreams of love, dreams of family, dreams of tenderness. Because instead of being wooed and won, Hira Dazirah had been part and parcel of a business agreement.

Her wrist jerked as the ribbon went taut. At the same time, the elder said, "He is bound."

On the other side of the wall, a single voice rose in the haunting cadences of the blessing chant.

Per the customs of her homeland, Zulheil, in a few more seconds Marc would be her husband. Marc with his slow smile and eyes full of temptation. Marc with his warrior's face and hunter's walk. Marc, who'd demanded her father seal their business deal with his daughter's hand.

She'd thought him different. From the first, his obvious strength had attracted her, as had the way he had of looking at her as though she was precious. Then he'd smiled at her in that slow, sexy way. Unable to resist, she'd softened inside and out, responding to the glittering passion in his eyes.

Believing that their shared smile augured the beginning of something priceless, she'd waited for him to court her. For the first time since Romaz had trampled on her heart, she'd felt the bloom of new hope.

Two days later he'd offered for her hand, *without having spoken to her,* and her illusions about her American stranger had shattered. Instead of wanting to know the woman, Marc had been entranced by the shell of her body, the beauty of her face. The staggering pain of her bewilderingly intense disappointment had yet to leave her. It sat like a heavy rock on her heart, crushing and unable to be ignored.

"It is done," her mother, Amira, said. "The blessing chant has been completed. You are married, daughter."

Hira blinked and nodded, none of her anguish showing on her face. They sat in a sumptuous room filled with the women of the Dazirah family, women whose sharp eyes missed nothing. She would never shame her mother by coming apart at the seams.

Amira stroked her cheek. "I know this is not what you wanted for yourself, but it will be all right. Though your new husband is scarred, he doesn't appear cruel."

Not unless cruelty could be defined as inciting hope and then crushing it. "No," she whispered. "He doesn't."

But that told her nothing. Romaz hadn't appeared cruel, yet he'd ripped out her heart and laughed at her while he'd done it. She'd thought herself in love, so much so that she'd left her home and ran to him, ready to marry him without her father's consent.

It had been the only time in her life that she'd considered an action that would've brought the scorn of society on her proud family. That fateful day, her happiness had been as iridescent as a summer rainbow, joyous and pure.

The minute he'd seen her in the doorway of his humble apartment, Romaz's dark-lashed eyes had lit up in surprise. "Hira. What are you doing here?" He'd glanced over her shoulder, as if expecting an entourage.

She'd walked in, brushing past him, sure of her welcome. After all, he'd told her that he loved her. "I have come to stay," she'd said, excited and a little afraid but so glad to be with the man she loved.

He hadn't embraced her as she'd anticipated. "Your family?" he'd asked, a frown on his handsome face.

She'd thought his reserve sprang from displeasure at her forwardness and had been sure that once he heard what she had to say, he'd forgive her for taking the initiative. "They won't miss me till dinner. We have time to marry. They cannot stop us after that."

Some of her nervous joy had started to fade at his continued lack of a response. "Romaz?" She'd glanced at the still-open door, wondering why he didn't shut it so they could have privacy to make their plans.

He'd given her a strained smile. "Your father will disown you. You must think this through."

"I have! He'll never agree to our marriage. *Never.* Already he seeks other matches for me." She'd wanted to touch him, but there had been an unfamiliar hardness in his eyes that had stopped her. "We don't need my father's money. You work hard and I'll get work, too. We'll survive."

The bitter smirk on his face had confused her. "You? You wouldn't know honest work if it hit you in the face."

Shocked, she'd stood there, unable to understand his anger. "Romaz?"

"Do you think I'll be able to keep you in the style to which you're accustomed?" He'd glanced dismissively at the bracelets around her wrists and the baubles in her ears.

His response sprang from male pride, she'd thought, relief shooting through her body like cool spring rain, bringing renewed hope. "None of it belongs to me. It is the family's." Stupidly she'd thought that that would reassure him. "I don't need such things if I have your love." She'd been so earnest in her desire to nurture his self-confidence.

"Well you might not, but *I* do," he'd snapped.

Later she'd realized it was the very naiveté of her statements that had caused his charming veneer to crumble. Her attempt at salvaging his pride had instead proved the futility of his courtship. Financially Hira was worth nothing without her family.

"What's the use of marrying you if I don't get access to the Dazirah coffers?" He'd raked her body up and down. "You might be beautiful, but in the dark, one female body is the same as another."

She'd been so badly wounded by that unexpected blow that she'd frozen, her feet rooted to the floor. "You won't marry me unless I come with my father's money?"

He'd shrugged. "How else do you expect me to move up in life? Unlike your wealthy family, I have only one asset—my looks." He'd pointed to a face so handsome it routinely caused women to stop and stare in the streets. "I intend to use them to my advantage. I don't want to labor all my life like my father."

His sneer had destroyed her final illusions about him, for his father was a respected and skilled man. His family wasn't as rich as hers, but they weren't poor, either. Zulheil looked after its own, but no man could expect to gain wealth without work. Her father, too, spent much time "laboring" in his businesses.

Yet, even after Romaz had said those horrible things, even after she'd seen the truth of his nature, she hadn't wanted to give up the tattered remains of her dreams. Hadn't wanted to admit she'd made such a horrible mistake. She'd been so foolishly innocent of the ways of the world, so untutored in deceit. "But…you said you loved me."

His expression had turned into a leer. "Any man would love a body like yours. Of course, I'll take that part of you if you're offering it without charge. Marriage is too high a price to own just you."

He'd crushed her with that dishonorable proposition. Barely able to function, she'd run from his apartment, wandering the quiet back streets for three hours. Just be-

fore darkness fell, she'd returned home by the same secret route she'd used to leave, and no one had ever
learned of her attempted elopement. They just knew
that suddenly all the fight had gone out of her. In one
afternoon Romaz had achieved the outcome her father
had been aiming for, for twenty-four years.

Now, almost six months after Romaz had cast her
aside because her body alone wasn't enough, it was the
greatest irony that she found herself married to a man
who cared nothing for her money and only for her body.

"Daughter?"

She jerked up at the sound of her mother's voice. "Yes."

Amira smiled. "Come, it is time for you to wait for
your husband."

Time to allow a stranger to touch her, Hira thought,
anger spiking. Fascinated with him from the first, his act
in bargaining for her like an object had turned her budding desire into fury. How dare he reduce her to nothing more than the sweetener for a business deal?

As she followed her mother up the stairs, her eyes narrowed. Marc Bordeaux might've married her, but he
would not *have* her. Not like this. Not without joy and tenderness. Not until she knew the heart of the man he was.

Marc leaned in the open doorway, his body thrum-
ming with anticipatory tension. "Why the face? It's your
wedding night, not an execution." He tried to keep his
tone light, but it was hard when temptation sat right in
front of him.

Hira occupied the middle of a canopied Arabian bed
that screamed decadence. Hung with rich velvet curtains
in a warm gold and made up with sheets of silken white,

it invited sin and seduction. The luxurious hangings whispered softly in the heavy heat of the desert breeze wafting in through the open balcony doors, full of murmurs of welcome.

It was as if Zulheil itself was urging him to indulge his hunger for his wife. To complete the invitation, her slender feet rested on pale-pink rose petals, petals that echoed the delicate pink of her wedding garments.

She should've looked like a dream. *His* dream.

But instead of welcome, there was only cool distance in her eyes. The woman who'd captivated him with a single smile was subsumed under the crystal hardness of icy sophistication.

One aristocratic eyebrow rose. "What did my father promise you in the deal? Tell me and I'll deliver." That cultured voice with its exotic accent swept along his bloodstream, inciting him without intent. Her voice flared at the end, a stab of heat that was quickly smothered by the ice, leaving him uncertain that it had ever appeared.

He clenched the fists he'd shoved into the pockets of his tuxedo pants, a feeling of dread infiltrating the joy with which he'd begun this night. "You agreed to this marriage, *princess*." What could've been an endearment came out as a taunt, her coldness stoking his temper. "I never wanted a wife who wasn't happy to be mine."

He'd starved for this moment since he'd first seen her on the balcony of her family home in Abraz, Zulheil's biggest city. Her face had been upturned to gaze at the stars, a wistful and somehow hungry smile gracing that lovely face.

"Your father refused to let me date you," he told her.

"You must know how old-fashioned he is. It was marriage or nothing, and you were asked your choice." He'd been startled by Kerim Dazirah's decree that no man was going to be allowed near his daughter without the ties of marriage, but had made his choice in an instant.

Driven by feelings he barely understood, he'd agreed to a marriage without courtship, chanced forever on the strength of one shared smiled, one instant of pure happiness. No woman had ever made him react with such impetuousness. No woman but Hira.

"Yes," she said softly, her strange light-brown eyes fixed on a point beyond his shoulder. "I had a choice. As much as any woman does when she has no independent means of income, no way to fight for her freedom, no chance of escape." Her tone was as emotionless as a doll's. "You were better than the alternative." The final line was heavy with disgust.

"Who?" He didn't like the idea of her with some other man, though he hadn't known of her existence until barely a week ago. From that moment, she'd become his. Only his.

Her full lips twisted. "You've met him. Marir."

"He's a relic." Marc recalled his one encounter with the oily merchant who was a crony of Hira's father. He'd disliked the man on sight because his eyes had kept straying to Hira, who'd been acting as hostess for Kerim's banquet. Marc had almost been able to see the old lech fighting the urge to lick his lips.

Simmering with possessive anger he hadn't then had any right to, he'd barely walked away without punching Marir in his florid face. "Why would your father consider him a suitable match?" In spite of his lack of a beautiful face, Marc knew he was of value to the Dazirah family because of his wealth and business status.

"He has royal blood. Many times removed, but present nonetheless." Her mouth curved in a humorless smile. "My father always wanted to claim royal connections."

Another blow against him—he was no more royalty than the lowest bayou rat. "Then why did he accept me?"

"In my father's eyes, you are American royalty. As well as being a man of considerable wealth, you do business with our sheik and are welcome in his home—close enough to royalty to please him."

Marc clenched his hands even tighter, frustrated and angry. And *hurt*. Why did it hurt that this beautiful woman was rejecting him? Why did he feel like something indefinably precious was slipping out of his grasp? "So that was all that was going for me? I wasn't old and fat?" He didn't spell out what they both knew. He might not be old and fat, but he was disfigured.

Scars ran in fine white lines down the left side of his face. His body bore far deeper marks. He'd become used to them long ago, his confidence founded on more substantial things, but this beautiful ice princess would surely have noticed. When she'd agreed to his proposal, he'd thought that the scars didn't matter to her. Now he saw that he'd been deluding himself. There was no welcome in Beauty's eyes for this particular Beast.

She gave a regal nod and the shimmering light from the tiny, perfectly detailed chandelier caught on the diamonds dripping from her ears. "I do not know you. You are a stranger. My father may have refused to allow a courtship, but you didn't even try to talk to me once!"

In fact, Marc had asked to speak to her several times before the wedding but had accepted her father's explanation that such things were not done in Zulheil. Unfamiliar with the marriage rituals of this country, he'd been wary of giving offence and losing his chance to claim Hira. Not that that was any excuse, he thought harshly. He should've tried harder.

"Are your feelings going to change as we get to know each other?" Despite everything, he continued to ache for the gift of warmth she'd tantalized him with just once before. But he had no intention of taking something that wasn't freely given. Not even when desire was digging into him with razor-sharp talons and his body was heavy with passion so hot, it was almost pain.

A sudden shadow dulled the almost-golden brilliance of her eyes. "I once loved a man." Her long lashes lowered. "And I don't think I will ever love again."

Her words formed an arrow aimed at dreams he'd barely acknowledged but now knew were vital to his existence. "Why did you marry me, then? Why make us both miserable?"

She raised her head and he caught a glimpse of red-hot anger in those changeable eyes. "My father said you wouldn't sign the agreement unless I married you. The deal with you is very important to the clan."

He swore under his breath. "The central agreement was signed and sealed *before* I asked for permission to date you. Nothing but the most minor ancillary matters remain." He wondered if she'd believe him, this beautiful, dusky desert rose. It was his word against her father's.

To his shock, he thought he saw a glimmer of tears in her eyes. "I thought he cared for me a little…but my worth to him has always been determined by my looks." The pain in her was so tightly controlled, it wounded him just to hear her. "Now I know he feels nothing for me, if he can so cold-bloodedly manipulate me into marriage with a man he wishes to do business with."

Marc couldn't stand to see this proud woman so humbled. This was not how his haughty beauty was meant to sound, lost and alone. Striding to the bed, he sat down beside her. When he reached out to touch her cheek, she froze. "I have no intention of doing anything against your will, so stop looking like a deer caught in the headlights."

Her head jerked up. "Don't snap at me like that."

This was the woman he'd fallen for—this woman of fire not ice. Desire flared again, deep and heavy. Without conscious intent, his fingers trailed down her face to rest on the delicate skin of her neck. She shivered at his touch, and hope blazed inside him. Driven by dreams he'd never thought to experience, he found himself leaning forward to taste her.

Harsh reality intruded when she turned her head away in sharp refusal, giving him her profile.

He dropped his hand and got off the bed. Walking to the door, he tried to tell himself it didn't matter that she'd rejected him. "Do you even desire me, Hira?" It was a question without subtlety, but he needed the truth, and from the lush look of her and her confession of involvement with another man, he knew she had to be experienced.

He *hated* the idea of those long, sun-kissed limbs intertwined with another man's, though he'd never been a man who judged a woman on her sexual history. He was no hypocrite. Except, it appeared, with this woman. Tonight had been full of unwelcome surprises.

Eyes wide, his new wife looked up from her intense perusal of the white-on-white embroidered bedspread, her fingers crushing a single fragile petal. The sweet scent of roses shimmered into the air. "All you know of me is my face and my body—there is nothing more to tie us together. I don't believe in lying with a man unless there is emotion between us." Her voice almost trembled at the end.

And she'd said she would never love again. The pain in his chest was nearly overwhelming. "You expect me not to touch you all our married life?" He wanted to be very sure of her meaning, very sure of what he'd surrendered to his inexplicable but raging need to possess the woman he'd glimpsed by the light of a delicate sickle moon.

She continued to crush rose petals in her elegant fingers. "My father had another woman always. Can American men not do the same?"

He rocked back on his heels. "Is keeping a mistress common in Zulheil?" He'd thought that this was a land of honor and integrity, a land where a man could find a woman who'd be loyal as well as beautiful, a woman who could find beauty in the night sky *and* in a scarred man's face.

"No." Hira's acknowledgment only gave him a moment's relief. "It's considered dishonorable, and most of our women will not stand for it. If they cannot fight for their right to be honored as a wife, their clan will fight for them, even if that means dissolving the marriage." Her eyes met his, fierce in defense of her country.

Yet when she smiled, it was a parody of beauty. "But it's done in my family. My mother's clan does not help her because she does not ask. My father has her well under his thumb. He only lay with her long enough to gain heirs—my two brothers. You can do the same." Ice coated every word.

It was a blow to the most masculine core of him. "You obviously have no desire to be with child." He ran his eyes down her perfect form, something she'd hate to lose to a belly swollen with his child.

What a fool he'd been. Even after his long-ago emotional mauling at Lydia's hands, he'd married a beauty thinking that something far more precious, something the lost boy from the bayou had been searching for all his life, was hidden beneath the outer layer. Instead he'd gotten exactly what he deserved. "Don't worry. I won't need heirs for a while."

Turning, he tugged open the door with unnecessary force. He was so disgusted with his own folly that he didn't trust himself in the same room as her. Or perhaps it wasn't his anger he was afraid of but the dangerous sliver of hope that continued to dig into his heart, insistent that he fight for his wife. That sliver wouldn't let him end this marriage, not until he'd discovered the truth about the woman he'd married.

Who was the real Hira? An icy sophisticate or a warm-hearted innocent who'd once looked at him with shy welcome in her eyes?

Hira stared after her husband, her stomach in knots, her uncaring mask threatening to crack at any moment. The instant his footsteps faded, she jumped up and locked the door with trembling fingers, almost blinded by the light reflected off the diamond bracelets around her wrists.

Only when the bolt slid home did she crumple to the floor, stuffing her knuckles into her mouth to muffle her sobs. Tears streamed down her face, but she didn't bother to wipe them. Who was there to see if beautiful Hira Dazirah looked less than perfect?

You obviously have no desire to be with child.

Marc's—her husband's—disgusted pronouncement ran through her mind over and over. Like every other man before him he'd wanted her for her body and yet he blamed her for it. Even worse, he blamed her for something that was untrue.

She'd once dreamed of having as many children as her body would allow, with a husband she'd love. A husband who'd love her back. Those thoughts had belonged to a young girl full of hope and joy, a girl long since buried under the pain of a heart crushed so completely she wasn't sure if it would ever heal.

Her experience at Romaz's hands had left her easy prey for her father's machinations. Kerim had used her sense of family honor to get her to marry, saying that they couldn't afford to have Marc renege on the deal. From what her new husband had said, clearly it had been Kerim who'd pushed for marriage, not Marc. Her father no doubt believed that Marc would favor family in matters of business; Hira already knew that the man she'd married would never succumb to such manipulation.

Kerim's lies had achieved no purpose but to bind her to a man who didn't want her now that he had her. She wasn't even to have the comfort of thinking he'd fallen for her with one glance.

So why had Marc acquiesced to her father's wishes? Only one answer came to her—he wished to own her. It didn't matter to him what kind of woman she was, whether she had a good heart or mind. He'd seen the outer package and liked it enough to go along with Kerim's demands.

Her father had sold her to cement an alliance, and Marc had bought her because he liked the look of her. Between them, they'd reduced her worth from woman to chattel. She wasn't surprised at her father's actions. No, it was Marc whom she was angry at. Marc who'd betrayed the awakening thing between them by marrying her without courtship or romance. According to all she knew, he hadn't even *tried* to get around Kerim's orders.

There had been more than simple desire between them the night they'd first met, but with his act, Marc had crushed that wild and tender emotion.

Two

Hira woke later than usual, courtesy of slumber riddled with nightmares. Dressing quickly after a hurried shower, she girded herself to go down and face her husband's temper, for what man wouldn't hate the woman who'd denied him their marriage bed?

It had been a shameful thing for her to do, but she couldn't bring herself to regret it. An emotionless coupling with a man she'd barely spoken to would've made a mockery of all her beliefs about the meaning of the most intimate act between a man and a woman.

Even though the man she'd denied made her body heavy with desire so hot and blinding, it rocked the foundations of her understanding about her own heart.

Shivers raced up her spine at that traitorous thought. Blinking furiously, she fought them off, though she knew that this blazing heat wouldn't disappear so easily. Not when she was wife to the man who was the cause of her confusion.

Expecting a fight, she set her jaw and forced herself to leave her room. But what she found on the lower floor was far more unsettling than an angry husband. Suitcases lined the hallway, several of them hers.

Shaken, she walked into the living room and saw Marc bent over a table, signing something. "We are leaving?"

His dark-brown hair gleamed in the sunlight angling through the windows as he glanced at her before turning back to his papers. "Yes. In an hour." With strong strokes, he signed his name on another line.

Inordinately crushed by his dismissive attitude, she managed to ask, "Where?"

"My home. Louisiana. Near Lafayette." His words were curt, holding no welcome.

She thought for a moment. "That state has much water but also pra…prairies and its borders touch the Gulf of Mexico. Lafayette is near Baton Red… No, Baton Rouge. It is sometimes called Cajun Country, is it not?"

The man she was joined to was staring at her. "What, you read encyclopedias in your spare time?"

Since that was exactly what she did, she scowled at his sarcastic tone. "They are very informative." And she was starved for information.

Her father didn't believe in higher education for females, but she'd managed to educate herself, first through books and later through clandestine use of the Internet-linked computer in the study. As a teenager, she'd railed against the unfairness of being denied the educational opportunities lavished on her two uninterested brothers, but had soon realized the futility of her pleas.

"What's your favorite subject?" It was the lack of sarcasm in Marc's question that startled her out of her dark mood.

"You're not making fun of me?" She didn't understand his curiosity. Her husband was not reacting as she'd expected. Instead of nursing his anger over their disastrous wedding night, he appeared to be trying to facilitate a conversation between them.

Those piercing eyes seemed to narrow. "No."

"Well then. It is economics, theories of management, things such as that." Aware that it wasn't a feminine type of subject, she stared right back at him, defiant.

"Sure, princess. I believe you." He appeared to be fighting a smile.

Suddenly her frustration erupted. "How dare you… what is your word…*patronize* me? You see only what you think to see. You cannot recognize what is beneath the surface for you are a man who buys only on outward appearance!" She turned on her heel, the wind generated by her dark skirts buzzing angrily around her legs. "I will be ready to leave within the hour."

His arrogance made her angry, but beneath the anger the broken edges of lost dreams rubbed her raw with pain. Despite everything, she'd dared to dream that her American husband would be a man who'd allow her to spread her wings and fly. That hope was now forever lost.

He was just like her father, intent on caging her in the box he'd set aside for her in his mind. She'd fallen for his slow, seductive smile—so rare on that brutally masculine face…a warrior's face—forgetting that being akin to a warrior was no guard against male failings.

Marc frowned as he watched his wife storm out of the room, as regal as a true princess. He'd learned long ago that appearances counted for nothing. Had he committed the cardinal sin and judged his wife on her beautiful face rather than what lay within?

It took him only a minute to discard that idea. If she was so damn smart, what was she doing living in her father's home, on his charity? Zulheil wasn't a restrictionist culture. Sure, the women were well protected and cherished, but they were allowed the same opportunities as their male counterparts.

If nothing else, Hira could've gained the money she needed for study by joining the modeling world. The minute she walked into an agency, the bookers would've crawled on their hands and knees to sign her up. One of his best friends had clawed her way out of poverty using her face, and he respected her for it.

Snorting at almost falling for his spoiled new wife's tricks, he continued to sign papers relating to a minor outstanding matter. He'd have to return to Zulheil in a month or so for a further set of negotiations, but right now he was needed in Louisiana.

Truth to tell, he missed his watery homeland. All this stunning golden desert and too-blue sky could get wearing on a man used to humidity and mosquitoes and the occasional gator.

Hira didn't speak to Marc again until they were winging their way through the clouds, seated side by side in the first-class cabin of a commercial jetliner. Having never flown before, she was feeling more than a little lost and wished Marc would talk to her instead of working on his documents. He might be stubborn and inclined to snap, but at least she knew him. All these other people were strangers, even the flight attendants who smiled at her so nicely but whose eyes were cold.

They thought her nothing but a pretty face, a rich man's newest toy. Marc's dismissive attitude toward her had undoubtedly strengthened that belief. Her anger at the way she was always labeled without being given a chance was a pulsing wound inside her, a wound that grew each time she tried to protect herself by showing a cold face instead of shattering with rage.

Even the times when she'd broken down and cried, she'd done so in the dead of night, in silence. Who could she tell? Who wouldn't laugh at her and call her a "poor little rich girl," as if her looks and her father's wealth meant that she was never to be accorded any real sympathy?

Yet all her life, how she'd envied those plain girls who were adored by their husbands for their laughter and their wit; girls who would never have to worry about being forgotten once their skin wrinkled and their bodies changed. Girls who could joyfully confess to gaining a few pounds, safe in the knowledge that in their husbands' eyes they'd remain forever beautiful.

Despair and hurt tangled inside her soul, making her want to scream and cry at the same time. But she did neither. She'd been brought up to be the perfect daughter and the perfect wife. Seen, not heard. *Never* heard.

The blond flight attendant passed by again, giving

Marc a subtly interested glance. He didn't look up. At least he wouldn't humiliate her by openly flirting with other women, though it was likely that many would throw out lures.

He wasn't a man who could be described as handsome, but there was something compelling about him. Power and strength, buried passion, depths without end—he had the kind of charisma women found irresistible. She'd been pressured into marrying him, but in the privacy of her mind, she admitted that he was a man who made her blush with impure thoughts.

The first time she'd seen him, he hadn't been aware of her scrutiny. She'd been standing in a hidden alcove on the upper floor of their home, looking down onto the banquet hall to check that everything was in order. Barely after she'd arrived, her eyes had landed on Marc, drawn by his magnetic presence.

He'd been standing alone in one corner, his determined and ruthless nature stamped on his features. She didn't fear ruthlessness—all the truly strong males she knew had that element in their makeup. It was part of what made them the powerful men they were.

When he'd moved, she'd imagined him as the most predatory of hunters, all dangerous grace and barely contained power. Her eyes had followed him across the room, unable to drag themselves away. Disturbingly, he'd paused midstep and looked right up at the alcove, as if he'd known she was watching.

Shaking from the impact of those ice-gray eyes, she'd retreated with her hand pressed over the thundering beat of her heart. It had taken her half an hour to calm down enough to finally join the banquet…where Marc had smiled that slow, secret smile at her and turned her whole world inside out.

In short, her husband was a very sexy man.

But even concentrating on Marc's undeniable sexual allure wasn't alleviating her fear. Aware that she couldn't expect sympathy from the man she'd frozen out of their marriage bed, she forced herself to reach for a magazine. Moments later she watched in dismay as the glossy paper slid out from between fingers numbed by the desperate way she'd gripped the armrests.

Without saying a word, Marc put down his pen and picked up the magazine, placing it atop his papers. Eyes wide, she waited. Before she could ask for its return, he reached over and closed one big hand around her trembling fingers. She froze.

"Not a good flier, princess?" There was no mockery in his expression, only concern.

She gave him a watery smile, stunned at his compassion. "It is my first...flying."

"Your first flight?" His surprise was clear. "I've met your father several times in Munich, L.A., even Madrid."

She knew all the facts and figures for those places, could name streets and landmarks, but never had she seen them in reality. "My father believes in unmarried women remaining at home." She tightened her grasp on his hand. "But he never took my mother, either, so perhaps he really believes in keeping all women at home." Expecting to be reprimanded for her disloyalty, she nonetheless gave him an honest response.

For a moment she thought she saw anger flare in the suddenly dark mists of his eyes. "I didn't think that sort of thing was accepted in Zulheil."

"We are a people with much history. Some stay with the old ways and we do not judge." Except sometimes she wished someone would judge.

In fairness to her homeland, Hira knew that if she'd spoken out, she would've been accorded education, perhaps even an independent life. The sheiks for the past three generations had passed laws to ensure all women had the right to follow their own path. But if she'd brought such attention to herself, her clan's honor would've been forever besmirched in a land where honor was everything.

The Dazirah name was a proud one, with centuries of integrity behind it. Just because her father imprisoned his women with his old-fashioned beliefs didn't mean that the rest of the clan had to be tarred with the same brush. Her uncles had never stopped their daughters from reaching their full potential.

Marc gave her a sharp look but didn't pursue the topic. Instead, surprising her once more, he talked with her of his home. Every word was filled with a smile.

"I'll take you to see the French Quarter once we've settled in. Princess, there are things round there that'll blow your mind." He seemed delighted at the prospect, his eyes turning liquid silver. "I might even treat you to a trip through the bayou, if you ask real nice."

Hira's heart melted at his teasing words, delivered in that deep voice that was as smooth and tempting as hot honey. It was clear that despite the enmity between them, he was attempting to distract her from her fear. Seduced by the light in his eyes, she couldn't help but remember the first time they'd met face-to-face. It had happened at the same banquet where she'd become aware of his existence.

Catching her eye from across the room, he'd smiled at her in that way she now knew to be rare for him, and she'd felt the bottom drop out of her stomach. Her lips had curved of their own accord and she'd found herself smiling back at him, drawn by the fiery warmth in his gaze. Yet when he'd bridged the distance between them, she'd turned away with a haughty look. It had only made his smile wider.

At the time she'd told herself that her response arose from her dislike of the proprietary gleam in his eye. Now she accepted that it had had a deeper root. The feminine heart of her had known that Marc was dangerous to her in the way that only a strong, sexy male could be to a woman. Even knowing that, she'd agreed to marry him.

She felt ashamed that, motivated by fear and anger, she'd put the whole blame for their marriage on him when in truth, she *had* had a choice. It wouldn't have been easy to go against her father, but she could've done it—she'd done it before. She hadn't been a very good wife to him so far, but despite everything, he was trying to help her.

Hope blossomed in her heart. Perhaps, she thought quietly, she'd married a man with whom it might just be worth building a life. Her mother had worried that he was scarred, but the lines on his face did nothing to lesson his raw masculine appeal. If anything, they gave him an even more dangerous male air, enticing the feminine core of her to thoughts that shocked her with their flagrant eroticism.

What did a man's face matter, anyway? Her father was a truly beautiful man, as were her brothers. Romaz could have been a movie star. She had no use for handsome men.

But for a man with a heart?

For such a man…she might risk everything.

As they climbed up the steps to his old plantation-style house, its edges softened with hints of Spanish architecture, Marc took his first true breath in weeks. The moist richness of the bayou air swept into his lungs, welcoming and accepting.

From the corner of his eye, he could see the line of cypress trees forever trying to sink their roots into the tiny stream that angled past the edge of his property. As he turned, their branches shivered in the soft breeze and he found himself smiling.

Located far from the bustle of New Orleans, southeast of Lafayette, his extensive block of land, bought to nurture a very private dream, hugged the lush green wetlands that sang a song of welcome to him each time he breathed. He was a bayou brat and damn proud of it.

"Your home is lovely."

Hira's sultry voice broke into his thoughts, an unwelcome reminder that this homecoming was different. He'd brought a wife with him, an untouchable Beauty who wanted nothing to do with the Beast she'd married. Despite their truce on the plane, a truce that had tormented him with images of what could've been, he knew nothing had truly changed.

Fueled by resentment that she was going to turn his solitary haven into a battleground, his response was curt. "Thanks."

He unlocked the door without glancing back at her and walked through with two of their bags, deliberately keeping his hands full. Hira would hardly appreciate being carried over the threshold, even though some primitive part of him wanted to ritualize her entrance into his territory. When she didn't immediately follow, he dropped the bags to the floor and turned around.

She was pulling one of her cases from the back of his rugged all-wheel-drive truck, which he'd had parked at the airport. Her manicured fingernails, painted a soft bronze, looked incongruous doing manual labor. The vividly embroidered hem of her wide-legged cotton pants dragged in the dirt, the golden yellow turning brown as her heels sank through the soft earth.

He considered standing back and watching the show, but some idiotic male instinct refused to allow him to let her hurt herself. No matter what, she was his wife. And Marc Bordeaux looked after those who belonged to him.

Shoving a hand through his hair, he called out, "I'll do it, princess."

She ignored him and began lugging the case up the steps, using both hands. "I can carry this. It is small." As she walked, her midnight-and-gold hair moved around her face, looking soft and silky and touchable.

He'd never seen hair like hers, inky black except for the hidden strands of almost pure gold. Somehow he knew the colors were without artifice, her beauty hypnotically real. The ends had curled in the humidity and he wanted to wrap those curls around his fingers and tug her to him. His body was suddenly heavy. *Needy*.

He'd never needed anyone.

"What's in it?" he asked, to distract himself. Hadn't Lydia taught him anything? Beautiful women were mirages—there was nothing beneath the glittering surface. Yet he'd married this lovely creature expecting her to be more. He still did.

He hadn't begun annulment proceedings because he couldn't bear to let her go without trying to plumb the depths of the woman behind the sophisticate—the woman he'd barely glimpsed that night when she'd thought herself alone. What he'd felt for her at that moment had been brilliant, and so pure it had shocked him. He wasn't going to give up on that feeling until all hope was lost.

Her face turned pink as she stepped up to the verandah. "N-nothing. Just clothes."

Suddenly he knew she was lying. His anger was as cold as a chilling frost. Blocking her entry into the house, he stood as close as the suitcase allowed. "Don't lie to me. What—did your lover give you a going-away present?"

She blinked at him with those absurdly long lashes and if he hadn't known better, he'd have thought she was trying very hard not to cry. He fought the protective impulse that urged him to haul her into his arms.

"No. *No* lover gave me any presents. These are my books." Her gaze was mutinous, but he could see the faint tremor in her lush lower lip.

Her little dig about getting no presents from him hit the mark. He'd taken one look at her, at the secrets in her tawny mountain-cat eyes, and wanted her. Her father's scheming had only speeded up his plans. "Why the hell would you lie about books? What's really in there?"

She glared at him and dumped the case on the wooden planks of the verandah, then knelt down to unlock it. He waited. What did she hope to prove? After the final tumbler clicked into place, she threw him a rebellious look and flung open the lid.

"Books," she said, smoothing the faded cover of one. "I tell you no lies." Her voice shook.

Confused by the vulnerability he could hear, he went down on his haunches beside her. "Why did you try to hide them from me?" He was almost jealous of the reverence with which her slender hands touched the cracked spines and dog-eared pages.

She closed the lid as if to conceal them once more and relocked the case. "My father didn't think that women should have much learning. He threw away my books when he could find them." She wouldn't look at him, shielding herself behind a waterfall of shimmering hair.

Well, hell, that was one answer he hadn't expected. Very carefully, with all the gentleness he had in him, he stroked her hair aside so he could see her face, his hand cupping her cheek. She flinched but didn't move away. "You don't have to hide your books from me."

He felt the shudder that shook her frame. Finally she raised her head, her gaze wary. "Is that true or are you…playing with me?"

The guarded look in those eyes was one he recognized. She expected to be kicked when she was down, to be humiliated and laughed at. That she should expect it of him was infuriating, but he understood that the lessons of a lifetime couldn't be forgotten in a day.

"I promise you it's true." In apology for the way he'd jumped on her, he told her something of himself. "I know the value of books. As a child, I read everything I could find. I'll never begrudge you knowledge." He removed his hand. "There's a library on the first floor. Use it whenever you want."

Pressing her lips tight, she gave a jerky nod. "Th-thank you…husband." It was the first time she'd acknowledged his claim over her, and there was no taunt or barb in her voice. Instead he heard a bone-deep vulnerability that threatened all his beliefs about her.

Unsettled, he stood and offered her a hand. After the tiniest hesitation, slender feminine fingers slipped into his. As she rose, his eyes dropped unintentionally to the skin bared above the modest neckline of her sleeveless top. Sheened with sweat, her golden skin glowed. Heat flickered to life within him. No matter what his mind knew, his body couldn't understand why he was keeping his distance.

He forced his gaze to her face. It didn't do much good. It was as sensual as the rest of her. Full lips, sharp cheekbones, eyes a strange hypnotic shade of lightest brown that gave her a slightly feline look.

"You are so beautiful," he found himself saying, unable to believe the reality of her.

She gave him a tight smile and tugged her hand away. "Yes. People always tell me that."

It should've sounded conceited. Instead, her tone held such sorrow that he stopped her from heading inside, putting his arm around her waist when she tried to walk past. The heat from her body passed through her cotton top and over him like a secret caress.

"And you don't like that?" He frowned.

She looked at him with those amazing eyes. "I am more than a face and a body. I am Hira. But no one wishes to know Hira. Please, I'm tired."

He released her. Stubbornly clutching her precious case, she moved past him in a wash of soft perfume and an indefinable scent that was uniquely her. As he retrieved the other bags, he wondered if she placed him in the same category as those other people. And, if she did, was she right? He'd brushed aside her claims of interest in economics and thought she wouldn't know one end of a book from another. He'd been wrong on at least one count and that indicated he might be wrong on the other.

Or his beautiful, spoiled wife was playing games with him, trying to mess with his head.

Of all the possibilities, that seemed the most likely. First she freezes him out of their bed, then she comes across needy and scared on the plane, now he sees this tenderhearted hurting creature. Who was the real Hira? Marc hadn't yet made up his mind. He hadn't reached where he had in life by making snap decisions. Then again, he'd asked for her hand before he'd spoken a word to her.

Perhaps, he accepted, there was some truth in her complaint. When he'd seen her on that balcony, had he wanted to know Hira? Had he fallen for the soul of that lovely woman who'd seen magic in the moonlight?

Or had he wanted to own that beautiful creature, wanted to show the world that the upstart Cajun with a patched-up body and face could own something so exquisite, most men would never even dream of it?

It.

His blood chilled. When had he become the kind of man who treated a person as a commodity? When had he become like the rich men he hated, the ones who collected beautiful young women as expendable accessories?

No, he thought. *No.* He wasn't like them. If he were, he wouldn't have experienced such disgust at his momentarily aberrant thoughts. If he had nothing emotional invested in this marriage, the visceral pain he felt at the thought that he might have to dissolve it wouldn't exist.

Perhaps he could be accused of arrogance, but he'd been treated as a nonperson once. As a *thing.* He would never do that to another human being.

Not even to his ice queen of a wife.

Three

They'd just finished a largely silent take-out dinner later that evening, when he received a phone call from Nicole, a childhood friend.

"I'll be awhile," he told Hira. "Nic needs some advice on a contract." Used to his help, Nicole had begged him to fly up to New York, but no way was he leaving his new bride to go to another woman's aid. That would be killing his marriage before it began, and the lost, lonely boy inside him continued to catch tantalizing glimpses of his dreams in Hira's eyes.

His wife had no way of knowing that Nicole was like a sister to him. From what she'd revealed of her parents' marriage, he'd bet she'd think he was going to his "other woman."

No curiosity enlivened her closed expression. "As you wish." Despite his attempts during dinner, she'd refused to soften in any way. It was almost as if she were willing him to forget the woman he'd glimpsed in that instant's vulnerability on the verandah.

"You've probably seen Nic on the ads for Xanadu Cosmetics." React, damn it, he wanted to say. Show me you care about this marriage…about your husband.

"She is lovely."

Cold as ice, Marc thought once again, furious at himself for hoping for something more. "Perhaps I should've just married Nic instead," he muttered under his breath as he left the room, not intending his new wife to hear the wholly facetious comment.

Hira felt his words impact like sharp stones against her heart, wounding and so incredibly hurtful that she couldn't breathe. She sat there, unable to move for what seemed like forever. Marc had stalked into the spacious living area abutting the kitchen but had left the door open. Though she couldn't distinguish the words, she could hear the deep rumble of his voice.

And occasionally she could hear a low male chuckle.

Clenching her hands on the arms of the chair, she made herself take deep, calming breaths. The feeling of betrayal persisted. She didn't know why, but she hadn't expected that kind of cruelty from the man she'd married. He'd been so gentle, so *tender* with her feelings on the plane that he'd fooled her completely. And on the verandah…his rough understanding had been her undoing.

So quickly, so suddenly, he'd threatened to win her trust. Terrified of his power over her, she'd retreated behind the only protection she had—an icy facade that was as brittle as summer frost. The whole time that they'd sat across from each other at this table, she'd ached to place her faith in him, but the part of her that had grown up watching her father ambush, then degrade her mother's pride, had cautioned her to wait before she made an awful mistake. And that bruised part of her had been right. If Marc could cause her such torment now, how much worse would it have been if she'd taken those first halting steps?

Feeling lost and alone, she finally stood, searching for something to occupy her mind and her stupidly trembling hands. How had it happened that she'd become so vulnerable to this man she'd married, when she'd learned to protect herself from cruelty after growing up under Kerim's rule?

She couldn't bear to go up to her lonely room and shut herself in. She'd been shut in most of her life. No more, she decided. Her eye fell on their dinner dishes. Glad to have something concrete to do, she gathered them up and took them to the sink. Cool air whispered between her legs from the sway of the ankle-length skirt she'd changed into. Teamed with a white cotton blouse that had an elasticized neckline and little puff sleeves, it made her feel free. She vowed no one would steal that feeling from her.

Midway through the chore, her husband returned, apparently finished with his "Nic."

Perhaps I should've just married Nic instead.

The painful words rocked through her again. She wanted to throw something and ask him why he hadn't married his precious Nic! Why had he brought her out of the desert if he didn't want her? But she didn't speak, too used to having defiance punished by harsh measures.

The punishments hadn't destroyed her fire, but they'd taught her to be very careful as to whom she trusted with her thoughts and emotions. Sometimes those closest to you promised the least safety.

Marc was taken aback to see his princess of a wife efficiently doing the dishes. When she placed the washed dishes in the drainer, he grabbed a dish towel and started to wipe them, wondering once again if he'd been too hasty. For some reason, Hira made him react with quick-fire temper, when he had a reputation for steely control under pressure.

She sent him a startled glance out of those slanted eyes. "You do women's work?"

He grinned. "*Cher,* I used to be a dishwasher in a restaurant when I was a sprat."

That gave her something to think about, because she didn't speak until the work was complete. Despite the disaster the evening had been so far, he'd hoped that they might have coffee together, but she started to head upstairs to her bedroom.

"Hey." He grabbed her arm, careful of his strength on her fragile flesh. "We have to talk." He didn't know what he was going to say. He just knew that something had to be said. They couldn't keep living like this—two strangers who'd said some vows and now found themselves locked in the same cell together.

"Why? Do you wish me to come to your bed?" Arctic frost coated the question. Standing a couple of steps above him, she looked down on him as if he was a lowly slave, her expression as cold as a desert dawn.

He dropped her arm with a sound of disgust, all his

newfound warmth lost in the chill emanating from her. "Damn it, I don't do unwilling women."

"Then you will never 'do' your wife." Her fists were clenched by her sides, her lips pursed tight. It was the first hint of emotion she'd revealed since those moments on the verandah.

He was too furious to decipher the message blazing in her suddenly dark gaze. "What, my hands too dirty for you, princess? Did you realize that my money isn't enough to make you forget my roots?" His voice was harsh. What the hell was he doing? He was a man hunted by many women, but for some reason he wanted this one who held him in contempt. *Only* this one.

She frowned at his hands, as if not understanding the metaphor. "I don't know anything of that. I only know that you have shown your disregard for me by saying you should've married this Nic. I don't wish to remain here with a man who finds it so easy to hurt me."

The bluntness of her words rocked him out of his anger, while the shadowy fear she quickly hid made his next words tender. "Aw, hell. I'm sorry." He raised his hand again and with a gentle grasp on her left hand, tugged her down a step, wondering at the cause of that flash of sheer panic. What scars was Beauty hiding?

"I didn't mean for you to hear that." God, he was an idiot. No wonder her back had gone rigid the instant he'd returned to the kitchen. "It was just my temper talking, baby. Nic's like my kid sister."

"You give me an apology?" Astonishment rang in every syllable.

Her hand in his was a warm token of trust he hadn't

expected. "I acted badly. You have my humblest apologies, princess."

"I... That is all right." She was looking at him as if she couldn't understand him, her eyes tawny with surprised warmth, no hint of ice in sight. This was the woman who'd smiled at him shyly across a crowded room, lovely and vibrant and everything he'd ever wanted.

"What's wrong, *cher?*" The endearment slipped out—her perplexed expression was so very innocent.

Not fighting him when he used his free hand to move a strand of hair off her face, she said, "My father never apologized. He said it was not the husband's role to take blame." Her eyes met his, at once confused and daring.

Marc raised a brow. "What if he was wrong?" He shoved his free hand deep into his pocket to keep from reaching out and stroking the curve of her cheek, from luxuriating in the feel of that golden skin stained with softest pink. There was too much wariness in her gaze to chance the intimacy.

"He said he was never wrong."

"One heck of a way to win an argument." Pulling his hand out of his pocket, he rubbed the back of his neck instead of her cheek. "Takes the fun out of fighting, doesn't it?"

"Why would an argument be fun?" She frowned.

He couldn't help the smile that curved his lips. Leaning close, he deliberately crowded her with his body, the devil in him winning over. "Because then you get to make up, princess." His breath sent the tiny tendrils at her temples dancing. His lips were a whisper from hers, his senses awash in the sensual woman scent of her. Giving in to temptation, he raised his free hand to cup her face, wondering at being able to touch someone so soft and delicate.

Eyes wide, she jerked her hand from his and turned to run up the stairs so fast he had no time to react. His smiled faded with each step she took. What had he expected? That his scarred face would entice her into his arms? Though he refused to admit it, her rejection hurt in a soul-deep way that left him no room to hide. As another one of his dreams crumbled to ashes, he followed his beauty far more slowly up the stairs.

Always a loner, tonight he found his bed cold.

Hira lay awake late into the night. It was her husband's fault. He'd done something to her. Every time she thought she might fall asleep, ghost-gray eyes prodded her awake, asking her for something she had no knowledge of.

She knew he desired her. Most men desired her. It wasn't something she was proud of. It hurt to know that they wanted her only for her body and face. Not one of them would be able to tell her anything of her true self. Had she married just such a man?

He saw her as a "princess," a woman who had no redeeming qualities or many brains. But he wished to lie with her. It wasn't flattering to her to be compared to those American bimbos she saw with their rich, old husbands. Sniffling, though she wanted to be haughty and unaffected, she gave up trying to sleep and rose.

After snuggling into a sunny yellow robe adorned with a single red rose on the back, she sneaked downstairs with the intention of making hot chocolate. In the foreign books she'd read, it had been called "comfort food," and comforting was just what she needed.

She felt alone, adrift. It was as if her mind and body were disconnected. The smart part of her knew that if she allowed herself to feel tenderness for Marc, the hunter in him would seek total surrender. Her first impression of him had been of danger. Every time he came near her, every time he threatened to tear down the walls that had protected her from hurt all her life, that impression was cemented. Yet the sensuous heart of her nature found his masculinity hypnotically compelling. What was she supposed to do with these strange feelings?

And why hadn't her husband come to her tonight? She'd been terrified that he would, unaware how to cope with the sudden heat flooding her body, but she'd accepted the inevitability. She was his wife. He'd left her alone last night because she'd shown him anger, but tonight he'd wanted her and he had to have guessed that she wouldn't deny him again. Not when she'd reacted to his touch as if she'd been struck by lightning. Yet he hadn't come.

He confused her, her big husband who moved like a desert hunter with his lean body and watchful gaze, and who smiled at her as if they shared some secret.

Marc heard Hira leave her room. He wondered what she was doing wandering around the house at this time of night. His heavily aroused body was keeping him awake, but she had no such excuse. From the way she'd run, the woman had no more desire for him than she had for a rabid gator. Grunting, he got out of bed, pulled on a pair of gray sweatpants and started downstairs. To hell with caring for her sensibilities. If she couldn't handle the scars that marked his body, they might as well find that out right now.

He'd never had trouble drawing women, but they'd been tough women, women who prowled for men and knew exactly what they wanted when they got him. And it wasn't tenderness. Gentle, pretty women like his wife tended to find his patched-up body and face distasteful. If he knew that, why was he putting himself through this? he asked himself bleakly.

Shaking his head, he walked downstairs. When he entered the kitchen, Hira was pulling down the tin of hot chocolate from a high cupboard. Her hair fell thick and straight over her shoulders like a black-and-gold mirror, shimmering against the vibrant yellow of her thin robe. Lord, but she was beautiful. If only if he could figure out whether that beauty was also of the heart, he might yet survive this marriage.

"Hungry?" he asked, walking into the room.

Startled eyes in that strange shade of lightest brown met his. She blinked as if to ensure he was real. "I couldn't sleep." It was a grudging admission.

He deliberately crossed his arms across his chest, wanting her to look at him, really look at him. Despite her sophistication, even she wouldn't be able to hide an instinctive reaction. "Neither could I."

Her eyes refused to budge from his face. "Do you want some?" She put down the tin and opened the fridge door. "There is no milk!" Clearly frustrated, she glared at him over one shoulder.

He grimaced. "We'll get some more groceries tomorrow."

She closed the door and put the tin away, scowling at him. "But I don't have what I wish now."

"A little delayed gratification never hurt anyone." Now, if only his body would understand that, they'd both be far more comfortable.

Pursing her lush lips, she started to walk past him, nose in the air, hips swinging in a way that was utterly natural and sublimely female. The same devil that had got him in trouble before made him reach out and grab her upper arm, warm through the cool material of her robe.

Those almond-shaped eyes, mysterious and layered with secrets, clashed with his. "Let me go."

"Why?" he asked, encouraged by the slight blush in her cheeks, the fire in her eyes.

"Because I don't wish to do this and you said you wouldn't use force."

Was that fear in those magnificent eyes? No, he thought, gentling his voice nonetheless. "But what about persuasion?" His breath whispered over her lips, his tone husky. He made no effort to hide his honest desire for her. The sexual awareness between them couldn't be one-sided, not when every breath he took burned with passion.

She reared back. "You wouldn't be able to persuade me to do something distasteful to me." Her words were like swords, stabbing into him, adding to the scars on the inside, scars so bad that it was better they lived in darkness. "If you try despite knowing that, it will make you no more than an animal in heat."

Hurt more than he would've believed by that verbal shot, Marc dropped her arm and turned his back to her. At least now he knew that this hasty marriage had no hope of ever surviving. Then why couldn't he reconcile himself to walking away? "Good night, princess."

Hira stood there staring at Marc's rigid back, aware that she'd hurt him. She had never intentionally hurt another human being in her life. Conscience told her to apologize; the part of her that he'd been taunting was smug, but the biggest feeling was confusion. For there was nothing distasteful to her about her husband. Despite trying to keep him at a distance, she'd allowed him close. Romaz had never made her feel this chaos of mingled joy and terror. And she'd thought she'd loved him.

Overwhelmed and unable to understand what was happening to her, she whirled on her heel and escaped to her room. Inside, she paced across the small space over and over, shocked at the heat that had flooded her body at her husband's proximity. Her mother hadn't told her of these things. All she'd said was that if her husband was a gentle man, he would be careful of her fears.

Hira herself had learned long ago how things were in the marriage bed. However, she had no practical experience. Even with Romaz, she'd behaved with the utmost decorum. It had been easy to resist his attempts at seduction.

Too easy.

Her mind and heart urged her to accept the truth she'd been avoiding since the moment she'd met Marc—she hadn't been in love with Romaz, had instead been attracted to the dream of freedom he'd held out. If she'd loved him, it wouldn't have been so very easy to keep him at arm's length. If she'd loved him, she would've burned for him as she did for Marc, this husband she barely knew.

Faced with a man a hundred times more masculine than her only other would-be lover, a man who she believed would be demanding and impatient with her inexperience, she was lost. Brought up in a cloistered environment, she'd never been allowed to mingle with males such as her husband. Though her family had tried to make a match for her with the sheik, they'd never allowed her to be alone with him.

But tonight she was all alone with a man who wished to exercise his rights as a husband but didn't believe in forcing his bride. That meant that if she wanted to make this marriage more than words on paper, more than two strangers sharing a house, *she* would have to get over her cowardice and approach him, for she knew he wouldn't come near her again. He had too much pride, pride that she'd slashed at tonight with her panicked response.

He'd been so close, so overwhelmingly male, so *potent* that her entire body had seemed to go up in flames. She'd been almost dizzy with the sudden, shocking desire to place her hands on that magnificent chest and stroke until his control snapped, though she had no idea what she would've done with an uncontrollable male on her hands. Even more scandalous was the way she'd ached to rub herself against that steel-hard body.

She'd just *wanted* like she'd never wanted.

And her own desire had so frightened her that she'd struck out at the cause of her unease, wounding him when he'd done nothing to deserve it, when he'd apologized for hurting her with his earlier burst of temper. He'd been so sincere that she knew he'd told her the truth.

It had been easy to forgive him, for she didn't mind living with a man who had a flash-fire temper. In fact, she preferred it to her father's coldly judging silence. But tonight Marc hadn't shown her temper but such emotionless rigidity that she knew she'd caused serious damage.

With her actions she'd shattered the already fragile support base of their marriage. Now she was the one who'd have to rebuild it. Scared, not knowing how a woman went about seducing a male as strong as her new husband, she curled up in bed, thinking she'd never get to sleep.

She dreamed of silken sheets and a hunter of a male with eyes of liquid mercury. A demanding, hungry and powerful lover who refused to let her keep any part of herself back from him. A man who gave as much as he took and left her drenched in sweat, her body aching for a possession she had no knowledge of.

Four

Midmorning the next day, Hira stood at the kitchen window watching her husband chop wood in the back-yard. He'd ignored her since she'd come downstairs. It was likely that he was only outside because she wasn't. Not that it would do him much good to ignore her if she didn't wish to be ignored. Her father had often cursed her for being as stubborn as an old camel. She'd taken it as a compliment.

It would be Marc's own fault if she followed him out. After all, he shouldn't have dressed only in those blue jeans if he hadn't wished her to watch him. What woman could resist running her eyes over that muscled form, as lean and dangerous as a wolf in its prime? And she'd found that watching him led to wanting to touch him, just as she'd wanted to stroke him last night when he'd appeared before her only half-dressed.

Her burning hunger for him continued to startle her, for she didn't think of herself as a passionate woman. Her experience with Romaz had strengthened that belief. She'd *never* been so intrigued by the sight of a male body that she simply wanted to watch the flow and shift of muscle and tendon. Just watch and savor the idea of all that masculine power belonging to her.

What would it be like to be given the right to explore that unapologetically male body as she wished?

Even more unexpected than that secret craving, was the way her body grew hotter and needier with each moment she spent indulging her desires. Her knowledge of the way things were between a man and his wife in the marriage bed didn't account for this melting warmth in her navel...or was it lower? she thought, scandalized. And yet it felt so good she didn't want to fight it.

She wanted to explore it.

Perhaps she'd been sheltered, but she'd never been a coward. Well, at least not until she'd married this man who confused her and made her speak without thinking. Right now her muscular American husband was very angry with her.

Every time he slammed down the ax, chopping the wood to bits, she could feel the power of his anger. But, she thought wonderingly, no matter how angry he was, he never took it out on her the way her father did with her mother, berating and humiliating her. The times that Marc *had* lost his temper, any hurt she'd felt had been fleeting and she'd given him enough sharp words in return that they were even on that score.

And he was man enough to accept blame and apologize when needed. Unlike Kerim Dazirah, Marc seemed to have no need to crush her under his boot so that he could feel stronger. Last night he'd turned his back to her. Back in Zulheil, he'd given her a cold look and left her to a lonely wedding night.

She'd decided that he didn't care. Now she saw that he did. His passionate heart was there to see in every driving blow of the ax. Something quietly powerful bloomed deep inside her heart. If he felt this much anger toward her…maybe he could feel just as much affection, tenderness, even love?

Was it possible that she could find a way to make this marriage of hers more than glimmer and shimmer? Make it *real?* Make it so he saw Hira, saw the woman behind the face and body? To do any of that, first she'd have to reach him. And, she accepted, the easiest way to reach him would be through touch. He reminded her of the desert men of her homeland—while he'd let her close to his body, he'd guard his heart and soul until she'd proven herself.

But if she were brave enough to bury her pain and humiliation at Romaz's hands and fight to make true the sacred vows she'd spoken, she might one day gain the kind of marriage she'd always dreamed of. It was better than this emotional limbo which would inevitably lead to divorce. Her heart kicked in pain. For some reason she didn't want to be separated from this dangerously masculine creature she'd married in haste.

Squaring her shoulders, she took a deep breath and straightened from her leaning position against the kitchen sink. The misty skirts of her clothing floated around her ankles. In her home she'd decided to dress the way she'd done in Zulheil, with some modifications that might help her reach her growling male of a husband.

Her snugly fitted top ended just below her breasts, cupping and shaping a part of her that she usually tried to downplay. The rose-colored silk also exposed the length of her arms, the sleeves being mere puffs on her shoulders. Finally, the waistband of her skirt hugged her hips, leaving the curved plane of her midriff scandalously bare. Her father would never have tolerated such an outfit in his home, would have termed it immodest. For once, she would've agreed with him. Such dress shouldn't be worn by maidens, or out in public.

But between a husband and his wife…

When she'd given in to the urgings of the seamstresses who'd worked day and night to ready her clothes for the wedding, she'd never thought she'd be wearing such an overtly sexual outfit so soon. Perhaps she was taking this step too quickly, but with all that lay between them, waiting any longer could irrevocably damage their marriage.

A marriage she couldn't bear to give up on.

So today she'd dressed to tempt, wanting her husband's admiration of her body. It was the only thing she had with which to fight for a real marriage, the only part of her that had a hope of reaching Marc. She couldn't allow herself to think how pathetic that was. It was the simple truth, and she accepted it because she had no desire to be a divorced woman with many husbands. That was never what she'd wanted for herself.

Mouth dry and feet bare, she rubbed her palms on her skirts before walking out of the house and across the lush grass of their backyard. Marc continued to chop wood, though she knew he was aware of her approach. Her husband had the instincts of the great hunting beasts that had once roamed his homeland. Stopping a safe distance away, she called out, "Husband! Marc!"

He kept chopping.

Scowling, she started to walk closer, not heeding the flying chips of wood, trusting his protective instincts. He didn't disappoint her. Slapping the ax blade down into the stump he'd been using as a stand, he turned to her, all rippling muscle and gleaming flesh.

"What the hell are you up to, princess?" He didn't bother to hide his fury. "Come to flaunt your body in front of your animal of a husband?" His eyes raked her exposed skin, already sheened with a fine layer of perspiration.

Her lower lip quivered. She caught it with her teeth, aware that she deserved his harsh words, for she'd been very unkind last night. Her fear had made her behave in a manner that shamed her. "I have come to confess that I let you believe an untruth."

"And what would that be?" He shoved a hand through his sweat-damp hair and gave her a sardonic glance. "That I'd be getting a real wife, not a porcelain doll?"

She winced but forced herself to keep talking. "I was not disgusted by your approach. Neither do I see you as an animal." He wasn't behaving as she'd expected. Many men would've been satisfied by now, more than happy to take the body she was offering in garb that screamed a sensual invitation. Yet Marc seemed to want far more from her than just her body.

He narrowed his eyes. "What game are you playing now? I know a woman recoiling when I see one." His voice was a harsh denouncement.

Suddenly it was too much. "I was afraid!" She folded her arms across her chest, goaded into honesty. "I bring shame to the good name of my family."

"I'm not a violent man," he snapped, as if she'd insulted him. "Why the hell would you be afraid?"

Perplexed by his lack of understanding, she snapped back, "I am a maiden, husband. My mother said if I had a gentle husband, he would be careful of my fears. You are *not* gentle! You growl and snipe and are very ungentle!"

Marc felt as if the ax had jumped up and knocked him on the back of his head. He could barely comprehend what Hira was telling him. Lips pouting in accusation, she was standing there looking so sexy in her little pink nothing of an outfit that he wanted to lick her up, and she expected him to believe she was virginal?

And yet, as he'd seen last night when she'd told him why she didn't want to talk to him, she had the oddest way of telling the absolute truth at the most disconcerting moments…as if she'd never quite learned the art of subtle lies and half-truths.

"What about your boyfriend?" he finally asked, hooking his thumbs into the waistband of his jeans. No way in hell was he going to touch her unless she asked for it.

"Romaz was not my husband." She sighed. "I shouldn't tell another lie." Her eyes were wide and she was twisting her hands together, but her gaze remained locked with his, determined and so brave that he felt like picking her up and telling her it was all right.

"And the truth?"

"He didn't make me wish to lie with him as you do."

"I turn you on?" He was dumbfounded.

She frowned. "I am not an electrical switch."

"You want to lie with me?" he rephrased. The sun shone bright overhead, but this was the most surreal conversation he'd ever had.

"I have just said that." Her brow knit. "Why do you make me repeat it? Have you lost your desire for me?"

Couldn't she see exactly how much desire he felt? Then he caught himself. No. She'd kept her eyes firmly above the waist—shy innocence or a beautiful woman playing with a scarred man's mind? At the end of his patience, he walked closer. Her cheeks bloomed with a delicate blush at his nearness, but she didn't back away.

"You don't want me," he stated, his voice hard.

He wasn't going to allow some pampered little princess to make fun of him. Not again. Never again. Memories of being humiliated by Lydia Barnsworthy, daughter of Trevor Barnsworthy III, shoved their way to the surface of his mind. He'd been good enough to clean her car, cut the grass and do other menial chores, and over a summer of flirting, she'd made him believe he was good enough to date her.

When he'd finally asked her out to a school dance, she'd said yes. Using some of his hard-earned cash to rent a tux and buy a corsage, he'd shown up at the doorstep. The maid had informed him that Lydia had gone to the dance with someone else, leaving him only a message. "It was just a bit of fun. I never thought you'd actually think I might go with you. Sorry."

That was all the apology he'd received, and he'd known it was meaningless. She'd intended to do this from the first. Fuming, he'd gone to the dance and seen her laughing at him from the arm of the school's star quarterback. In spite of working so many jobs, Marc had managed to be picked for the baseball team. He'd played not because he loved it but because he'd known it would get him through college on a scholarship, allowing him to pursue what he really wanted to do.

But being a sporting hero hadn't been enough to touch the perfect tennis-toned body of Lydia Barnsworthy; he had to have the money and the pedigree, too. As he'd watched her dance, he'd found a new maturity born out of cold rage. To her clear disappointment, he hadn't caused a disturbance. What he'd learned that night was that a beautiful woman was worth nothing if her heart was cruel. Unfortunately, the two seemed to go together.

His wife gave him a fiery look, shattering the memories. Lydia was a hag compared to the woman he'd married. Yet, as he'd already discovered, Hira's beauty wasn't enough. If she'd remained the ice queen he'd met on his wedding night, he would've ignored her and eventually annulled their marriage. He'd had enough coldness and pain in his lifetime. But she'd kept him on the verge of hope with those fleeting moments of vulnerability that teased him with hints of the woman beneath the ice, the woman he'd seen on that moonlit balcony.

"Why should I lie to you?" She put her hands on her hips and moved closer. They were both in bare feet and she had to tip her head back a little to meet his gaze. He wondered if she realized her breasts were pressing against his sweaty chest. "I do not lie...perhaps sometimes I try to lie, but then I always tell the truth!"

What the hell, Marc thought, bracing himself for a blow. The worst she could do was reject him. Perhaps then he'd finally accept that the hope had been a mirage, an illusion sent to torture the vulnerable part of his heart, the part that held the soul of the bayou boy used to surviving unbearable hurt.

He clamped his hands on the exposed skin above her skirt. Smooth and warm under his touch, her body invited him to satiate himself in any way he wished. The hunter in him growled that she was his mate, his to do with as he wished. The civilized man barely managed to keep the instinctive reaction in check.

She shivered under his touch, a smooth whisper of soft skin against callused flesh. "That is odd."

"Odd?"

Those exotic eyes looked at him in accusation. "Why do your hands make parts of me burn that you don't touch?"

Marc moved his hands up and down the curve of her waist, still not certain of her desire, trying to scare her off with his nearness and undeniable masculine arousal. Instead of backing off, her lips parted and she put her hands on his shoulders, pressing close.

He wasn't convinced. Not when she hid her face in the curve of his neck. Calling on every ounce of control he possessed, he ran his hands up her torso and boldly cupped her breasts. She jerked at the accelerated intimacy.

"Husband," she whispered against his skin. "What... do you do to me?" Her voice shook, but when he went to remove his hands, she moved just the tiniest bit closer, as if not wanting to lose his caress.

"Do you like this?" he asked in her ear, letting her continue to hide her face because he could feel the pebbled hardness of her nipples.

Her hands clenched on his shoulders. *"Yes."*

If she really was a virgin, there was no way she could be faking the needy ache in her voice. "How's this?" His voice was a husky whisper as he released her breasts and moved down to gently squeeze her bottom.

Fingers digging into his shoulders, she pulled away, eyes big and worried. "Husband, these things shouldn't be done outside."

"There's no one to see." And he wanted to take her under the cerulean-blue sky, because he'd just figured out that she was telling the truth. His bride wanted him. There was a shocked innocence in her eyes that couldn't be fabricated. He knew that in his desire to test her, he'd touched her far too boldly, but he intended to make up for it by pleasuring her any way, every way she wanted.

She drew her head away. "Please." For a moment he saw such deep vulnerability in those tawny mountain-cat eyes that he was shocked. Never had he imagined that his sophisticated princess had a heart so very soft. What else was she hiding behind that hauteur of hers?

His interest in her multiplied again. At the same time, an almost painful tenderness took root in his heart, barely a bud but powerful despite it. "All right, *cher.*"

He kissed her once, lingering at the mysterious taste of her, at the sweetness of her tentative response. When he asked for entrance into her mouth, she hesitated. "It's okay, baby," he whispered, his tone gone rough and low, "let me in."

Her body shivered under his hands as her lips soft-ened, giving him what he sought. Fighting the urge to conquer, he tasted her just enough to have him craving more. When they parted, she was staring up at him, roses blooming on both cheeks. No woman on Earth could've counterfeited the passion clouding those magnificent eyes. "Let's go inside. I need to shower, anyway."

"I will help bathe you." Her voice was soft, almost lost on the whispering bayou breeze.

His arousal became excruciating. "What?" Maybe he was still asleep and this was one hell of an erotic dream, because only there would a maiden wife make a suggestion like that.

"In my clan, it's the oldest of traditions that wives help their husbands bathe." She was biting her lower lip, her guilt obvious in the way her body had gone tense. "I've been shirking my duty because I knew you didn't know of it."

And, he guessed, because she was a virgin. How could he have expected an untutored girl to understand the barbarian hunger she'd probably seen in his eyes last night? Tenderness that he hadn't known he could feel made him move his hands up and down her back, gentling her.

"Would it be such a chore?" he whispered. Despite a lifetime of confidence, he found himself waiting for her response, armoring his heart against pain.

Her cheeks tinted again with that rosy shade that made her golden skin glow. "No." It was the softest of murmurs. Her lashes drifted down to hide her eyes from him, but he continued to feel her arousal in the way her nipples pressed against his chest. "You make me wish to touch you," she confessed, mouth almost on the skin of his chest.

"What about the scars?" he asked bluntly. Painful

truth was better than a fantasy like the one he'd built around Lydia. The eventual shattering of fantasies tended to wound a man far more than honesty.

She ran a slim finger across one of the ragged scars on his chest. "In Zulheil, desert chieftains participate in a ceremony to show their loyalty to our sheik." Her fingers floated down to trace the faint lines that ran across his abdomen. "They mark their bodies with pride. You are a hunter like them and these are your scars of battle." She pressed a kiss to the jagged scar that cut across his collarbone.

He shivered. "I suppose they could be considered battle scars." His childhood had been a battleground and he'd come up against his father's belt and his mother's fist more times than he cared to count. His hand stroked the bare skin of her hip. To his surprise, she cuddled closer. There was a softness to her body that spoke of true welcome.

"They make you…sexy to me." Her voice was almost indiscernible. "I see the men in your advertising and they are too pretty. Who would wish for a husband who couldn't protect them?"

Once again, he was reminded that his wife was a woman from another land, a land that for all its sophistication, had a primitive core that lay very close to the surface. "And you think I could?"

She tipped up her head. "Despite your civilized front, you're a hunter at heart." Her hand trailed up his chest, the languid stroking fuel to the slow burn of desire within him. "You see me as your property, and you'd never let anything hurt what is yours."

Her intuition startled him. Whatever the state of their

marriage, in saying vows, he'd made her his and he would die protecting her if it came to that. Clenching his fist in her abundant hair, he tilted her head. "How do you like being my property?"

Mountain-cat eyes narrowed. "I am no man's property. I simply said that that is how you view me."

His lips quirked. "A subtle distinction."

"A distinction nonetheless. But, I will accept this—as your wife, I belong to you." Then she did something totally unexpected. She gripped the curling hairs on his chest with one hand, making him wince. "And, husband, if we lie together, you become *mine.*"

Well, well, well, Marc thought, at once amused and intrigued by the possessive interest in his wife's eyes. "The princess doesn't want to share?"

She pulled at the hairs in her grasp. Hard. "The princess will *never* share. Decide."

He untangled her hand, fighting his grin. "My tigress." He had no intention of cheating. If he couldn't keep it in his pants, he would've never taken a wife. His father might have been an abusive tyrant but even he'd never sunk that low.

Ten minutes later Marc decided he was insane. Why wasn't he inside his wife's tight little body right now? Because she was naked, wet and slippery, and slowly soaping his thighs. His arousal was blatant, but she avoided looking at that part of him, the possessive tigress suddenly turning shy. It was the reminder he needed that he was the experienced party. She'd only go so far before halting in confusion.

"Enough. I'm clean. Your turn." He took the soap

from her, desperate enough to be completely unsophisticated.

Her eyes went wide. "That is not custom!"

"It is in America." He turned her away from him so he could soap her back. "I, too, have been shirking my duty."

Her body was so lovely that he thought he was dreaming. The slender waist he'd savored outside, flared into womanly hips that would cradle him deliciously when he drove into her. Those long legs of hers could make a man beg for mercy. Thankfully she didn't appear to like wearing shorts or she'd cause traffic accidents.

"This wasn't told to me in my lessons on American culture." She threw him a suspicious glance over one wet shoulder, water-darkened lashes delineating her tawny eyes even more sharply.

He grazed her skin with his teeth, deciding he liked the taste of his wife. Later, after she was more at ease with him, he intended to take his own sweet time tasting all the secret places of her body. "It's for a husband to teach his wife, not for everyone to know."

"Oh." She wouldn't look at him, but he let her face the glass wall. The hunger in his eyes was likely to scare her.

He'd kept his mouth shut when she'd shyly undressed before following him into the shower, though he'd wanted to swallow his tongue at seeing her naked for the first time. Even after her maddening "help," he wasn't going to push her to do something she wasn't ready for, and it had been obvious that getting into the shower with him had taken every ounce of courage she had.

When he hadn't forced anything on her, letting her become used to his body and his strength, she'd begun to relax. But she was still far from giving him the welcome he needed if he was going to take her to his bed. As he'd told her, an unwilling woman held no joy for him. However, he had no intention of letting her do all the work in this mutual seduction.

With her hair pinned atop her head, the vulnerable line of her nape was bared. He pressed a kiss to the tender skin, giving her the gentleness she'd accused him of lacking and had the pleasure of feeling her tremble against his hands and lips.

"Will I truly be your only lover?" he whispered close to her ear, his palms flat on the shower walls on either side of her head. She was enclosed but in walls that would break the moment she displayed any resistance. It was his way of teaching her not to fear either his passion-rough voice or his desire-taut body.

"Yes." Her murmur was as soft as the feel of her skin.

Taking a chance, he slid a hand down the front of her body and cupped one heavy breast. She gasped, her body going taut. He squeezed gently, his mind whirling at the feel of her, the sensual weight of her in his palm. The things he was intending to do to her sweet flesh would probably curl her toes. "Princess, if we do this, no more separate bedrooms."

Silence.

"What? Don't like the terms?" He kept his hand on her breast, proprietary as hell. She'd given herself to him. Now she had to take all of him. No playing by arbitrary rules. Either they were husband and wife or they weren't. "If you don't, we stop right now. Right here." Reining in the possessiveness driving him, he gentled his demanding tone. "This is enough for today, if you're not ready."

The only urgency lay in the desire that had a stranglehold on his body. And that he could control if Hira was unwilling. She'd shown such courage in coming to him despite his anger that he'd grant her all the time she needed.

"I... My parents never... Is this acceptable?" It was a hesitant question.

The flaring possessiveness within him calmed at the innocent explanation. His wife led a sheltered life, her only example of marriage being what she'd seen between her parents. It was becoming very clear to him that he'd have to fight those memories to claim her as his own.

Only then did he realize that he'd decided to fight for more than a marriage based on desire and practicality. He wanted the real thing. "I'm your husband and I say it is. Do you doubt me?" Smiling, he kissed the side of her neck.

A short pause. "No." But she didn't sound utterly convinced by his dominance in the relationship. He didn't want her to be. A wife who always agreed with him would be no fun at all. A real marriage included disagreements as much as it did loving, laughter and loyalty.

Grinning against her, he released her breast and soaped up his hands before putting the soap in the holder. A question shimmered into his mind. "Should I get protection, sweetheart?"

He felt her blush heat up her skin. "No. I visited a doctor before our marriage."

Delighted at not having to halt his exploration, he took a step back and ran his hands from her shoulders to the tops of her thighs. Her buttocks tightened under his touch and he stroked up to rub the soap in circles, blocking the spray with his body so that she remained soapy for his pleasure.

She made a tiny, woman sound. "Am I very dirty?"

He was fascinated by her smooth bottom, very aware of the heat and silky pleasure that awaited him below the curve he was caressing. Voracious and impatient, the rush of need was almost savage, but he controlled it with ruthless force. This time was about teaching his princess that she now belonged to the American she'd married. Without compromise.

"Filthy," he whispered against her neck. "The front of you is going to need extra attention."

She shook her head in desperation. "No, I'll do it."

"Uh-uh," he disagreed. "My privilege."

"Husband, what you make me feel may drive me crazy. You do not wish for a crazy wife."

Her panicked words made him want to tease her some more. Wrapping his arms around her body, he closed his hands over her breasts and then pressed his body flush against her back. In an effort to escape, she squeezed herself against the glass wall of the shower. He followed. His erection lay between them, hot and throbbing.

"Husband, please." The husky plea asked for mercy…not for an end to this highly charged game of pleasure but for completion.

"Don't you like this, *cher?*" She wiggled her body in response, settling him even more snugly against her.

"Stop that, unless you want me inside you right here, right now."

"Okay." She nodded vigorously. "I'm not afraid. You have been very careful of me. I'm ready. Truly, I am."

He chuckled. "You're not getting away that easily."

"Why do you torture me?"

"Maybe I'm taking revenge for all the bad things you've done to me." He nipped at her neck again, aware that she reacted each time he indulged himself that way. She was a quiet lover, but he was a man who'd grown up with the whispers of the bayou. He knew how to listen for the softest of his wife's sighs, how to read the sweet tension in her feminine muscles, how to smell the scent of her desire. Hira was telling him what she liked, and he was paying damn close attention.

"I have not done such things!" She pushed back in rage but he was far stronger.

Fighting an urge to laugh in delight, he moved his hands until her nipples were between his fingers. At the same time, he nudged one leg between her thighs. She gasped. "Are you wet for me, Hira?" He pinched her nipples gently.

"I..." Her whole body trembled.

"Maybe I should check." He slid one hand from her breast down her damp stomach to the curls at the juncture of her thighs. Because his thigh was between hers, she couldn't close her legs even if she'd wanted to. He went slowly, watching for any sign that she wanted him to stop, even going so far as to start to slide his thigh out. She squeezed her legs together, not to halt his hand, but his withdrawal. His mouth dry with anticipation, he thrust his hair-roughened thigh between her smooth ones once more, his hand resting below her navel.

Whimpering, she let his fingers slide through her curls and into the delicate folds between her legs. So unbearably soft that she made him feel incredibly male, she shuddered as he stroked her sensitive flesh in search of heat. When he found it, he gently pushed a single finger inside her, just enough to tantalize, to tempt. She cried out, her slender frame racked by tremors. His own body went taut with desperation.

"Yes, you're wet." Voice beyond rough, he removed his hand and her body tried to follow. Chuckling hoarsely, he drew back and turned her in his arms, letting the water wash over her. "Wet all over."

Eyes almost blind with desire met his. "You must finish," she ordered.

"In a while." He had no idea how he was remaining in control. Perhaps it was the fact that despite her natural sultriness, she was an innocent and didn't know how to push him to the edge.

Then she made a sound of utter frustration and her hands clasped his erection. "Now!"

Pleasure splintered through his body as her hands held him with expertise that belied her claim of virginity. Experience he could accept, lies he despised. Growling, he thrust a hand through her hair, scattering the pins to the floor and sending that black-and-gold waterfall cascading down her back. "Who else have you held in your hands?"

She scowled at him. "No one!" Then to his shock, she leaned forward and bit his lower lip, a sharp little snap that rocked him. "You have made me crazy as I warned."

It was the edgy remark that calmed the hunter. Perhaps he had pushed her to take this bold step. Hira, he was beginning to learn, was a very strong woman. A woman who went after what she wanted. A woman who acknowledged her mistakes and called on him to explain his own actions.

Reaching down between their bodies, he removed her hands, though she didn't go quietly. Moving them up above her head, he pinned them against the glass with one hand. She tried to escape, her eyes wild as she watched him soap up his free hand. Dropping the soap to the floor, he began to lather her breasts.

Her body shuddered. "Marc…"

"That's it, baby, say my name." He moved enough that the spray washed away the soap on her breasts. Then he leaned down and took her nipple into his mouth.

She bucked and screamed. "Marc! Please! Please!"

He wanted to give in to her, his body aching for release, but he knew the importance of seducing her properly. Once he had her, he'd want to taste her passion again and again, and she had to want him just as much. He released her hands and lifted her by the hips. She wrapped her legs around him, clasping him to her and opening herself to his penetration.

"Not yet, *cher.*" When she parted her lips to protest, he kissed her.

Because her mouth was already open, it began as a much more carnal kiss than the one they'd shared outside. But despite that, he didn't ravage her. Instead, he teased her with short strokes and licks of his tongue that barely ventured beyond her lips. Her hands clenched in his hair. For a few moments she didn't respond, then her tongue shyly stroked his lower lip. He couldn't stop his body surging into her.

He was inside her before he could breathe, lodged just barely in her heat.

She tried to push forward and impale herself. He

clasped her hips and kept her still, though sweat was pouring down his face, mixing with the shower spray. "Kiss me, *cher*. Kiss me like you want me deep inside you, touching you in a place no one else has ever breached." It was a sensual demand that pushed at her innocence but he needed her with him all the way, needed her to feel the same raging fire that was scorching him. His hunger would be satisfied with nothing less than her utter and complete participation, followed by her absolute, unflinching surrender.

She gasped, tawny eyes almost swallowed by dark pupils. Then she leaned just a tiny bit forward, held his face in her hands and kissed him. It was the tenderness of her hold that rocked him. Before he could find his feet, she was obeying his order, kissing him with such passion that he felt her desire all the way to his toes, a sizzling heat that made every nerve ending he had fire in rapid sequence.

Her tongue stroked his, shy but determined. "Husband…"

The single trembling word shattered his control. Entwining his fingers with hers, he pressed their joined hands to the glass wall and slid another inch into her. Her whole body shook, but she didn't break eye contact.

"Ready?"

"Yes." Sensual determination was stamped in her features, her lips lush and just barely parted.

He rocked against her, giving her time to get used to this absolute intimacy. She shuddered, and the tight sheath of her body gave way. "More?" he whispered, releasing her hands to stroke his over her buttocks while his body held hers pinned to the wall.

It didn't surprise him that she understood. Her breasts heaving against his chest, she swallowed. "I'm sure, husband... Marc, *I want you.*" No prevarication, no hesitation, just the truth of her desire.

He read that truth in her exotic gaze. Though her pupils were hugely dilated, she was still with him, riding passion's currents. She was, he realized, his perfect match in this arena. Fire rippled through him, urging him to surge forward and brand her with his possession.

Gritting his teeth against temptation, he held her wriggling hips still and nudged another tiny bit into her. Despite her open hunger, she was a novice at this—it was his task as her husband to prepare her, soothe her...and then storm her. Another tiny nudge.

He did the same again and again, moving slowly deeper until he hit the feminine barrier he'd known was waiting for him. Some wholly primitive part of him growled in approval. She was his. *For always.* It was right that he was the one to initiate her into this. The only one. Fighting the grip of the primitive within, he took her lips in a voracious kiss and nudged again, this time with more force. That fine barrier stretched and then broke. Hira's fingers dug into his shoulders but she didn't pull away.

Instead she returned his kiss with fierceness that destroyed him. Sure of his welcome, he pushed fully into her almost-shocking heat. The pleasure was indescribable. Lips locked with hers, he moved one hand to her bottom, squeezing and caressing as his other hand moved up to her breast. He could feel her fighting the multiple sensations, trying to control her senses.

"Let go, baby. Let go for me." His husky demand

was whispered into her mouth, almost drowned out by the water.

But she'd heard. When he rolled her nipple in his fingers, her body jerked and then she cried out against his lips. Her surrender was apparent in the way she clung to him as ripples of pleasure tore through her body. In the deepest, most feminine part of her, she clenched around him again and again, an intimate caress that brought him to the edge of insanity. He clung to that edge with every ounce of strength he possessed, determined to hold her safe through her first ride into the firestorm of pleasure.

Almost sobbing with the fury of her ecstasy, her legs locked tight around his hips, she wrapped her arms around his neck and buried her face against him, as if she wanted to crawl into his body.

It was the final straw.

He started moving faster, speeding his rhythm in a way designed to stroke her already sensitive inner tissues into shuddering abandon. He felt her shock as her body began to react again, felt her mouth open on the skin of his neck as she kissed him there, touched him, stroked her fingers into his wet hair. But she didn't back away.

Her lush body accepted the pleasure he lavished on her. It was all he'd wanted, but she gave him more. With her lips and her hands and the way she held him to her, she not only accepted but actively participated, telling him without words that his pleasure mattered to her. It was his last thought before the spiraling void he'd been circling sucked him in.

He took her over the edge with him, took her on another incandescent ride into a realm where pleasure was the only currency. His and hers.

Five

Hira wasn't sure she was functioning properly. Moving her head with care lest it fall off, she looked beside her to the hunter sharing the bed. Yes, she'd once thought him a civilized man, but that had been a complete delusion. He was about as civilized as a mountain lion. His taking of her—and it had been a taking in the most basic sense—had been domineering, controlling and very, very sexual.

This very uncivilized man thought he owned her even relaxed in sleep. She was pinned down with one heavy arm thrown across her waist and a muscular thigh across her lower legs; now that she'd given herself to him, he wouldn't allow her to back away from their sexual joining.

But was it making love?

No, she thought with a little pang of loss. It hadn't

been making love. He desired her but he didn't love her. And as for her? She didn't know what to make of her own emotions. She'd been so sure she'd loved Romaz, and yet she'd never felt this desire to mate with him that she did for her American husband.

From the first moment she'd seen Marc, her feelings had spun as wildly out of control as a desert storm. Turning, she raised one hand and brushed his dark hair off his face, unable to stop the tender caress of her fingertips across his strong jaw.

He fascinated her, this hunter with his scars and his eyes full of shadows. She'd never seen a more magnificent man, and she came from a culture far more primitive in its beliefs about men and women than her new home. Zulheil's history had made its men toughened, somewhat wild creatures who had to be coaxed to trust a gentle feminine hand.

Had she misjudged her husband and dealt with him in the worst possible way? If he were like the men of her homeland, then he would have to be treated with the same wary tenderness, for wild creatures didn't trust so easily as their civilized brethren. She'd thought him an American millionaire but that was merely a mask. He was far more like Zulheil's desert chieftains, who sometimes took women for the simple reason that they wanted them.

Eyes the shade of aged silver were suddenly looking into hers. "How long have you been awake?" he demanded.

"Hours and hours," she lied. Like those chieftains, he must never be given all he wanted, or he'd become a total dictator.

His lips curved in that slow sexy smile that never failed to weaken her virtue, and he rolled over to lie on top of her, his arousal nudging at her. Shocked, she felt her eyes widen. "Already?"

"The first two times were mere entrées, baby. I'm working toward the main course." He pushed into her.

Gently. Oh, so gently.

Surprised by the tenderness she could feel in the care he took with her well-loved body, she was undone. To her further shock, she accepted him easily, without pain or discomfort, feeling only sweet, hot hunger. He was slow this time around, moving with languorous ease that gave her much pleasure. As passion built, she rode the tide with him, clutching the sheets and letting him kiss and suck her breasts as he would, giving herself to her hunter.

Marc watched Hira move sinuously beneath him and could barely believe she'd been a virgin only hours before. He'd been merciless, not letting her recover from that first joining before taking her again, stroking her to incoherent passion as morning turned to afternoon, his appetite for her and her pleasure out of control. But she'd been with him every step, a sensual, gorgeous creature whose body reacted to his touch like dynamite to fire. He'd never had his hands full of fire before. It was an education.

Though he would never tell her, she'd spoiled him for other women. They damn well were going to stay married forever because he had no intention of going without, now that he knew what was possible. In bed she was his perfect mate, honest and giving with just a whisper of wildness. He wanted to coax more of that wildness from her, in the bedroom and out.

Her breath hissed out from between her lips as he touched her deep in her heat, his engorged flesh stretching her swollen tissues. Slowing the tempo of his hips, he stroked and kissed and caressed, giving her the tenderness he'd denied her earlier. "Was I too rough, *cher?*"

Exotic eyes of lightest brown met his. "Did I complain?"

He grinned. "You said I made you crazy."

She reached up and cupped his face in her hands. Obligingly he moved close enough for her to kiss him. "Yes. I am insane and that is your punishment."

Chuckling, he inserted a hand between their bodies and caressed her where she was most sensitive. She moved against him, surprising him with her acceptance of the intimacy. To his delight her curious honesty apparently translated into open sensuality in bed. He gave her what she wanted and she returned the favor, locking her long legs around his hips and holding him to her.

Watching her eyes go almost golden as she reached her climax, Marc wondered why this day felt more momentous than their wedding ceremony.

After that incredibly pleasurable day with her husband, Hira decided to truly fight for their marriage. She had taken vows. Though they hadn't been made with full freedom of choice, they had been made. She had many faults, but she wasn't a promise breaker.

Her husband didn't love her, she thought as she walked along a stream that ran near the house. But neither did he treat her with the lack of courtesy that her father always showed her mother. It wasn't much, but it was better than the life she'd expected on her wedding night.

For the past three weeks, ever since she'd admitted her desire for him, he'd been warm and indulgent. Whenever he could delegate work, he'd been teaching her about *his* Louisiana. Wide-eyed, she'd visited a voodoo practitioner's temple, gorged herself at a backwoods crawfish restaurant and ridden through the gator-infested bayou country that Marc loved so much.

It was a lush land, full of surprises and hidden glory that easily enchanted. Attempting to appreciate this vivid, green country was not the hardest thing in her life. Especially when she saw it through her husband's eyes.

But there was one thing that gave her pause. Every Wednesday night and Sunday afternoon, Marc disappeared. When she'd asked, he'd said that it had to do with some important business. But while he'd been out last week, his secretary had called looking for him, unable to get through to his mobile phone.

Hira had given the woman a plausible excuse, but she couldn't help wondering where her husband went when he left her each sunny Sunday, and what he did that made him arrive home so very late every Wednesday.

Though it was a painful thing, she accepted that despite the risk she'd taken in giving herself to him, he might have another lover. Romaz hadn't been satisfied with her—why should she be enough for this far more magnificent man? Clenching her fists, she took a deep breath of the wet air. Everything in this land was wet. Even her eyes.

Rubbing her tears off her face with the backs of her hands, she decided that she wouldn't suffer in silence. She wasn't going to spend the rest of her life ignoring her husband's infidelities the way her mother did. Perhaps it had allowed Amira Dazirah to live with some semblance of happiness, but it would never suit her daughter.

Walking out of the woods surrounding their extensive compound, she strode to the house and made her way to the master bedroom. The sound of the shower in the en suite bathroom only gave her a little peace. She knew she shouldn't spy on her husband's affairs but she couldn't bear to simply ask him, couldn't bear to tear open her soul that way. If he told her face-to-face that he had a lover, she wouldn't be able to hide her pain.

She felt ashamed spying, but she would rather feel that than the crushing humiliation that would surely come if she went into a confrontation with no knowledge whatsoever. She needed some shield against Marc, some way to protect herself. As he'd shown her last night, when his hands touched her body, she became his in a way that defied her own mind and soul.

Ears perked to catch the slightest sound, she reached into Marc's jacket pockets and pulled out everything in them. The wallet and keys went straight back in. She started going through the handful of receipts in one pocket. No matter that this was wrong, she had to know, for the idea of her husband finding succor in some other woman's arms was unbearable.

"Gas," she muttered, scanning the receipts. "Groceries. Clothing…from a boys store? Electronic equipment. Flowers." That was all there was. Brow furrowed, she put the receipts away just as the shower shut off.

Giving a soft gasp, she whirled out of the master bedroom and padded quickly into her own. Though she hadn't spent a night there since she'd lain with Marc, it was still her room, full of feminine things and her favorite books, a place of retreat when her hunter of a husband became too dominating or overwhelming. However, she'd rarely been pushed to use it in the past weeks.

She'd found herself drifting into the relaxed living room to sit with Marc, without ever consciously planning such a domestic scene. He never asked her to be with him, but if she was away from him for more than an hour, he came looking. Until now she'd thought that implied growing care for her, and her heart had bloomed. But what if it had been nothing more than a proprietary search for the woman he considered his property?

The instant Marc walked out of the bathroom, he knew that someone had been in the bedroom. Barely a second later he knew it had been his wife. Her elusive scent tantalized his nostrils and threatened to arouse him when he had no intention of being made a slave to desire.

As he dressed, he thought over her distant behavior of the past week. He'd wondered if she was trying out her fledgling sensual wings, seeing if she could control him by withholding her full self from their intimacy. If she was, he'd shown her last night that she was a novice in that game.

He frowned. Had he been too demanding of her? He hadn't let her hold back an inch, asking more and more and still more, not letting her sleep until she'd begged him for rest. Even then a part of him had raged to keep taking her, stamping his mark on her, forcing her to remove the distance he'd glimpsed on her face even in the darkness.

He swore under his breath. Despite her sensual nature, she really was an innocent in that particular arena. His gut twisted at the thought that he might've scared her with his intensity, even though she'd ridden every wave with him.

Hira sat in her room, unable to stop thinking about what she'd found. The groceries, clothing and computer equipment hadn't come to this house. Neither had the flowers, and that hurt most of all. Her husband had never given her flowers, never so much as a tiny trinket to show her that he felt some affection for her. That wasn't to say he was a stingy husband. No, in some ways he was far too generous.

A racy little sports car had been delivered for her personal use a few days after her arrival in America, and just last week, his secretary had accompanied her on a shopping trip to a number of designer boutiques where Marc had set up accounts for her use. But despite his generosity, he'd never once given her anything that might be interpreted as the least bit romantic. Perhaps he didn't wish her to get the idea that she meant more to him than a pleasurable face and body.

So where had the flowers gone?

Who had they gone to?

Her heart felt as if it was slowly breaking into a thousand little pieces. Could it be that her husband had become more than just a lover? Could it be that she was the trophy to show off, while his heart belonged to a woman he couldn't marry for some reason?

It wasn't such a ridiculous idea. Her father's longest-serving mistress was a twice-divorced Parisian dancer whom he'd known since before his marriage. She'd once heard him say to her brother, Fariz, that though he couldn't let the woman go, he'd never considered marrying her—a man of his standing needed a wife with a pristine past.

Pain beat at her temples as, for the first time, she realized that this hunter of an American with his quick mind and compelling eyes meant far more to her than a convenient husband. In her heart she'd claimed him as hers the first time he'd teased her with that slow smile. And that had been back in Zulheil.

She didn't know if she loved him, but she did know she felt things for him she'd never felt for any other man. He was her husband and she wouldn't sit aside and let him betray her. She wasn't a toy he could play with, as he'd played with her last night, and then put back in her box when she became inconvenient.

Gulping, she considered confronting him right then and there. Only a second later she thrust that idea aside. He was half-naked right now and would surely see her entry as an invitation to seduction. No, she couldn't let him touch her body while he thought of another woman.

The past few days had been torture, last night had been pure humiliation, given that she'd been trying to keep her distance while she decided whether or not he was cheating on her. With hands that caressed and teased, lips that lavished attention on every secret corner and husky whispers that rasped along her skin, he'd made her give up all her precious dignity and taken his pleasure in her shuddering climaxes.

She could accept his lack of loving, but it was unbearable that he might be giving some other woman the
very affection he couldn't find in his soul for her. She
had to know the truth. But how?

"Hira." Marc's deep voice came through the door.

"Yes?" Startled, she stood and walked over to stand on
her side of the wooden barrier, hoping he wouldn't ask her
to open it. Today he'd have no trouble seeing past the ice
princess to the very human woman underneath, and she
couldn't bear that, not when he might be in love with another woman—someone whom he adored far more than
her beautiful face and sexually enticing body. Marc might
pity his jealous wife, and that would be the greatest cruelty. Alone in this new land, her pride was all she had.

"Get dressed, *cher*. We'll go grab dinner—I'll introduce you to the best jambalaya in town."

Her husband's voice held infinite gentleness. After
the way he'd tamed her last night, he probably felt as if
he could be gentle, for what weapons did a woman so
capably taken have?

"I do not wish to." Even to herself she sounded as
welcoming as winter frost. It was the only way she
knew to protect herself, the only way she'd ever been
able to bear her father's treatment of her mother and dis-
missal of her own dreams.

Silence from the other side. Then a short, "Suit yourself. Don't wait up," he added sardonically.

Ten minutes later when she heard him drive away,
she suddenly realized how she could find out the truth.
Her husband was *always* out on a Wednesday and Sunday. Tomorrow was Wednesday and to her knowledge
Marc wasn't planning on going into his city office.

* * *

At around four the next afternoon, Hira sat behind the steering wheel of the sleek sports car Marc had given her, wishing it were any color but cherry red. She'd told her husband she was going for a drive, but instead she was hiding behind a curve in the road, her ears straining for the sound of his truck. It was shameful but she was going to follow her husband.

Perhaps if he'd come to her upon returning home, she might have broken down and confronted him. But when he'd come through the front door late last night, he'd stalked into the master suite without pausing. She'd thought that despite his dictate that she share his bed, he hadn't cared enough to search her out.

Inexplicably hurt, she'd lain awake for hours, missing him and thinking about the other woman who was keeping him satisfied. But if she were to be honest, her pain had been filled with a great amount of anger. It was that anger that had given her the courage to do what she was about to undertake.

Anger *and* frustration, for her stubborn husband had come to her last night, deep in the darkest hours when her defenses had all been down. He'd aroused her body, had her whimpering even before she'd fully wakened. Then he'd taken her, storming her senses with fierce purpose.

There hadn't been anger in his touch, but something far more dangerous—a possessive surety that indicated he viewed her as belonging to him, a situation he'd never allow to change. He'd driven her to erotic ecstasy and then he'd started over, giving her another look at the wild male underneath the civilized man. As far as that hunter was concerned, she was *his*. Full stop. End of story.

By the time he'd finished with her, she'd been so exhausted with pleasure she hadn't been able to speak. She'd barely registered the fact that he'd carried her to the master suite, hauling her possessively close to his side. This morning he'd wakened her with that same intense hunger, watching her go over the edge, allowing her to hold nothing back.

Though she'd felt the raging desire in him, his steely control hadn't broken. That control had hurt her already bruised heart—she'd thought them equal in their desire for each other. Yet he'd given her no chance to seduce him, controlling their sensual dance till the end.

A throaty rumble sounded. Mouth suddenly as dry as dust, she started her own engine and crept around the corner. Marc was just turning right. Swallowing, she followed. As the immediate area around their property was trafficless, she had to hang back until his car cleared each tree-lined curve. After more than ten nerve-racking minutes, they entered a comparatively busier area, but given her distinctive car she knew she couldn't chance getting closer.

Strung taut with nervous tension, she lost track of time as they drove out of their isolated patch of bayou country and north toward Lafayette. For a while they hugged the Vermillion River, but soon even that landmark disappeared, leaving her solely reliant on following Marc.

Relief came as they headed into Lafayette proper. Marc remained on the outskirts of the city, near a large park, but the streets were busy enough to allow her a chance to relax from the constant fear of being spotted. It helped that not a single road in this place seemed to go in a straight line.

The last five minutes of the journey were the most difficult. Because the streets were quiet and contained many turnoffs, she had to stick closer than she liked or lose her line of sight. But at last he turned into the drive of a large house.

She parked her car a few doors down, behind a black van, her eyes drawn to the house. Children's toys lay here and there in the yard, and a swing set was just visible on the other side. Her hands squeezed the steering wheel and she almost forgot to breathe as it hit her that he might have children. In her pain over the flowers, she'd forgotten the receipt for clothing from a boys store.

When she finally dared to walk down the street to look at the faded sign near the gate, she was startled to see the words Our Lady of Hope Orphanage for Boys.

An orphanage?

Mind in turmoil, she returned to the car. It appeared that her aloof husband wasn't meeting another woman, but what was his connection with an orphanage? And why had he kept it secret from her? Turning the key, she went to start the car. A big male hand reached inside and jerked it out.

Crying out, she whirled around and looked into the furious face of her husband. "Marc!"

"Get out!" He pulled open the door.

She obeyed, shaken by the visible rage on his face. Once she was standing in front of him, she didn't speak, waiting for his words. And his punishment. From what she knew of men she didn't believe he'd let her go this time without trying to humiliate her pride.

"You think I didn't see you following me?" he demanded, eyes glittering. "What kind of game are you playing?"

"I thought you were meeting another woman," she admitted, her throat dry. She'd never seen him this openly furious, this out of control.

He seemed to get even angrier. "You want to see what I'm doing? Then come with me. Let's see what happens when you're faced with something that's not so pretty and pampered like the rest of your life, princess."

She didn't point out that she was only pampered because he wanted it that way. *He'd* been the one to set up accounts for her at the most exclusive boutiques, the most expensive stylists, as if she were an accessory that needed to be polished, she thought with a stabbing pain inside her stomach. Well, she'd always known where her worth lay. And she'd walked into this relationship with her eyes wide open. It did no good to rail at fate.

Now instead of arguing she went with him, the full skirt of her sunny-yellow dress whispering around her ankles. He tugged her up the stairs of the orphanage and pulled her inside the run-down building. An old man looked up from a desk in a room just off the entrance… A room that held a huge vase of wildflowers.

"Father Thomas." Marc's tone conveyed the deepest respect. "This is my wife, Hira."

The man smiled and stood. "My dear, it's lovely to finally meet you." Father Thomas walked over to the doorway and held out his hands.

Though Zulheil's ways were ancient and unlike those of her new home, there was such wisdom and peace in this man's faded-blue eyes, Hira knew he was close to divine grace. Awed, she went to him and bent down so he could kiss her cheeks. The hands that held her own were wrapped in papery-thin skin, but as strong as a young man's.

"I am honored, elder." She gave him the honorific of her land, wishing she wasn't wearing a sundress. In Zulheil, respect would demand formal clothing for such a meeting. Some of the old ways were worth following.

He chuckled. "You are a lovely young woman. A gentle soul."

The compliment brought tears to her eyes, for despite his ability to pinpoint their location, she could see that he was almost blind. This man *saw* Hira, not just the face and the body that were her trappings.

"You've done well, my son. I suppose you want to show her off to the boys. Off you go, daughter. I expect to see a lot more of you."

Hira smiled, feeling more warmth from this frail old man than she ever had from her own father. "You will." She turned and let Marc lead her away, leaving the elder to his ruminations.

The second they were out of earshot, he said in a cutting whisper, "Good performance, babe, but the boys won't be fooled so easily." Suddenly he paused. "Damn it, what the hell was I thinking? I shouldn't have brought you here—they've suffered enough." The bitterness in his tone startled her. "It's too late now. *Don't hurt them.*"

Before she could ask him to explain the deep and uncompromising care she heard in his tone, they walked into a large kitchen. Ten boys of different ages, from a skinny five-year-old to a gangly youth of about fourteen, appeared to be trying to cook. Flour had turned the floor white but it was the childish laughter and the joy on their faces that held her attention. Then they saw her.

And the laughter died.

Six

"**B**oys, this is my wife, Hira." Marc's tone held no hint of anger but she could almost feel his tension.

Immediately Hira was aware of the wariness in the boys' eyes. "I'm pleased to meet you." She smiled, but there was no response, not even from the youngest of them all.

She didn't panic, conscious that they had no reason to trust her, but even so, she was at peace. She adored children and they'd always been her friends when older women had rejected her. Children didn't judge a person on anything but their heart.

Ignoring the flour that dusted the floor, she knelt down in front of the youngest. "What is your name, *laeha?*"

His eyes widened at being singled out, but he didn't look away. "Brian." It was a whisper.

"And what are you cooking, Brian?" He was so thin, she wanted to put him in her lap and feed him.

"Apple pie...for dessert."

"I have never eaten apple pie," she admitted.

Someone gasped. "Never?"

She rose to her full height. "I'm not from America. Your apple pie is not made in my homeland."

"Where are you from, then?" another boy asked.

She looked across at the dark-haired child. "Zulheil. It is a desert land. I find your, uh, Cajun Country too green. There are growing things everywhere." It still disconcerted her that flowers bloomed in the grass. She kept trying to avoid stepping on them, for flowers were precious in the desert.

A bespectacled boy gave her a tiny smile. "I read about Zulheil on the Internet. You look like the pictures of the people, but you're dressed different."

"I am trying to... Husband, what is the word?" She glanced over her shoulder, wondering who'd hurt her Marc so very much that he couldn't find it in his heart to trust her with his secrets. Secrets like why these orphans meant so much to him.

"What?" He looked like an immovable wall, arms crossed over his chest and eyes narrowed watchfully.

She smiled at him, treating him with the same gentleness as the children—she was beginning to see that he carried scars on the inside just like these wary babes. "For trying to fit in here?"

His eyes narrowed farther. "Blend."

"Yes." A smile broke out in her heart at his warning glare. Teasing her arrogant husband could be fun. "I've been trying to blend in. Do you think I will succeed?"

she asked the children, once more turning her back on Marc.

Yet she could feel his presence like a physical touch, the tiny hairs on her nape standing to attention at his nearness. Her husband had branded her with his mark and her body knew it. She just had to keep him from finding out. The minute he discovered just how vulnerable she was to him, he'd stalk in and take full advantage. She wasn't ready to allow that, not while he refused to share the most important pieces of his self with her.

The bespectacled boy shook his head. "You're too pretty and you talk different."

She made a face at him, at ease with his honesty about her looks whereas adult comments made her bristle. "I do not wish to be the same as everyone else, anyway. Do you?"

He thought that over. As he did, she saw that though he was small, he appeared to be the leader of this troop. "No," he finally said. "Only pod people are all the same."

Confused, she looked to Marc for help. "Pod people?"

But it was the tall boy who answered, "Have you got a lot to learn! We're watching that movie *again* tonight because Damian can't get enough. You can watch, too."

"I have no idea what you are talking about, but I agree to watch this with you." Hira laughed at the grin that crossed the tall one's shy face. "So how do you make this apple pie? There must be flour on the floor, yes?"

At that, everyone but her stubborn-male of a husband laughed. When little Brian's hand slipped into hers, she picked him up and set him on her hip, uncaring of the flour and little-boy dirt on him.

Unable to stifle her concern and unwilling to do so, she asked, "Do you not eat, *laeha?*"

He wrapped skinny arms around her neck and laid his head down on her shoulder. "I'm sick. What is a *laeha?*"

Stroking his back, she said, "It means darling child." The literal translation was darling baby but she had a feeling that none of these boys would appreciate knowing that. Walking over to the bench, she saw the somewhat abused-looking dough. "I will make this apple pie with you. I saw it once on a television show. They had ice cream with it."

A groan from behind her. "Don't you go putting ideas in their heads."

Delighted to have provoked a reaction from Marc, she opened her mouth to respond. The boys beat her to it.

"Too late. Ice cream sounds good," a voice piped up.

"Yeah, yeah. Who wants to go with me to the store?" There were two volunteers.

"Husband, can you also bring back almonds?" She thought and then added cinnamon and cardamom to the list. "And also vermicelli."

He didn't ask her why she wanted the odd ingredients. "Sure. We'll be back soon." His eyes turned flinty and focused on the boys around her. "Don't eat my wife."

The drawling warning made Hira scowl. "These lovely children won't hurt me. You must not say such things."

He just raised his brow. After the door closed behind him, she turned to the remaining boys. "My husband believes you will behave like wild camels while he is gone. I wish to make him…"

"Eat his words?" said Damian.

"What does that mean?"

"Prove him wrong."

"Yes." She nodded. "Yes. He's always right. It's most annoying. Let us prove him wrong."

They grinned at her. And she knew the little devils were well aware she liked them. In her arms, Brian wriggled and settled in more firmly. She saw a few of the boys' eyes go to the littlest boy in hunger. So, she thought, they were not cuddled much.

Her husband likely gave them his strength but wasn't much of a cuddler. Even in bed he rarely gave the comfort of simply being held. Starved for it herself, she knew how much it meant to be touched in simple affection. Reaching out to the boy closest to her, she ruffled his hair. He didn't move away as most children his age would have.

His eyes looked into hers, too old in that young face. "You must be okay if Marc married you."

Ah, she thought, understanding their willingness to trust her. "Or I could be as the dragon in the tale of the 'Secret Princess.'" Her big, brooding husband might be a most unaccommodating male, but he'd done something good here, given these boys a sense of safety in what was undoubtedly a shifting world.

For that she could forgive him his secrets, give him the time he needed to learn to trust her. Like these children, his guard would only drop when he was certain of her, when he was convinced that she was *his*...body and soul. Where that certainty came from, she didn't know.

"Huh?"

She dragged her mind away from Marc. "It is a story

of my homeland, of a princess who was also a dragon. I will tell you this if you show me how to make apple pie."

It took a few more minutes of tantalizing bits from the story, but she soon had them hooked. One boy swept the floor clean, and then they showed her how to make apple pie. Brian fell asleep in her arms sometime during the story. Damian offered to take him from her.

"No, I wish to hold him." She smiled at him, thanking him for his concern. "He's so very light, I worry."

"He's sick a lot. I think he misses Becky."

"Becky?"

"His twin. When their ma and pa died, they put Brian here and Becky in some girls orphanage," Damian explained.

"But that is wrong! In Zulheil, it's said that two who are born together are each other's heart. They are not to be torn apart." No wonder the boy was so frail.

"Marc's doing something to help him."

Hira thought to ask her husband about this later. For the moment she'd enjoy the children's honest company, and try not to think about the depths of tenderness this place revealed about the dark and moody man she'd married and was only now beginning to know.

Marc returned with Larry and Jake, carrying six containers of ice cream. What the boys didn't eat today would be savored later. He expected to find the kitchen in chaos, his princess overwhelmed by these tough kids who'd known more hurt than humanly bearable and yet had survived.

When he'd realized that she was following him, he'd let his temper drive him into a situation that could mean terrible pain for those who least deserved it. Furious at her lack of trust in him, he'd reacted without thought, a strange experience for a man known in business circles as having a will of iron and a heart of ice.

He hoped he hadn't damaged the boys' trust in him by leaving them with a woman who could destroy with one scathing comment. To her credit, she'd never disparaged either his scars or his background as a dirt-grubbing child, but even after he'd loved her this morning, her eyes had looked at him with such distance that he'd felt taunted into trying to tame her.

He'd wanted to rub off some of that aloof sophistication and find out if there really was a living, breathing woman beneath the ice. He didn't want her to be only a beautiful shell who could shut off her emotions as easily as she'd shut him out of her bedroom last night. *But,* a part of him whispered, *she hadn't locked the door.* And he'd taken full advantage of that lapse.

"Let's hope for the best," he muttered to himself, shouldering through the swinging door.

He walked into a kitchen filled with laughter. Little Brian was fast asleep in his wife's arms, and tall and shy Beau was blushing but trying to tease her about something. The other children were gathered around her.

She had flour on her nose and elbows. There was a streak of dirt on her designer yellow dress from Brian's shoe, and handprints on her skirts from other little hands. She'd begun the afternoon with her hair pinned on top of her head, but Brian had pulled strands loose. She looked disheveled and messy, and her face was full of such joy that his heart stopped for a minute. Lord, she was beautiful when she was all prettied up; messy and with a child in her arms, she was devastating.

Painful tenderness cramped his heart. His hands froze around the bags he held. This was no ice princess. Despite all the times her facade had cracked, how had he failed to spot the truth about his wife?

"What's so funny?" One of his ice cream helpers asked.

Damian looked over. "Hira's been telling us stories."

"Oh, man! We missed it," Larry grumbled.

"Don't worry, I'll tell more."

Marc couldn't believe the way she had them all in the palm of her hand. As the late afternoon progressed into evening, he expected her to wilt under the emotional demands of the attention-starved boys, but she seemed to glow. Much later, after dinner and the supervised completion of various pieces of homework, they sat down to watch the first hour of a video, a midweek treat the boys only got for good behavior.

However, it quickly became clear that they weren't enjoying it. Despite the nonchalance they tried to portray, they were very worried about Brian. Once again he'd barely eaten anything. After settling the boys down, Hira went into the kitchen and made something with milk, sugar and the other ingredients she'd asked him to buy. Cuddling Brian into her lap on her return, she lifted a spoonful of the mixture to his mouth, her other arm holding him carefully.

"Come, *laeha,* you must eat this. I have made it just for you," she coaxed, her voice holding the exotic music of a faraway land of desert and sunshine.

The sad-faced little boy opened his mouth and let her feed him a spoonful. His eyes widened. When a second spoonful was raised, he made no protest. Carefully, while the other boys ostensibly watched their movie, she managed to get a whole bowl of the rich mixture into Brian.

Drowsy after eating, he snuggled into her body and fell asleep again, his thumb in his mouth. The habit had developed after the traumatic separation from his twin.

Marc took the bowl and spoon from his wife, his chest tight with pride. "Thank you."

Worried eyes met his. "He is too small."

"I know, *cher*," he whispered. "I'm trying to find his sister." He touched her hair once and then walked into the kitchen, finding that she'd made more of the sweet treat than had been needed for Brian. Deciding the rest of the boys would like a taste, he took out small servings. "Here, extra dessert thanks to my wife."

Soon, sighs of repletion sounded around the room. When he looked to see how Hira was taking this, he found her fast asleep, Brian's head cushioned on her breasts. In sleep, his princess looked as guileless as the child lying trustingly against her body. If he only knew which face—the sophisticate or the innocent—was her true self, he might have a way to understand the woman he'd married.

Hira woke when Marc took Brian from her. "We are leaving?" she asked, rubbing at her eyes.

He nodded. "The others have gone to bed. They said good-night and come back soon." His eyes looked at her with a gentleness she couldn't understand.

While he carried the sleeping boy upstairs, she went to the kitchen to tidy up, only to find it sparkling clean. Smiling, she located the shoes she'd kicked off, and stepped into them. When she went to say goodbye to the elder, it was to find the study disappointingly empty.

A big hand came to rest on her hip. "Father Thomas didn't want to disturb you when he went to bed."

She turned to look up at her husband, feeling drowsy and happily tired. "He is a nice man."

Marc pressed a kiss to her forehead. It was so far from his usual passion, so tender that she just stared.

He chuckled at her dazed expression. "You are not driving home. I've moved your car to the parking lot behind the orphanage. We'll get it later."

Nodding, she let him lead her out to his truck.

The drive home went quickly because she was exhausted. The next time she woke, it was to find Marc carrying her up the stairs to their bedroom. When she blinked and pushed at his shoulders, amused gray eyes looked down at her.

"Did I sleep?"

His grin was bright in the warm light of the small lamps he'd apparently switched on, on his way up. "You dozed off against my shoulder, just like Brian did on you."

She yawned and then, without thinking about it, snuggled her face against his neck and went back to sleep. She was vaguely aware of him undressing her and laying her down on their bed. He didn't put her nightgown on her, but she'd expected that. But, though he slipped in naked beside her, he didn't do more than hold her tight.

"Sleep, princess." A kiss on the pulse in her neck.

He was cuddling her, she thought, smiling into dreams that were soft and pleasant. It was nice to be cuddled by an American hunter who was pleased with you.

* * *

The next day Hira went in search of her husband, feeling confident enough to ask him for something that was important to her. Unless she'd imagined his tenderness of the night before, Marc had changed his mind about her. Her heart bloomed with joy. Perhaps, after seeing her with the children, he no longer thought of her as a spoiled "princess" but a woman with a heart.

Once more she found him the backyard, chopping wood. But this time a slow, seductive smile eased her passage to him. "Good morning." His eyes ran down her demure mint-green top and skirt, made in the way of her homeland. There was definite male approval in his gaze.

"Good morning." She felt herself blush with sudden shyness. "Why do you chop wood when a fire does not appear to be required in this area?" she asked, trying to ground herself with mundane matters.

His eyes seemed to brighten. "I prefer it to lifting weights. I give the wood away to the people who need it." His eyes flicked toward the bayou.

"Oh. I understand." Her husband was a man with a big heart, she thought, trying to stop twisting her hands in front of her. "I wish to ask you for something."

He slammed the ax into the tree stump and faced her, hands on hips. The ridged musculature of his abdomen held her spellbound for an instant. She knew exactly what those muscles felt like under her hands. "Shoot."

Alarm rocketed through her. Did he think she was a violent woman? "Why would I want to?"

She could tell he was biting back a smile. "I didn't mean literally, princess. It's a figure of speech. It means, go ahead, speak what's on your mind."

"You Americans are very strange." She looked down at the ground rather than the magnificent expanse of her husband's chest. "I wish to pursue some studies."

"You want to take some classes? Pottery or something to occupy your time? That's fine with me."

She told herself she'd imagined the patronizing tone of his voice. Surely, after everything, he didn't still see her as a pretty toy? "I wish to study management theory and economics. There are classes in those subjects taught at the University of Louisiana in Lafayette.

"And since this is my new home, I thought I would also take advantage of the Center for Louisiana Studies and learn about Acadian culture."

Her husband's bark of laughter had her jerking her head up. "Sure, princess."

"Why are you laughing?" She couldn't bear to be laughed at, especially by this man who was so smart and loyal to the people whom he'd taken under his wing.

His smile faded. "You expect me to take that request seriously?" He shoved a hand through his hair. "Honey, I know you're intelligent. I said I'd never stop you learning and I won't, but to be honest, I don't think you're up to the rigors of intensive study. You were raised to be a pampered wife, not an academic."

She should have been glad that he wouldn't stand in the way of her dreams. Instead she found she wanted not only his permission but also his support. "I'm more than just smart. I'm determined," she insisted. "These things come to me naturally. I helped my older brother many times when he was stuck, but we didn't tell our father for he would've punished Fariz for asking my help."

"Look, I said it's fine. Send the bills to me."

He was already turning away from her, *dismissing her.*
Rage choked her throat, blinded her vision, as years and
years of being ground under a male's boot took its toll.

A small hand pushed at Marc's chest, forcing his attention back to the woman in front of him. He expected
to find her in a feminine sulk because he hadn't immediately supported her sudden desire to study seriously.
If she'd wanted it that much, she could've pursued it in
Zulheil, which had a world-class university and no re-
strictions on the entry of female students. There were
also any number of scholarships she could've applied
for if her family hadn't wanted to finance her.

He didn't see what he'd expected. Hira was standing
there, her hands clenched at her sides. Fury vibrated
through her entire body. She was like a high-tension
wire strung as taut as it could possibly be and not snap.

"You are a…horrible man! You hurt me and do not
even care to say sorry!" Pure anger sparked in those
stunning eyes. "You don't care to get to know me. I'm
just some toy to you, like o-one of those windup things
that children play with.

"Look," she said, imitating the voice of an infomer-
cial presenter, her face strained white, "push this button and pretty little Hira will shatter from the pleasure
of your touch, then touch this lever and she'll return to
her place as a stupid, polished toy with no more brains
than a vegetable!"

He was frozen. This wasn't the calm, composed princess he was used to seeing. This woman looked as if her
heart had broken, and she spoke to him with bluntness
that sent him reeling.

Seven

His wife turned on her heel and stumbled. Reaching out, he grabbed the backs of her arms, stunned to find fine tremors shaking her entire body.

"Let me go. *Let me go,*" she repeated softly. "Just… let me go." Her voice hitched as she lost the battle with her tears.

Deep inside, where nothing was supposed to reach, a lost part of him found its way to the light. "Don't cry, Hira. Please, don't cry." He pulled her trembling body back against his chest, his chin on her hair, his arms around her waist. "I'm sorry. Hush, *cher*. Hush." Emotion brought the boy who'd roamed the bayou back to the surface.

She sniffed, keeping her back to his chest. "What do you always call me? Is it a bad word?"

He found himself smiling. "No. It's an endearment."

One that he found himself saying more and more, when he'd never been a man who threw the word around, charming women and breaking hearts.

"Why are you being nice?"

The question rocked him. "Am I not nice to you?"

"No." Bluntness again. "You treat me like... What is the word that Damian used yesterday to Larry?" She raised her hands and he could tell she was furiously wiping her eyes. "Yes, you treat me as if I am a nitwit." She sounded very proud at remembering that derogatory term.

"You send me shopping so I'll be out of your way while you do real work, and you get your secretary to make me appointments at these beauty salons where I'm so bored I complete all the crossword puzzles in every one of their silly magazines."

He winced because she was right. He'd asked his secretary to arrange outings for her so that he could work in peace and quiet at home. The strange thing was, he'd found himself missing her. When she was home, he tended to go searching for her. That realization made him take a hard look at his actions. Was that why he'd sent her out? So he could pretend he wasn't falling for her?

"You have my most humble apologies if you think I treated you like a nitwit." He turned her in his arms and she came, though the face that looked up at him was defiant. "I don't think that of you."

She narrowed her eyes. "Perhaps."

There would be no easy acceptance of his apology from this woman. Marc found he didn't mind. He didn't want a wife who hid her emotions the way Hira's mother did to placate her husband. "What can I do to make it up to you?"

He knew that if he didn't fix things now, his wife would sublimate her pain and anger just like Amira, and he'd lose a piece of her. Tomorrow she'd be gracious and forgiving, and all the while she'd be living her own life in her thoughts and dreams, a life that he'd never again be invited to share. He didn't want that. He wanted *all* of her—spirit and soul, passion and heart.

"Nothing." She squared her shoulders. "I need nothing from you, husband."

His temper ignited, overwhelming the remorse. He was suddenly furiously angry at the way she refused to give him any rights over her, as if he weren't good enough. As if he should beg for her attention. She was treating him like another beautiful woman had a lifetime ago, and he'd had enough, more than enough.

"Except my money, you mean," he taunted. "If I wasn't keeping you in the style to which you're accustomed, you'd be out on the street."

This time there were no tears. Hira's face paled under that golden skin and then she whispered, "And you say you are nice to me? I'm alone and without family in this land. You know I have no one and so you can say these things."

His gut roiled, the burst of anger buried under an avalanche of self-hatred. "Hira…"

She kept talking. "I thought, maybe, you were a good man but you are just like my father."

He bristled. "I'm nothing like that tyrant."

"My mother always had to beg him for money." She damned him with those exotic eyes. "Oh, she was given expensive clothes and jewels. Father made sure they were delivered to her like clockwork. We had to keep up the—what is the word—yes, *image*.... We had to keep up the image of the rich merchant."

Marc just stood there, letting her talk in that soft voice that was so unlike the vivid woman he'd come to know, feeling more and more despicable with every word she spoke. Until he'd married, he hadn't known he had such a volatile temper. No one else had ever made him angry enough to be cruel.

"But she had to ask him for every cent if she ever needed spending money or money to buy her children gifts, or even to go out to have lunch with a friend. Because of their uniqueness, she couldn't sell the jewels without destroying the reputation of the family, so she was dependant on him." Her eyes were distant and pain filled, as if she were reliving the humiliation her mother had gone through day after day.

"He'd sit in his study chair like a pasha and have her stand there like a supplicant, with no rights. He'd make her beg for money as if it was not her entitlement as his wife, who worked so hard to make his life agreeable. As if she hadn't borne him three children, even though she was a fragile woman whom the doctors had advised to stop with only one." Sadness filled every word, ripping at his heart. "*And yet he made her beg.* Even the lowliest servant was ensured of his weekly wages but not my mother of her income." Her chest was heaving, the only sign of the anger she'd subsumed so well.

"Okay," he said. He'd never been a man who ran from the harsh reality of his own flaws.

"I don't understand." Her eyes remained wary, the haunted shade of a wild creature who'd been captured and was waiting for the pain to begin.

Guilt twisted like a knife inside of him. "I agree that I was a complete and utter jerk. There's no excuse for what I just said."

She seemed taken aback. "Why do you say this?"

He blew out a breath. "I wish to hell I didn't have a temper but I do. I'm as mean as the gators that roam the waters around here, and you got bit. But I can tell you that you aren't ever going to have to beg." The image of her proud spirit being crushed infuriated him.

The next time he went to Zulheil, he'd ensure that his mother-in-law had a separate account with enough funds in it to allow her to live in peace. He knew Amira wouldn't take the money from him but she'd accept a gift from Hira. Such a gift would likely rock the foundation of Marc's relationship with Kerim Dazirah, but he didn't give a damn.

He put his hands on his hips in an attempt to keep them off his wife. He wasn't much good at finding the words a woman needed to forgive a man, but when he touched his wife, she became his in the most raw sense of the word. And right now the temptation to make her his was almost unbearable. "An account was set up for you when we married and money transferred into it. Monthly payments will be made into it automatically."

"What is the money for?" she asked quietly. There was such fragile dignity in her that he knew she still expected to be hurt by him. And the hell of it was, he couldn't deny that he had hurt her, that she had a right to look so shell-shocked. But, damn it, he wanted to wipe that look off her face. He wasn't a saint but neither was he a man who enjoyed the suffering of others.

Especially not of his wife.

"It's yours to do with as you wish. Invest it, use it for your education, blow it in Vegas, whatever you like." He could tell Hira wasn't quite sure how to take this revelation.

"Why didn't you tell me earlier?" she asked.

"I forgot." The truth was, he'd liked paying the bills for his wife's purchases, liked the proprietariness of such an act. Liked knowing she *needed* him for something. "The documents for your bank account are in my office."

He began to walk to the house. She followed with barely a sound. Once in his study, he found the passbook and charge cards and handed them over.

She gasped when she saw the amount that had already been deposited. "Husband! This is far too much money." Her eyes were darker than he'd ever before seen.

He shrugged. "I'm very rich."

Putting the passbook and cards on his desk, she looked straight at him. "You must take it back."

"What? Why? I thought you'd appreciate the independence." He scowled.

She didn't back down. "I've done nothing to deserve it."

"You're my wife." A wife he wanted with more than simple lust. The way she'd held his boys, the way she'd laughed with them, the way she challenged him with her wit and her honesty, wasn't something he wanted to lose.

"And yet I do nothing that a wife does." She didn't break his gaze as she made that confession. "I don't run this house as it is run very well by the strangers who come in on schedule, do their silent cleaning and leave.

I don't help with your business. I am not the mother of your children." Her shoulders squared. "My mother isn't a strong woman, but she does many things to earn her income."

God, he thought, she was so proud and so very vulnerable because of it. His Hira, his *wife,* could be hurt by a well-placed barb that would strike her pride before anything else. Taking a deep breath, he made a decision that might either save his marriage or expose the cracks in the foundation to the bright light of day.

"And so will you. Things have been quiet on the business front since we married, but they're about to heat up." He frowned, thinking of one particular acquisition. "When negotiations take place in informal settings, such as this house, you'll act as a second pair of eyes, ears and even hands, for me.

"I'll expect you to know the finest of fine details and get me any information I request, ASAP. I won't cut you any slack just because you're my wife. I'll be demanding as hell and I won't tolerate any mistakes. Such negotiations are worth millions. Think you can handle that?"

The offer wasn't just a sop to her pride. A lot of deals were in fact completed here, away from the often virulent media interest. He'd never allowed anyone but himself to be privy to the final stages of those sensitive deals. Until now.

"You would trust me with this?" Nervous excitement glittered in her eyes, but her words were hesitant, as if she wasn't sure she could believe his offer.

"I may be a jerk but I'm not stupid. Not only are you too proud to ever betray my confidence, you're a very intelligent woman." He knew that, had known it almost from the day they'd married, so why had he hurt her like that outside?

Was he afraid that she'd discover a tempting new world of academic grace and forget her bayou beast of a husband? Despite his wealth, he'd never quite lost the rough edges of his upbringing, but until he'd married Hira, he hadn't given any thought to them. Yet lately he'd begun to wonder if his lack of refinement was one of the reasons his wife maintained her emotional distance.

Shock that his motivations might be rooted in jealousy and fear made him curse himself in self-disgust. He'd crawled up so far, and yet he was still the boy who'd pressed his nose against the windows of the Barnsworthy house and declared that one day he'd be on the other side of the glass. That boy had believed that once you had something, you clutched at it with all your strength. Setting something free only meant you'd lose it for good.

"You'll have to prove yourself with your studies," he continued, fighting the clutching fingers of that abused and lonely boy, "but that's something every student has to prove. I've never seen your work, so I can't judge how you'll do. I'm sorry I tried to do that outside."

Slowly she nodded. "Withholding your judgment is not a terrible thing, for you have no knowledge of my skills. I can see how you would worry that I might not understand these subjects, but I'll show you otherwise."

He nodded, belatedly becoming aware of the steel spine beneath that delicate golden skin. Perhaps he could chance trusting her with something far closer to his heart than a business deal. "The orphanage is pretty run-down."

She adjusted to the change of topic with ease. "Yes. There isn't much room for growing boys."

"No." He perched on the edge of the desk, trying to make himself less threatening to his wife. If he tried, maybe she'd approach him, even after he'd hurt her. It was a bitter pill to swallow for a man who'd never relied on anyone, but he accepted that he needed more than hot sex from his wife. He needed tenderness, the one thing he could never ask for. Especially not after the way he'd let his temper rip into her. "In a few months, this house will be remodeled and made much larger, large enough to fit all of them."

Her eyes widened, but she remained silent.

"I don't want the boys institutionalized. I want to create a home for them." He gave her a wry smile. "But there will be a very large private wing for us. With soundproofing."

Her responding smile was shaky. "What will happen to other orphan boys?"

"I can't save every orphan in the world, but I can save these ten. And Becky, too, soon as we find her." He wanted to ask her what she thought of his plans, his dreams, but kept talking. "The old orphanage is going to close at the end of this year, to be replaced by a modern facility. I'll be funding that, but Beau, Damian, Brian and all the others are to be mine. The legal process is almost complete."

As he watched, his wife covered the distance between them in graceful strides and wrapped her arms tightly around his neck. Hardly believing, he embraced her slender length, luxuriating in the feel of her warmth against the skin of his shoulders and neck. Her exotic scent teased his nostrils and threatened to bring the more primitive side of his nature to the surface.

"So you don't mind mothering ten boys and one girl?" he asked, breathing in the freshness and sweetness of her. Lord, he needed this woman he kept catching fleeting glimpses of. The feeling of vulnerability rocked him but wasn't strong enough to make him release her. "I'll be hiring several full-time helpers, so if you're not comfortable with the idea, you can—"

Drawing back, she placed a finger on his lips, her smile bright. "I always wished for many children, but my mother had difficulty with birthing, so I thought I'd only have one or two if I was very lucky. Thank you for blessing me with such a great gift, husband."

Stunned, he remembered his cutting words to her on their wedding night. He'd never thought of her as maternal and then realized what a fool he'd been. What woman who didn't adore children would've won the trust of the boys so quickly? "Will it be dangerous for you to have children?" Keeping one arm wrapped around her back, he placed the palm of the other against her stomach.

Her eyes widened at the openly possessive action. "The doctors my mother took me to after I was old enough to understand the reason for her worry, told me that I should be safe but not to strain my body beyond two children."

He rotated his hand on her abdomen. He'd barely begun to understand her and already he could imagine her big with his babe. Lifting his head, he found those exotic eyes staring into his. Taking a chance that he'd won some forgiveness for his earlier burst of temper, he leaned in close and when she didn't move, brushed his lips over hers.

Electricity sizzled between them. On his shoulders, her fingers clenched convulsively. Groaning, he deepened the kiss and tasted the uniqueness that was Hira. She was a mix of sugar and spice, fire and ice, his desert beauty. Before he could prolong the contact, she'd pushed off his chest and was a foot away.

Startled, he looked up into a pink-cheeked face, wondering if he'd misread her, if she hadn't welcomed his touch. His gut twisted. As he watched helplessly, his wife raised her hands to her face and gave him a look that was a mix of shocked innocence and sheer desire. When he moved, she swirled on her heel and left the room.

Marc began to chuckle, his tenseness retreating. Hira had just discovered that he could turn her on even when she was steamed with him. He whistled. If he had that to work with, he'd eventually get his way. And his way involved long, sultry nights spent cradled in his wife's body.

He must've done something right because that was exactly how he spent the hours of darkness that night.

When he surfaced the next morning, the clock told him it was close to dawn. Hira was lying on her stomach, using one of his arms as a pillow. His leg and other arm were flung over her, as if even in sleep, she captivated him. He watched her sleep, stunned at himself for doing it. It betrayed a commitment beyond anything he'd ever before experienced.

He'd spent most of his childhood as a kid without any loving ties. As an adult he'd kept that cloak of aloneness wrapped around him...until the night he'd seen

Hira Dazirah on the balcony of her desert home, smiling up at the moon. Right then and there he'd fallen so hard and fast he'd had to have her. He'd been tied to her with passion's reins since that first moment, but yesterday something stronger had snapped into place between them, something born out of their willingness to fight rather than withdraw into silence. He was a little bewildered by the gentle strength of this feeling but could find no reason to fight it.

As if she'd been disturbed by his watching her, her eyes blinked open and she yawned. For a while, she lay there and watched him back, sleepy and apparently happy to be in the position she was in. Then one slender hand lifted to stroke his cheek.

"You appear sad, Marc. Husband." Her lips curved in a soft smile. "May I do something for you to give you joy?"

Her generous offer made his chest tight. No one had ever offered to do something for the simple reason of making him happy. "No, baby. I'm okay."

When he moved his leg off her, she rose up on one elbow and touched his cheek again. "Husband, tell me something of your childhood."

He couldn't help playing with the silken strands of her midnight-and-gold hair. "Why do you want to know?"

"It is said that the child will show you the man." She kissed his chin, the movement causing the strands in his fingers to slide away. Last night she'd been all woman, pure heat and passion. Later, when he'd tried to move away, she'd held on. He'd understood the silent message. His lover needed more than ecstasy. So he, a man who'd never been accused of tenderness, had spent the night happily holding his wife as she slept.

"You're a hard man to know so I would learn of you from your childhood."

"Did you ever learn to lie, *cher?*" Folding one arm behind his head, he ran the other down the warm curve of her back, lingering on the upward slope of her buttocks. When she didn't protest, he ran his hand back up and then down again, indulging his sense of touch.

Hira nodded vigorously in response to his question and didn't sound the least repentant when she said, "I told my father many lies."

He raised a brow.

"Like when he asked me whether I had told the housekeeper to give away Fariz's old computer. I told him I had." She propped herself up on her elbows, face cupped between loose fists.

"But?"

"But I kept it hidden in my room. He never came in there. Rayaz was young and spoiled, but Fariz wasn't a bad brother. He didn't ever tell Father my secret. He even used to lend me his software."

Marc frowned. "Don't females have the same educational rights as males in Zulheil?"

"Of course. My compulsory schooling was given to me, but after that…my father didn't believe in wasting college fees on a female who would simply be a pretty thing in her husband's home." She shrugged as if it hadn't mattered, though he knew it must've broken her heart.

"Why didn't you complain?"

"It would've shamed my entire clan. The Dazirah family is proud, but we're part of an even prouder clan. The clan is supposed to protect each member within it.

To speak out would've been to say that they had failed in their duty."

"They did fail." His voice was hard. Protecting the vulnerable was the one thing he'd never compromise on.

"Yes, but they had many successes. Last year they sent several students, male and female, to learn advanced mechanical engineering in Britain. If I had spoken out, their honor would've fallen in a land where honor is everything." She gave him a smile full of maturity. "Those who gave the educational fund assistance would've sent their money elsewhere. Now, say to me that a single woman's unhappiness is worth destroying the dreams of many."

He could see her point. "Was there no one you could've asked for help?" How could someone so bright and beautiful, someone with such a gentle heart, have spent a lifetime alone?

Her smile was tight. "I wasn't popular at school or with my cousins once I was no longer a child. They didn't want me near their boyfriends and lovers. The only girls who might've been my friends were the beauties who had no interest in study, and I couldn't bear to pretend to be like them. So there was no one." She paused, as if debating whether to share something else.

When she spoke, what she said sent spikes of temper arcing through his body. "The boys wished to be friendly with me but even the smart ones could never just be content to be my friends. They all wanted more."

"Did they—?" he began, his eyes locked on hers.

She shook her head almost immediately. "I stopped building friendships with boys very young, before they were old enough to try and do more than steal a kiss.

So the boys liked me too much and the girls not at all."
She was attempting to make a joke out of what must
have been some very painful years.

He could imagine that lonely girl learning to become
ice to survive the exclusions, the whispers behind her
back. "There is someone now. You'll tell me everything."

"Yes, husband." Her voice was meek.

He frowned. "Are you laughing at me?"

"Only a little." Her eyes lit up.

It was an effort to keep his lips straight—she didn't
need any encouragement. Pulling her head down, he
kissed her. "So, princess, you want to know about your
bayou brat?" he said, against those luscious lips that
made him want to bite. Deciding there was no reason
to resist, he gently nibbled on her lower lip.

"Why do you call yourself that?" she asked when he
released her, her voice breathless.

"Because it's true. I grew up in the bayou, living in
a shack that barely held together when the waters rose.
My parents were both alcoholics who didn't give a
damn about me, so long as they had enough money for
booze."

"And if they didn't?"

He could still remember the blows, the pain and the
darkness. "They amused themselves by knocking me
around."

Hira made a sound of distress.

He soothed her with his hands and his voice. "It was
okay. I could run pretty fast so I usually just hid out until
they were drunk again."

Gentle feminine fingers traced a scar on his chest, so
tender that the touch felt like the brush of a butterfly's

wings. He should've been amused that she thought she might hurt him. Instead, his heart thundered as a hint of some powerful understanding hovered just over the edge of his horizon.

"You didn't get these because you were a fast runner. They hurt you badly." Her eyes dared him to explain the scars away. This woman he'd married wouldn't be soothed so easily when someone she cared for was hurt.

It took him a moment to overcome his astonishment at the realization that both his wife's words and her careful touch arose from a belief that he was hers. He wanted to force her to tell him how strong Beauty's care was for her Beast of a husband, but restrained himself, unwilling to destroy the fragility of their new accord.

Instead he contented himself with answering her question, telling her something very few people knew. Her unhidden expression of care deserved to be rewarded with honesty. "Actually, I did get them for being a fast runner." He made a wry face. "When I was about seven, they were desperate for money. So they sold me."

Eight

Hira jerked up into a sitting position, holding the sheet to her breast. "People cannot be sold! Not in my country and not in yours."

He ran a hand up her arm, undone by her distress. "It wasn't so bad. You can imagine the kinds of things a depraved mind could do to a child."

She nodded, her face lined with worry. "I know."

His protective instincts urged him to change that look, to take the pain away from her. "Well, nothing like that happened to me. The reason Muddy offered money for me was that I could run like the wind. Thieves need to be quick on their feet."

Her eyes were huge and round in the early morning light. "You were sold to a thief?"

"An old thief. He couldn't pick pockets himself anymore but he took me to New Orleans and trained me to do it. We preyed mainly on tourists who wandered off the beaten path in the French Quarter. I was with him for two years and most of these scars come from that work. Not all. Some are actually courtesy of my parents and Muddy's fists, but the really bad ones are from running the streets."

He ran his hand over one ragged line that ran diagonally from his left clavicle to the middle of his ribs on his right side. "I got slashed by a knife once when Muddy sent me into someone else's patch—territory," he explained, rubbing his hand along the white lines on his face.

"As for these, a gang took offence at my being in their territory, and I had a bottle broken across my face. Both times I got sliced up pretty bad but the wounds didn't require stitches, which is why the scars are so ugly. No surgeon to make them pretty."

She laid her hand over his, lips pressed tight. "They are not ugly. I have told you so."

He turned his palm up and captured her hand, something primitive in him appeased by her lack of resistance. "Not exactly an honorable warrior's marks." His mouth twisted. "But I was a damn good thief."

Her hand squeezed his, her bones fine but strong in a very feminine way. "They *are*. How else could you have survived such a life without letting it destroy you, if you didn't have the soul of a warrior?"

He looked up into that intent, loyal face and found himself believing her. "You're far too innocent for the likes of me. But I'm keeping you." That primitive part of him rose to the surface, hotly possessive.

Her smile was pure sunshine, calming the primitive.

"You are welcome, husband mine. What happened after two years with the old thief?"

"I was in a really bad street fight. Muddy sent me somewhere he never should have—into drug territory. Anyway, I got opened up pretty bad." The memories were hazy because of the blood loss he'd suffered. "Muddy disappeared, never to be heard from again. I don't know if the drug lords got him or he just escaped when I was wheeled into intensive care. A couple of cops found me lying half-dead on the street."

"But you survived." Her fingers traced the fine white lines of scars across his abdomen.

"Yes. The doctors did a good job—those scars are the least visible."

"And yet there are so many. You were not just cut once." There was such anger in her eyes. "What happened after you recovered?"

"When the cops asked me how I'd ended up in the city, I lied and said I'd run away. So they returned me to my parents, instead of sending me to a foster home."

Hira frowned. "Why did you wish to return to your parents? They may have tried to sell you again."

"I knew they wouldn't, because I'd become their meal ticket."

"You stole for them?" There was no disapproval in her tone, as if she respected what the boy he'd been had done to survive.

Another sliver of his heart fell into her careful hands without his conscious volition. He just knew it was forever gone. Forever hers.

It was an effort to speak without demanding she give him something to replace what he'd just lost. "No. I stopped stealing as soon as I left Muddy. I got work, any work, and I gave them enough to keep them happy. That's why I went back. I knew that as long as they were boozed, they wouldn't care what I was up to, whereas a foster parent might've actually made an effort to discipline me."

Hira lay back down beside him on her side, propping her head up with one arm, her other hand still intertwined with his. "What were you doing that you didn't wish for discipline?"

"I had plans. I decided in the hospital that I'd never again be anyone's whipping boy." Even now he could feel that savagely beaten boy's grim determination. "That meant I had to have money, and to do that, I needed to work. My parents didn't care that I was working far too many hours for a kid, working late into the night in factories where the managers ignored my age.

"It took a few more kicks before I got my head screwed on perfectly straight, but once I did, that was it." One of those kicks had been delivered by Lydia Barnsworthy. "I was young but determined. By the time I'd graduated high school, I'd saved over thirty thousand dollars from working and then investing that money. I went to college on a baseball scholarship. Even though I'd worked on instinct in investing, I knew that some of the men I'd be dealing with in the future would be impressed by a degree."

Hira began to nod, her midnight-and-gold hair sliding across her bare shoulders. "You started your business with the money you made from your investing."

"Yes, with a little help from the bank. The first company I bought was a dying little family outfit that produced these unique toys. I busted my gut with it and sold it when I finished college for a profit that was big enough to allow me to buy my next company. Within five years of graduation, I was a multimillionaire."

"And you did it by saving dying companies, not looting them," she murmured. "A harder road."

He shrugged, uncomfortable with the veiled praise. "It's the way I like to work." Not by ripping apart but by slowly, painstakingly, gluing a fractured masterpiece together. He'd spent too many years with people who'd tried to destroy him. He couldn't do that to anyone or anything else.

"You were a very determined boy." The admiration in those mountain-cat eyes didn't dim. "How did you get involved with the orphanage?"

He found himself wanting to tell her, when he'd kept his secrets from everyone else. "I met Father Thomas about a year after I returned to my parents. He gave me a steady job cleaning the church after school. He also gave me…hope." He'd taken a beat-up, hard-as-nails kid and taught him the value of compassion and integrity.

"Later, when I needed to borrow money from the bank to finance that first business, he guaranteed my loan. I tried to pay him back with shares in my next company, but he said that he wouldn't take money from one of his sons." Being called "son" by Father Thomas meant far more to Marc than any biological relationship.

"I begin to see why these boys mean so much to you," Hira murmured. "You wish to give them a chance in life as Father Thomas gave you. You're a good man, Marc Bordeaux." A gentle kiss on his cheek sealed her words.

"I'm a man, same as any other." His tone was husky, not from lust but from the light in her exotic eyes.

His wife smiled at him like he'd given her the moon, when he suddenly realized he'd never given her a single present that wasn't big and expensive and meaningless.

"Ah, but you're my man, Marc. That must mean you are blessed." Her lips curved in a teasing smile.

Chuckling, he rolled over, pressing her into the mattress. "Is that so, princess?" Nothing had ever felt as right as telling his secrets to this woman with her pride and her curious honesty. Perhaps this Beauty might just be willing to love her Beast.

Less than a week later, Marc found himself standing on the verandah, waiting for his wife to return home. She'd left early that morning for her first class and it was now after five. Despite the way the lost boy inside him had wanted to cage her with protection, despite the primitive in him who'd growled *mine,* he'd tried to be gentle when she'd left, because the past week had been the most wonderful of his misbegotten life. His wife had opened herself to him, heart and soul, mind and body.

It was the first time in his life that he hadn't been lonely.

Right then he knew that if there ever came a time when Hira rejected him, it would be because he'd decided to let her go. And quite simply, he never would. He'd fight to the death like some feral thing before he watched her walk away.

Second by second, minute by slow minute, his wife had worn down his defenses and made a place for herself in his heart. The vulnerability was so sudden and

ran so tearingly deep he didn't dare release it to the light
of day. He just knew that only Hira could calm the ache
within him.

But in spite of the new depth of their commitment to
each other, a part of his wife remained out of his reach.
The crazy thing was, he knew exactly why she sometimes acted as wary as a wild deer. If he could wring
Kerim Dazirah's neck, he would. Hira's father had
planted that fear of trusting the one you married in her,
a fear that even now shadowed her eyes.

An engine sounded, snagging his attention. A second
later his wife's cherry-red sports car came around the
corner. Parking in the drive, she exited and ran up to him,
leaving her books in the car. Dressed in a long denim
skirt and plain white shirt, her hair pulled back in a tight
braid, she glittered like a perfectly cut diamond.

Delighted when she ran into his waiting arms, he
swept her off her feet and spun her around, her laughter wrapping around them like a silken whisper. When
he finally slid her slowly down his body, her sparkling
eyes had him leaning down to savor the taste of her lips.
She opened for him, warm and welcoming. Her fingers
spread on his white T-shirt. "I like the way you welcome
me home," she whispered, her tone husky.

The sight of her well-kissed lips, wet and luscious,
made him want to ravage her. "Did you have a good
day?" He was trying very hard not to demand her where-
abouts for the last few hours, since her lecture had finished long before.

She smiled and wrapped her arms around his waist,
raising her face for another kiss. Tightening his embrace, he indulged both of them with a slow slide of lips

and an even slower stroking of tongues. It was a kiss of lovers, one that left them both breathless.

"My day was interesting but strange." One hand slipped up to lie against his heart. "I learned many things at their big library, made a friend—" her smile was both surprised and delighted "—and found out that young men today have no morals."

His whole body tensed at that disapproving sound, the arms around her turning into steel bands. "And how did you learn that?"

"They kept trying to court me when I'm clearly a wife." She raised the hand with her wedding band on it. The fine gold sparkled in the light of the setting sun. At the same moment, a cool breeze ruffled the fine curls at her temples, causing goose bumps on her arms.

He tugged her inside. "What did you do?" Closing the door, he led her to the living room sofa and sat down. She cuddled up next to him, one hand on his abdomen, while the fingers of her other hand drifted up to play with his hair.

Her look would've done justice to a particularly self-satisfied cat. "I told them I was yours and I used your name. They stopped."

He bit back a grin. "You used my name?" He loved it when she touched him like this.

"Yes. Apparently they are scared of what you might do—it didn't take me long to find out that you have a reputation, husband." She scowled, and he knew she'd question him on that reputation later. "Now I'll have peace. I said that—" her voice dropped a few octaves "—my husband would not be *pleased* with their attentions."

He gave up trying to hold in his laughter. "God,

you're amazing!" He tugged her into his arms and kissed her smug little face.

"I am glad you understand that."

"So what will you do with your degree once you've finished?" he asked, hungry to learn her dreams, to be allowed into the secret world of her hopes and wishes.

"Well, I've only just started but…I thought I might like to be a teacher like the ones at the university."

He caught the uncertainty in her tone. "You'd make a wonderful lecturer."

Her smile bloomed. "Do you really think so? I'd have to do much more studying to become such a teacher. It will take a long time, especially since I want to spend a lot of time with the boys when they are ours, but I think I can do it if I work hard."

"I have every faith in your stubbornness, *cher*," he joked, touched by the way she was embracing *his* dream. "If you're not careful, you'll make us respectable. Can you see me at some faculty dinner, discussing business theory?"

She laughed at his horrified tone. "I shall try very hard not to tame you—it's fun having a husband with a reputation such as yours."

He grinned. "Tell me more about your day."

A frown marred her face. "Well…many people asked me if I was a model, as if a woman with a certain kind of face could be nothing else."

He moved his hand to her hair and undid her plait, sending that midnight-and-gold glory tumbling over his hands. "I suppose people think that that would be more glamorous than studying."

"Hmm."

"Why didn't you model? Wouldn't it have been a way out?"

"I thought about it." She settled herself more comfortably against him. "It will be hard for you to understand, coming as you do from this country of ultimate freedom, but I'm very old-fashioned. I don't believe in showing my body to anyone but my husband.

"I couldn't do it, not even to escape my home. It would've been a betrayal of myself, a surrender to my father's attempts to change me from the woman I am. I always thought I would think of something else."

"I like being the only one who's seen your body," he whispered, touched by her confession of her deeply held beliefs, of her determination not to compromise those beliefs, even in an attempt to escape the life she'd hated.

Her fingers undid one of his buttons and touched skin. "I know. Every time you look at me, I know you're congratulating yourself on acquiring me."

"Men don't acquire women. We woo them." He bristled.

"When did you woo me?" It was only when she met his gaze that he realized his lovely lady of a wife was enjoying herself by teasing him.

Grumbling, he captured her laughing face and proceeded to kiss her until she was whimpering and agreeing to his every demand. Then *he* teased her.

Things had been going a little too well as far as Marc was concerned. He supposed he should've expected it all to come falling down around his ears. He'd been kicked viciously by life too many times to take anything for granted.

"There's a letter for you in the mail my assistant just dropped off," he called out, striding into the kitchen the next day. After waking at 4:00 a.m. for an international telephone conference, he'd had no desire to head into his city office. The fact that Hira had had no classes, either, had cinched his decision to telecommute. "It's from within the States."

Hira's face was as curious as his when he handed her the pale-lilac envelope addressed to her, care of his company's post office box number. "That's strange. I don't know many people yet."

She didn't object when he walked around to stand beside her, one hand idly stroking over her curvy hip. At that moment he was simply interested in the unexpected letter, with no knowledge of the pain that could result from a single small envelope.

Hira tore open the flap and pulled out a card with the words *I Love You* emblazoned in red on a white background. Marc felt his whole body tighten in readiness for a fight. Who the hell had dared to send his wife love greetings?

"Perhaps it's one of the boys—they make me cards sometimes," Hira muttered, flipping open the cover. Almost immediately she slammed it shut.

"Who is it from?" he insisted, his hand clenching on her hip.

Her face was pale but her answer honest. "Romaz."

"The man you loved?"

"The man I *thought* I loved," she corrected. "He wasn't who I believed him to be."

But, Marc thought with a gut-wrenching shaft of pain, she'd cared very deeply for this man at one time and there had been no coercion involved. Not like their marriage.

"What does he want?" His wife was entitled to her privacy and he wanted her to trust him.

"He's in the country with his new wife, but he wishes to visit me." She sounded vaguely shocked.

"I see."

Her head jerked up. "What do you see, husband?" Her voice was soft.

He was furious at the gall of the man in contacting Hira through *him*. "You had feelings for this man once. Now you're my wife, so you won't be seeing him." It came out sounding like an order.

Her eyes narrowed and he knew he'd made a mistake. "Ah, so you never see the women who have been in your bed?"

He blinked. "That's very crude coming from you."

"Perhaps I've decided that with you, a lady will only get crushed into the dirt." She turned to face him fully, those wild eyes of hers furious. "You didn't answer my question."

"Tit for tat?"

"Do you really think me so shallow?"

He rubbed the back of his neck. "No. But I still don't want you seeing him."

"Why?"

There was no answer he could give her that wouldn't betray his snarling possessiveness. Hands fisted, he moved away. "If you're determined to meet him, I can't stop you." His tone was harsh.

Silence, then a quiet, "I'll write him a short note telling him a visit is not possible. Even he should be given a response."

She turned and walked away, leaving him shaken by the power of the relief he felt at her decision.

That night as they lay in bed Hira turned to her husband. "I've sent Romaz a letter saying that I'm happily married and have no wish to meet with him." She knew her husband would never ask her what she'd said, having too much pride. A woman who married a hunter of a man like him had to know when to bend, for a hunter's pride was part of his emotional armor, something no true wife would ever steal away.

He turned to her, arms folded behind his head, ghost-gray eyes glinting silver in the moonlight shooting through their bedroom windows. "Are you happily married?"

It wasn't a question she'd anticipated. "I suppose I'm happy."

"That's not exactly an avowal of joy."

"No, it's not." She sighed. "When I was a girl, I dreamed many dreams about the man I would marry, though I was aware from a very early age that my father saw me as a commodity. I always knew I'd be part of a business deal, so it wasn't such a shock to marry you."

"Ouch." Her husband rose to lean over her, a wry look on his savagely masculine face, a face that made her heart sigh and her stomach tighten in desire, no matter how hard she tried to resist. And when he smiled that slow smile…

"I thought you might've fallen for my charm."

"You tease me, for you know we didn't speak much before our wedding night." Marc had seen her one night, and the next day he'd agreed to her father's desire to seal the deal with her hand.

At that stage she'd met the American stranger who'd offered her a way out of her father's house exactly twice. And yet he'd seemed by far the better choice. Her womanly instincts had craved him from the first, though the dark intensity in his eyes had scared her.

Her husband brushed his lips across hers. "Thank you for telling me about Romaz." He paused. "I'm sorry you missed out on the big wedding girls dream of."

She was surprised at the genuine regret in his tone. "Do not be, husband. I never dreamed of a big wedding. I always hoped it would be a quiet affair, though I accepted that my father's business instincts meant it would most likely be huge. So you see, you gave me the wedding I wished for." She stroked his thick, dark hair off his forehead, unwilling to hurt him in any way if she could help it. Her man had known far too much hurt already.

To her confusion, he moved away from her. Reaching behind him to the small bedside table, he picked up something and returned. "Hold out your left hand."

Curious, she did as asked. Using one hand, he slipped her wedding ring off. She bit her lip and forbore to ask him what he was doing. Her patience was rewarded as the ring was slipped back on, with another below it.

Raising it to the moonlight, she saw a trio of jewels winking back at her. In the dim light, she guessed that the two flanking stones were small square-cut diamonds. Another stone sat in the centre.

"What is this for?" Her heart felt as if it would burst.

He stroked the delicate skin of her inner wrist. "It's the engagement ring you never received—a little romance to make up for the hurry with which I 'acquired' you."

The teasing reminder of her own words made her want to smile, but then she wondered if he'd had his secretary pick it and she shouldn't be feeling so cherished. "What's the stone in the middle?"

"A tigereye prism." Linking their fingers, he brought her knuckles to his lips in a kiss that was as possessive as it was tender. "Don't you want to know what the other two are?"

"They appear to be diamonds." She began to feel hope in her deepest heart. A tigereye prism wasn't something to be bought off the street. Found only in her homeland, it was almost as prized as its more famous sibling, Zulheil Rose. However, because its structure made it so very difficult to work with, it wasn't exported. Most jewelers found the investment of their time in creating pieces from the recalcitrant gem uneconomical.

"They're Zulheil Rose in the palest hue, with the tiniest hint of fire within. I thought they'd pick up the color of the tigereye, the color of your eyes."

Her thudding heart felt as if it were smashing against her ribs. "You chose this for me?"

"Yes. I contacted a jeweler in Zulheil and described what I wanted. And I put a rush on it." He ducked his head and kissed her again. "Do you like it?"

"Oh, yes, husband. Thank you!" Captivated by his attempt at romance, she threw her arms around him in an exuberant hug. "You're wonderful. I'm so happy." Joy bubbled up deep inside her. It wasn't the jewels that made her so delighted, it was the fact that Marc's act had clearly been motivated by the desire to make her happy. Coming from a man like him, such an action meant far more than words.

"Well then, what I'm going to tell you next will make you delirious."

"What?"

"I have to return to Zulheil in the next couple of days, for approximately two weeks, to tie up some loose ends and engage in some negotiations with your sheik. Do you think you can play hooky that long?"

Her eyes widened. "Yes!" Then to Marc's surprise, she frowned. "We will stay with my family?"

He gave her a smile he knew was smug. "I've bought us a house, *cher.*"

"Husband, you are most definitely in need of a reward." Her smile was sultry in the dark.

He wanted far more than just sex from his wife, but he'd take what he could get. Yet it hurt that she still saw him as such a shallow man, to be "rewarded" with her body, not allowing him to share in that indefinable something that made her such a unique individual. "Yeah?"

"I will sing for you." She pushed at his chest.

He blinked. "Sing?" He hadn't known she could sing. "Why haven't I heard you before?"

"Because I didn't like you as much as I do now." Her answer was as honest as always, and for that reason it touched him in a place even the scars couldn't reach.

"So how much do you like me now?"

She leaned up and kissed his nose in a playful way that startled him. "A whole lot. And not because of the ring but because of the reason behind it."

"I did good, huh?" He tried to make light of the heavy weight of emotion clogging his throat.

Pushing him off her, she sat up. Then without warning, she sang to him. An exotic, alien song in the language of her homeland; a beautiful language that seemed to sway like the trees and roll like the sea. He had no idea of the meaning of her words, but he knew that whatever it was, it was powerful and utterly beautiful. Her voice was crystal clear, with just a hint of sultriness.

Sexy innocence.

Just like his wife.

He lay there in the moonlight and let the purity of her voice wash over him. His chest filled with the power of her gift. For the first time in their married life, he felt as though she'd truly accepted him as her man.

"Husband, are you asleep?" She sounded offended.

In answer, he hauled her down to his body and captured her lips in a kiss that was far more than a mere fusion of mouths. Unable to say what he felt, he tried to show her how important she was to him, how very, very important. The kiss accelerated, and the next time he came up for air he found her lying below him, her body holding him deep within her. The naked emotion in her eyes almost tore him to pieces.

And he knew.

They'd gone beyond sex, beyond lust, beyond desire, into a realm he'd never before explored. In this place there was joy beyond compare and stunning pleasure that touched the heart before the body.

He couldn't fight the tumbling of his internal walls, couldn't fight that strange, wild, unknown emotion that clawed its way into his heart and refused to leave. Barely able to breathe, he stroked her cheek once.

Then, as moonlight washed over her beautiful face, he moved inside her. Her hands closed over his shoulders and her exotic eyes went blind with passion so intense it refused to allow him to separate himself. Somehow he was able to focus his mind for the moment it took to watch her go over the edge. Only when she was crying out did he allow the madness of that inexplicable emotion to overwhelm him.

Nine

They were almost ready to leave for Zulheil two days later, when Marc got a call that changed all their plans.

"Becky's been found," he told her.

Heart in her throat, Hira went with him to see the child, who'd been admitted to a hospital in Lafayette. Becky's new adoptive parents were there as well, out of their mind with worry for their baby girl.

"Mr. and Mrs. Keller?" Marc's voice was gentle. She could almost see him rethinking his ideas about how to reunite Brian and Becky. The woman sitting there with red eyes looked as if she hadn't eaten for days, and her husband's face was haunted.

"Yes?" Mr. Keller looked up, hope lighting up his eyes for a second. "Are you a doctor? Did she wake up?"

"No. But I might be able to help."

Mrs. Keller's eyes were bleak. "How could you? I

know who you are, Mr. Bordeaux, but your wealth can't help us. She's wasting away and no specialist can tell us why. God, my poor baby. She's so tiny, so fragile."

Hira moved to sit on a hard plastic chair beside Mrs. Keller and took her hand. "You must not worry. My husband can indeed help. Tell them, Marc."

He pulled up a chair to face the Kellers, his jaw taut. "This may come as a shock, but when Becky was placed in the orphanage from which you adopted her, she was separated from her twin, a little boy. It was the first time they'd ever been parted from each other."

Mrs. Keller gasped, the hand in Hira's suddenly bruisingly strong. "No, no! Dear Lord. She never said a word. Not once."

"Brian lives in an orphanage that we have a connection to," Marc continued, voice low and deep. If Hira hadn't known him, she'd have thought him utterly calm. But because she did know him, she could see the worry weighing down his heart. "And he's almost as bad as Becky. They need to be together."

There was no hesitation. "Anything. Do anything," Mrs. Keller said. "If you have to take her away to live with Brian, you can even do that. Just save my baby." Her husband nodded. "Please, just save her. *Please.*"

Hira felt tears prick her eyes. There was no question in her mind that these people loved their child. Looking at Marc, she knew he understood that, too. While she sat with the Kellers, he left the hospital. When he returned, Brian's thin arms were wrapped trustingly around his neck, that small body cradled in a protective embrace.

The Kellers took one look at that sweet face and love whispered across their expressions.

"They look so alike," Mrs. Keller whispered. "He's a bit healthier than her. Someone's managed to make him eat."

"I'll give you recipes for some things he likes," Hira offered.

"Me?" The woman's smile trembled. "You'll let us keep them both?"

"It's my husband's decision, but he loves Brian. He won't do anything to harm him." Her faith in the goodness of the man she'd married was absolute.

Marc walked straight into the hospital room. He emerged moments later without Brian. "He crawled into the bed, took her hand and started telling her to wake up."

Mr. and Mrs. Keller went to look through the glass partition into the room, unwilling to disturb the reunited twins, but clearly needing to be nearby.

Once they were out of earshot, Hira found herself in the odd position of having to comfort her aloof husband. He'd sat down on one of the plastic chairs, his strong body in a defeated posture, while she was standing.

"It's all right, husband." Hesitantly she dared to touch his bent head in a light caress. "You got to Becky in time." You saved two children's hearts, she thought, emotion choking her throat.

Marc didn't shrug off her hand but stared ahead at the white hospital wall in front of them. "She's in critical condition." His voice was flat, without emotion.

Biting her lip, Hira moved to stand right beside him, her hand on his shoulder. "But she's alive. That's what you must concentrate on. In my land, the old healers believe that the spirits of the injured can hear the prayers of the living. We must call out and bring her home."

Marc raised his head. "Do you truly believe that?"

"With all my heart and soul."

To her surprise, he wrapped one arm around her body and laid his head against her stomach. "Brian will die with her if she doesn't wake." His acceptance of her care shook all of her beliefs about their union.

"He believes she'll live." Hira stroked his head, praying both for the children and for Marc. Her husband was a good man. He didn't deserve such suffering.

"He's a child."

"Perhaps that is so. But he has a connection with her that we can't doubt after seeing them. There are those who say twins are not two people but two pieces of the same soul. If that's true, we must double the strength of our prayers." The warm weight of him leaning against her gave her the strength to be his hope. For once someone needed her for more than her face and body.

Her husband didn't say another word but neither did his face settle into those fatalistic lines again. When he walked off to get them coffee, he touched her cheek in a fleeting caress that she couldn't understand but felt the power of. Her American husband was no ordinary man.

To everyone's shock, Becky regained consciousness two hours later. The Kellers were incoherent with joy, and Mrs. Keller was cuddling Brian as if she'd never let him go. Though it hurt Hira, she saw that the little boy felt at home in her arms, as if he knew how much they loved Becky and would love him, too.

"They belong to the Kellers," she said to Marc, when they got home that night.

His face was tight. "Yes. Tomorrow, I'll begin the

process that'll ease their adoption of him. I'm going for a walk."

"In the dark?" Worry for him sparked inside of her.

Without answering, he grabbed his jacket from the hall closet. Desperate, she reached in and pulled out hers, too.

"Where the hell are you going?" he growled at her.

She'd never seen him look more forbidding. But she knew he'd never needed her more than he did at this moment. "For a walk."

He moved closer. "I want to be alone."

She knew he was deliberately crowding her with his body, trying to intimidate her. But he'd done too good a job of demonstrating that he'd protect her to his last breath. "Okay. I'll walk in the other direction."

"Don't be a fool. You'll fall into the bayou and give some lucky gator his dinner. It's dangerous out there." He grabbed her jacket and threw it back into the closet.

She put her hands on her hips. "Husband, if you leave now, you have no way of stopping me from leaving."

His jaw squared. "You'll stay put."

"You really think I'll obey?"

His eyes were suddenly bleak. "I need to…"

She pushed his own jacket out of his hands and took his face between her palms. "You need to stay at home and let your wife share your pain. It's my pain, too."

Her every heartbeat reverberated with his sense of loss. Marc wasn't a man who loved easily, but he loved Brian, of that there was no question in her mind. And now he was being asked to give up one of the precious pieces of his soul.

For a moment she thought he'd walk away, unable to

accept the tenderness she offered. Then his arms slipped around her body, and he held her so tight she could barely breathe. Uncaring, she wrapped her arms around him and silently promised that they'd get through this together. They weren't alone anymore, either of them.

Somehow the hurt boy from the bayou and the lonely beauty from the desert had become a unit, a pair, a single beating heart. Her dependence on him should've scared her, yet all she felt was the dawning of a hope so exquisitely powerful she was humbled by it.

Only seven days later Marc stood beside Hira in front of the hospital and watched the Kellers drive off with both Brian and Becky, after having been granted temporary guardianship of Brian. Even the bureaucrats had seen that the children needed to be together. His heart felt as if it were being ripped out of him, but he smiled. Not for anything would he spoil the children's joy.

After they were gone, he turned to Hira and pulled her into an embrace. As he'd known she would, she began to stroke his back. Despite the pain he could feel in her, she was trying to comfort him. Her generosity of spirit kept throwing him, systematically destroying all his old ideas about beautiful women and their icy hearts.

"Home," he whispered, his voice husky with pain.

She nodded against his chest.

However, home wasn't the haven he'd expected it to be. Hira disappeared while he was parking the car. Angry at her for teaching him to need her and then not being there when he needed her so desperately, he began to head out to the bayou. It had always held welcome for him.

That was when he heard the muffled sobs coming from the small formal sitting room they used for guests, the one place his wife knew he avoided, much preferring the relaxed parts of the house. The heart he'd protected for so long seemed to shudder at the hurt in her ragged tears.

Taking a deep breath, he turned the knob and entered. It took him a moment to find her. She was sitting curled up against one corner, her arms around her knees, her heavy fall of hair a curtain. She'd come to cry in private.

Perhaps, he thought, it would be better to leave her to her grief. Something in him rebelled against that course of action. This was his wife in distress. He could never leave her, just like she hadn't let him walk away that night after they'd come home from the hospital. Decision made, he strode over to sit down beside her, tugging her into the vee of his legs before she could stop him.

She jerked in surprise, and a tear-stained face met his. "Wh— Leave!"

"No." He forced her head back against his chest. "You cry as much as you want, princess, whenever you want. But you cry in my presence."

She hit his chest with her fist. "I do not u-use tears to get m-my way!"

"No," he acknowledged, his proud wife would never use tears to sway him. Apparently, neither did she trust him enough to be vulnerable to him. Well, damn it, from today, that was going to change. "I don't like you crying all alone."

She didn't speak again. Instead she lay against him, tears streaming quietly down her face. He held her and stroked her until there were no more tears and the birds outside were settling down to sleep.

"Better?" he asked, wiping her face with consciously gentle fingers. He was aware that he had calluses. He'd crawled out of the bayou but it still called to him. Being behind a desk was alien to him.

She nodded and turned her face a little, giving him permission to complete the job. He did, feeling a dangerous squirt of pleasure at the tiny gesture. It spoke of deep-rooted trust as her lonely tears hadn't. Perhaps, he thought suddenly, there was more to her crying alone than her acceptance or rejection of his help.

"I had begun to think of him as my own." Her voice was barely a whisper.

"Me, too, *cher*. Me, too."

Slim arms slipped around him. "They'll be happy with the Kellers. They're good people."

"I had them triple-checked. No problems in the marriage. No indications of violence. They adore children but they're infertile," he told her. "Brian and Becky embody their dreams. People cherish their dreams."

"Yes." Hira nodded. "Yes. Dreams are to be cherished."

"Why do you cry alone?" he asked. *Why don't you need me as much as I need you,* the wounded boy inside him wanted to ask.

Her silence went on until he thought she wouldn't answer. Then, "My father often reduced my mother to tears purely for his own amusement. I swore I would never let anyone humiliate me that way."

"I would *never*…" He was so blindsided by hurt he couldn't complete the sentence.

Slender hands cupped his cheeks, and when he glanced down, Hira's tawny eyes were looking into his, wide and startled. "No, Marc! I didn't mean… *I know,*" she whispered. "I know you would never, ever do that to me."

There was no way he could doubt the honesty of her desperate confession. "Then why?"

She swallowed. "Instinct. I've never had anyone to go to before." It was a simple answer but one that spoke of years of pain. Such habits didn't develop overnight.

The memory of seeing her eyes sparkling with withheld tears made him ache deep within. "Crying all alone isn't healthy." He didn't like the thought of her hiding away her hurts, or what such actions revealed about her past.

"Do *you* ever cry?"

He thought of the rock in his heart at the loss of a child he'd thought of as his own. "No."

"That is not healthy, either."

He was stumped. "I'm your husband. Aren't Zulheil wives supposed to follow their husband's commands?"

"Only the old ways state that. I've begun to explore the new ways that my father forbade. They say a wife can disobey her husband if she has good reason."

"Well, hell." He found himself smiling. "Are you going to turn into an American woman?"

"Perhaps partly. Would that displease you?"

He chuckled. "I have a feeling that even if it did, it wouldn't matter to you."

A pause. "You could make my existence difficult."

There were so many facets to his wife that she kept surprising him. "*Cher,* I make your life hell, anyway, so what would change?" He'd meant to make her laugh but she remained silent on his chest. Hugging her, he said, "Hey, come on. I'm not that bad, am I?"

"You're not cruel," she said a long while later. "As a husband, you're more than I could've wished for. But I wouldn't have chosen you for myself if I'd truly been given a choice."

It was a kick to his gut. "I see. Why?"

"Because you can't give me what I most desire."

"And what's that?"

"Love of a kind that's rare in this world. Love that will not stop or dampen when I am old and have wrinkles, when I'm no longer the beautiful woman men covet. Love that will cherish me though I may become ill or hurt. That is what I most desire."

The quiet declaration of lost hope hit him with the strength of a Mack truck doing eighty miles an hour. She'd put into words what he'd wanted but had never been able to articulate. "You've experienced such love?"

"It's the most wonderful thing in the world."

"Romaz?" he forced himself to ask.

"No." Her answer gave him some peace at least. "That was my first brush with love. 'Puppy love' as they call it here. No, I've never experienced that kind of love and perhaps I never will, but I've seen it in the love our sheik has for his wife."

Marc couldn't disagree. There was something between Tariq and Jasmine that outshone the stars. "Why can't you imagine me giving you that?"

She snorted. "Husband, you have something against beautiful women. I'm not stupid. I know you married me to show the world that you could own something this beautiful." There was no trace of boast in her voice, just blunt honesty.

"I will not argue that you cherish me, that you treat

me as a human being with thoughts and feelings and the right to live my dreams. But I can't forget that you selected me as a trophy, as if I were something to own.

"You acceded to my father's desire to have us wed, though you only knew my face. I've tried but I can't get over the fact that my worth to you is determined by my beauty alone."

"That's a big call to make." Anger vibrated within him. Perhaps he'd started this marriage the wrong way, but never had he thought of Hira as an object. Not even when they'd married. And in the weeks since they'd said their vows, powerful emotions had taken root in him, emotions that defied her summation.

"Can you say that it is untrue?"

"Yes, I damn well can. I don't see you as a thing. You're the woman who coaxed Brian to eat and you're the woman who held me when Becky lay in the hospital bed. You read encyclopedias in your spare time, watch music videos when you think I'm not looking and are addicted enough to strawberry sorbet that I have to make sure there's a new carton in the freezer every three days."

Hira's eyes widened at his recitation. She hadn't been aware he knew of her craving for that particular ice cream, had just assumed the housekeeper bought it from a standing order. As for the music videos...

"I don't see you as a thing. I see you as a woman unlike any I've ever known." Marc's tone dared her to disagree with him.

"But would you have married me if you'd known my love of books and economics?" she persisted. He'd wanted a beautiful wife, not a smart one.

He chuckled. "*Cher,* I'm damn glad you turned out

to be an intelligent woman. At the beginning of our marriage, I thought I might've let my hormones tie me to a woman who'd bore me within a week. Whatever else you might do, you'll never bore me."

"I see. I may have misjudged you, husband. For that I say sorry." A spurt of fire warmed her heart. It whispered that she could trust him with her budding emotions, that he'd cherish the love that had crept up on her while she'd been busy arguing with him.

"Don't." His voice turned rough. "You were right about some of it. I did want to show the world I could hold someone like you."

Ice froze the fire. "I see."

"No. You don't." He sighed and dropped his chin onto her hair. "I guess you deserve to know, after everything you've had to put up from me. I grew up poor. Coming from Zulheil, you can't imagine the kind of poverty into which I was born. I scrounged around for food, knowledge, anything. Even before Muddy, sometimes I stole so I could eat."

Hira hurt for the boy he'd been. His pride was so much a part of who he was that the stain on his honor would've hurt him terribly. "It pains me that your mother didn't hurt for you. I find it a thing I cannot understand."

"Yeah. Well, she was as mean as he was—most of the scars on my lower back are courtesy of her. When I was too young to get away, she used to beat me until she took the skin off my back."

"No mother would do such a thing!" Hira rose up on her knees, her gaze on his face. "No, husband. Please...no?"

Marc was stunned at the anguish in her eyes. "It no

longer matters—it's in the past," he found himself
saying.

Her hands rose to cradle his face. "But, outside *and*
inside you have scars from it."

"I guess." He shrugged. "Don't worry about it."

She frowned but to his pleased surprise, leaned forward and gave him a soft kiss. "I'll worry if I wish. Tell
me why you don't like beautiful women."

"Why did I think you'd be accommodating?" He kissed
her to forestall comment. "My story isn't very original. I
was a poor boy but a smart, athletic one. I also worked several jobs. One of them was as gardener and car washer to
the Barnsworthy family. They were, and still are, one of
the richest and oldest families in the area. I fell for Lydia
Barnsworthy and asked her on a date. Confidence has
never been my problem." It was a joking comment, an attempt to hide the emotions evoked by the memories.

"A date?"

"A high school dance," he elaborated. "Lydia said
yes, but when the day came, she stood me up and went
with someone else. And she made sure everyone knew
what she'd done."

"What did she look like, your Lydia?"

"Slender ice blonde." To the teenage boy, she'd been
everything that was gracious, but now he saw the cruelty
beneath the beauty. These days it was Lydia who chased
him, much to his amusement and total disinterest.

"I've seen a picture of her in one of your American
fashion magazines," Hira startled him by stating. "She's
quite beautiful…if one likes cold women."

He hid his grin at the catty comment. "That certainly
doesn't apply to you. You're the hottest woman I know."

It had taken him too long to realize that beneath the armor of self-protective ice, she had so much spirit it burned hot enough to keep him warm for life.

"So you wished to show the Barnsworthy family and others that you could aspire to a woman of beauty." Her husky tones pulled him back to his story.

"Put like that, it sounds adolescent," he grumbled. "But it's part of the truth. The second part is, I saw you and wanted you. Without reason or thought. I just knew that you were mine. So I took you."

His wife stared at him, as though she didn't know quite what to make of that. Then she narrowed her eyes. "But you haven't shown me off to these people. Am I not good enough?"

"I've found that I don't want to show you off. You're for my eyes only." His tone was hard.

Her eyes widened. "Husband, you sound very... possessive."

"Yes." He was, he realized, very possessive where his wife was concerned. So possessive that he didn't want to share her with anyone, certainly not with the bitchy crowd that frequented those glamorous parties.

Unfortunately, as if he'd conjured it out of thin air merely by thinking of it, it became impossible to avoid going to one of those very same parties. With their travel plans to Zulheil being rescheduled, they were going to be in town on the date when an illustrious member of the business community was being given an honorary dinner.

"We have to attend," Marc told Hira the night before the dinner, pulling off his shirt. He'd arrived home only an hour ago after an intense day at the office. To his delight, his wife had waited up to have dinner with him. Such a little thing, but it meant so much, coming from the fiercely independent woman Hira was blooming into. "I respect Artie and it'll hurt him if we don't go when he knows we're still in the city."

"That's fine, husband." Hira closed her textbook and put it on the bedside table. "I don't mind attending these functions. It's one of my duties as your wife."

He gave her an exasperated look, trying not to be seduced by the sight of her in that lacy black slip she'd shimmied into. "Do you do everything because they're duties?" He wondered if she'd worn the sexy garment to tempt him, and his heartbeat accelerated. A woman who purposefully dressed to pleasure her husband had to have some feeling for him. Some need.

She thought about it. "No. I lie with you because I wish to. We are together too many times for it to be duty." Then she gave him a slow, sultry smile. "I wouldn't dress this way for you if it was only duty." A teasing light in her tawny eyes, she shrugged a slender strap off one honey-skinned shoulder. "Oops."

He felt the bottom drop out of his stomach. "Hell, I guess I think of these things as duty appearances, too. At least you'll make it bearable." Keeping his eyes on her, he peeled off the rest of his clothing.

She held out her arms. "Come to bed, husband mine."

He walked over, determined to say what he had to before the light of welcome in her eyes reduced him to incoherent passion. "I want to warn you—the crowd at these parties will stab you in the back if they have the slightest indication that you're vulnerable."

"Me? Vulnerable?" She gave an exaggerated sniff. "I am ice, husband."

"I'd forgotten." He stopped by the bed, waiting for her to shift so he could climb in beside her, and begin doing things to her that would leave her drenched in sweat. Pleasing his wife turned him on like nobody's business. "You're so hot."

Instead of accommodating him, she moved until she was facing his erection. "Hot, hmm?"

His whole body shuddered as she dipped her head and took him to his own private vision of heaven. "Yup, damn hot." Those were the last words he said for a long, long time, because his desert beauty was in the mood to pleasure her husband.

Slowly.

Ten

The party was as he'd expected. Except for a few men and women he respected, the glittering ballroom was full of debutantes who did lunch and slept with other women's husbands, and those same husbands. None of them dared to approach Marc because he wasn't known to be kind to their species, but he noted the way they looked at his wife.

"Stay close," he warned her.

She gave him an amused look. "I can negotiate these waters. I'm used to being talked about."

He nodded. "Don't let them hurt you or I'll have to get mean."

"Yes, sir." Laughter lit her eyes.

Despite her words she did stay close to him for most of the night. Toward the end of the evening she whispered, "I'm going to powder my nose."

He nodded and watched her walk off. Lord, but she was stunning. The other men had been noticing all night. But, scared off by her ice-queen expression, none of them had had the temerity to approach her. He had to hide a grin. His wife was anything but ice but she could do ice extremely well.

At that, an earlier thought intruded. Underneath her glittering beauty, Hira had been just a little stiff ever since they'd arrived, though on the drive over, she'd been her usual warm self. It was hardly noticeable, but he knew her well enough, had seen her without her shields too many times to be fooled. The second they were alone, he'd find out what was bothering his wife. And then he'd dedicate himself to soothing her. Smiling, he turned his attention back to the party.

He got caught up in a conversation with the guest of honor for the next ten minutes, and when he looked around for Hira, he couldn't see her. Intuition had him heading out to the hallway, off which the ladies' powder room was located. His eyes narrowed when he saw Lydia walk out of the white-painted door, a smirk on her face.

Her blue eyes lit up when she saw him. "Darling!" She went to kiss him on the cheek. Behind her back, he saw the door reopen and a familiar figure walk through.

Without any hesitancy, he pushed Lydia aside. "What the hell do you think you're doing?" He hated being manipulated. Even worse, he hated being used as an instrument to hurt his wife.

Lydia wobbled in her high heels. "But, Marc, our relationship…"

He'd been trying to be gentlemanly, but when he saw

Hira's eyes darken in pain, he stopped pulling his punches. "Last time I saw you, you were showing me your breasts and asking if I'd like a taste. I believe I refused and told you to get your tail back to that old man you married. Isn't. That. Right." He made it a command.

Lydia's face went white. "You bastard."

"I may be, but I'm an honest one. Why the hell would *you* interest me when I've married a woman who outshines you by megawatts?" Walking over, he hauled Hira to him. She came without hesitation. "By the way, if I ever again catch you taunting Hira, I'll ensure that the tape of you propositioning me finds its way into your husband's hands."

"You're lying." Lydia sounded shaky.

"Do you really think I'd trust you an inch?" He turned and looked down at his wife's still face. She'd been hurt by Lydia. Without further words he headed for the exit.

Marc flicked on the light in their bedroom and turned to Hira. She hadn't said a word on the drive home and he hadn't pushed, though his simmering temper had demanded to know everything. Hauling her inside, he locked the door, shutting her in with him.

"Now, you'll tell me every lie that bitch spouted." He crowded her until she was pressed against the wall. Her purse dropped to the floor as he wrapped one hand gently around her nape.

"How do you know they were lies?" Her pulse pounded against his hand, but her tone was defiant, her eyes beginning to burn with inner fire.

"Because Lydia wouldn't know honesty if it bit her."

He crowded her some more until her soft breasts pressed against the jacket of his tux.

"Stop giving me orders," she hissed. "And back off."

"No." His woman had been hurt and he wanted an explanation as to why she'd let that happen.

She blinked at the uncompromising denial. "You are not behaving as American men are supposed to."

"How am I behaving?"

"Like one of the desert chieftains. They're known to be primitive."

"Is that so, *cher?* Then you'd better start talking. Us primitive types aren't known for our patience." His eyes drifted to the lushness of her lips. Before his civilized side could talk him out of it, he leaned down and kissed her the way he'd been wanting to all night. Pure heat and pure possession.

Her soft lips parted for him, inviting him into her mouth. He took the invitation and claimed her sweetness. His free hand went to her breast but he didn't like the feel of her sparkly dress against his skin. Without releasing her lips, he pushed the strap down and slipped his hand under the dress to close around one heavy globe.

Hira jerked, but her arms came around his neck in permission that he hadn't asked for. Rubbing his thumb across her nipple, he broke the kiss only long enough to allow her a breath and then he ravished her again, massaging her breast with a hand that knew exactly what she liked.

"What did she say?" he asked, raising his head.

Her lips were wet, her eyes sleepy looking but her mind sharp. "You're trying to seduce me to get your way."

"Yes." He plucked at her nipple before cupping her breast again. "I'm a bastard of a negotiator."

"No, you're merely determined." Her lips curved in an indulgent smile. "Lydia said much, but it all came down to the fact that you were sorry to have married me and were madly in love with her, that you had begged her to come to your bed despite the fact that she was married."

Raw rage whipped through him. Leaving her breast, he pushed both hands through her lush fall of hair. "And you believed her?" He was furious with her for thinking so little of him.

Her eyes narrowed. "I told her that you'd never lower yourself to trash such as she was."

He wasn't fully mollified. "Then why the hell did she look so happy?"

"I believe she thought to drive a wedge between us by planting seeds of doubt in my mind."

"Did she succeed?"

"You are a man with much pride. You'd never beg the favors of a woman who had rejected you."

"You know me." He pressed impossibly closer. Only her height in heels allowed her to meet his gaze. "But you believed some of it. You looked like hell."

"No. I was hurt at being reminded that though you say many things which make me think you value me as more than just a pretty face, I'm still a trophy wife to you, like Lydia is to her husband. Most of the couples there tonight were successful men with beautiful young women they treat as ornaments. *I fitted right in.*"

His control snapped. "Trophy wife?" he asked very softly. He'd been torn up at the sight of her in pain and she considered herself a trophy wife? He was sick of trying to get through to her. Maybe it was time to use nonverbal communication of the kind they were best at. Putting his hands on her waist, he lifted her. "Legs around my waist."

She obeyed. "What are you doing, husband?"

Good. She sounded wary. But beneath the wariness was trust that soothed the raw edges of his temper. "Teaching you that whatever else you might be, you're no trophy. Trophies get put up on a shelf and admired. I want you in my hands, to touch and please and *own* in a far different way." He reached under her dress and made short work of her fragile panties.

She gasped. "This is…" Her words were lost as his fingers probed her, testing her for readiness. Within a few strokes, he was rewarded with damp heat. The scent of her desire rose in the air.

"Yes, *cher*," he said. "That's it."

She hit his shoulder with a closed fist. "Do not talk to me as you would to a horse."

Some of his masculine possessiveness retreated under that sharp-voiced command. Only some. "But, baby, you respond so beautifully to a little coaxing." He slid a finger deep into her, gentle with her in spite of the desire running rampant through his body.

She cried out and clutched his shoulders. When her eyes opened, they were full of some feminine mystery he couldn't hope to understand. Clenching around his finger, she pulled his head to hers. He went, his free hand breaking a strap on her dress to give him easy access to her breasts. As one hand closed around her flesh, her teeth scraped his lips.

"Biting, Hira?" He grinned. "Tut, tut." Another finger deep within her.

Her eyes flashed, even as tiny feminine muscles rippled around him. "I will make you pay for this, Marc."

He started kissing her neck, wondering if she knew just how rawly sexy she looked with her dress tumbling off to half expose one breast and completely free the other, her hair falling wild and free onto her shoulders and her long, silky legs wrapped around his waist. Suddenly it was too much. She was hot and more than ready.

Removing his hand, he went to work on the fastening of his pants. Holding her gaze, he guided himself to her and then thrust. She gasped and blinked, and it was all he could do to stop with that first deep thrust sunk in the velvet heat of her body.

"Move!" she ordered, breathless.

Since he had no objection to the idea, he moved. Again and again and again until he couldn't think and there was such erotic pleasure, it felt as if his whole body was going up in flames.

Hira wondered how she had never, in all her researches, come across the mention of how erotic it was to be made love to by a fully clothed man when one was almost naked. Though she couldn't remember how they had got there, she was now in bed, completely naked. Her forest-green gown was hanging over the back of a chair by the vanity. Beside her, Marc lay sprawled on his back, one arm thrown across his eyes. He remained dressed except for his shoes, which he'd apparently kicked off at some stage.

Very carefully, she sat up and looked down at her husband. Over six feet of long, lean man, he was presently asleep. She was glad. Tonight something fundamental had changed in her thinking about their relationship and she needed time to come to terms with it. Her husband had behaved as an enraged male whose wife had done something that displeased him, rather than as a man annoyed with a woman he'd acquired for her ornamentation value alone.

It was a very sharp distinction. One was a reaction fueled by emotion, the other by logic. Whatever else it had been, their joining had not been logical. It had been decidedly out of control and that was something her husband guarded fiercely against. Tonight, at the party, she'd overheard people discussing his reputation of icy control in the most stressful circumstances.

Except, with her, he'd always been fire and heat.

The bruised bloom in her heart unfurled into full flower at the revelation that her husband was truly not indifferent to her. The hope she'd felt the night she'd realized they'd somehow become a unit, reawakened. She had yet to understand the depth of what Marc felt for her, but it was surely something far more than mere desire.

Perhaps the love in her heart wasn't doomed.

It had taken her a long time to accept that this wild hunter of a man had found a foothold in her soul, but she was a woman who knew herself. Marc Bordeaux was the one. The only one. In her deepest heart, she must've known that when she'd acceded to her father's demands; she was far too smart a woman not to have found a way out if she'd been desperate. She'd been stalling Kerim for months before Marc came on the scene.

Marc shifted on the bed, throwing his arm wide, and she realized he had to be uncomfortable. Experimentally she reached out, undid his bow tie and slipped it off his neck. He didn't react. Emboldened, she managed to get his jacket and shirt off him by moving him around when it didn't seem to wake him. Then, biting her lip, she got rid of his pants and socks, leaving him clad in plain black briefs. Still asleep, he turned over onto his stomach, and she couldn't help stroking his back, his skin hot and vibrant under her fingertips.

A glance at the clock showed that it was 2:00 a.m., but she was hungry, having eaten nothing but hors d'oeuvres since lunch. Carefully covering Marc with a light blanket, she pressed a soft kiss to the back of his neck, slipped into his formal white shirt and went down to the kitchen.

Marc chanced opening his eyes after a minute of silence. Groaning, he turned over in an effort to ease the pressure on his rigid arousal. Growing up as he had, never knowing when a vicious blow would shatter his rest, he slept lightly. He'd woken the moment Hira had but had kept his eyes closed, wondering what she'd do. And had learned that being undressed by a naked woman, whose breasts kept teasing you with every movement, was sheer torture.

He hadn't been ready to talk to her, uncertain of her reaction to what had happened between them tonight. Whatever else, she couldn't back away from this inferno. She was no more a trophy wife than he was a prize husband. However, his little deception had had an unexpected side effect.

His chest tightened as he recalled her tender kiss on his nape and the way she'd carefully covered him up.

They hadn't been the acts of an angry woman or even a woman who saw him as a duty. It had been care, pure and simple. He'd already known his wife had a big heart from seeing her with the children, but until now he'd never really felt the power of that heart. She'd done little things for him but they were all very wifely things, and he'd thought she felt duty bound to do them. But, tonight...tonight she'd gone far beyond duty.

Throwing off the blanket, he went in search of Hira, finding that he was greedy for her. He located her at the kitchen counter eating a piece of bread slathered with crunchy peanut butter. Her eyes widened at his entrance but he didn't stop, walking around to stand beside her. Leaning down, he bit off the other end of her bread.

She swallowed. "You are hungry, too, husband?"

He nodded. "Why did you put on a shirt to come down?"

Taking another bite, she offered him more. He took it, demolishing almost the entire remainder. She waited and fed him that last bit before turning to get another slice from the loaf at her elbow. It was another small example of her inherently generous nature.

"Because it would be immodest to walk around unclothed." With efficient movements, she spread peanut butter on the bread.

"But it's only us." He moved closer, rubbing her cheek with his knuckles, daring to display the affection that had changed his view of himself. "Come on, I dare you to take it off."

A soft smile on her lips, she raised the hand holding the piece of bread to his mouth. After a bite, he nudged her hand back to her own mouth. She took a small bite and chewed. Then, a smile flirting with her lips, she asked, "Why are you in such a mood?"

"Let's see, I had amazing sex with my wife a few hours ago and, since she doesn't appear to be holding my somewhat Neanderthal behavior against me, I'm raring to go again and I was hoping to create some sexy atmosphere. How's that?" He allowed her to feed him again. "Humor me."

She smiled and blushed. "But—"

"If we can't be free with each other, who can we be free with?" Even as he said it, he realized that it applied to more than sexual exploration. He'd never truly trusted anyone and he badly wanted to trust his wife.

She handed him the slice of bread. Then, nibbling at her lush lower lip, she lifted her hands to the buttons of his dress shirt. His eyes were riveted to those elegant fingers. She undid the first button. He took a deep breath. She did the second one. He groaned.

"Faster, *cher.*" He wanted to reach out and haul her to his chest, but no way was he going to interrupt this very private show.

"What would be the fun in that?" Her question held teasing laughter, and the look in her tawny eyes said she was enjoying herself.

"Did I indicate this was supposed to be fun for you?" He fed her a bite from the remaining bread. "This is sexual gratification for me alone."

"Is that so?" Another button. The valley between her breasts was a shadowed treasure, the softness of her belly a silky plain for his exploration. "What if I wish for some gratification, too?"

"You can have it later. After I'm done." Finishing

off the bread, he stood there, completely concentrating on her.

She laughed, the sound husky and intimate, and released the last button. The darkness between her thighs was an invitation he gladly took, cupping her gently. Sighing, she leaned closer. With a single lithe movement of her shoulders, the shirt went to the floor.

He ran his hand up from her heat to flatten over her stomach. "Damn, you're lovely." Her face fell. "No," he ordered. "None of that. Sure, your body is hot, but you know what makes you perfect?"

She shook her head slowly, wary eyes holding a vulnerability that made him want to cherish her forever.

"The fact that you adore my body despite my scars, say yes to playing with me at this ridiculous hour even after the stunt I pulled tonight, and have peanut butter stuck to your bottom lip."

Her hand flew to her mouth, eyes wide. He pulled the hand off and licked the spot off. "Yum."

She giggled and stepped back. As he watched, she put her finger in the peanut butter jar and dabbed a spot on her lip again. Surprised, he leaned forward and licked it off. Her hand went to her breasts and each nipple was coated.

"You sure know how to gratify this man." First, he sucked the finger she held out to him, cleaning it off. Then he made slow work of each morsel, his hands stroking her bottom. When he stood to his full height again, it was to face a woman with a passion-soft face, eyes heavy-lidded and a sweet, sexy smile on her lips. Reaching out a hand, she traced the shape of his mouth.

"Still hungry?" Her voice was a husky whisper.

"A little." He backed her up until her bottom hit the edge of the counter. Then he lifted, setting her down on the marble. She spread her legs and he stood between them. Reaching to the right, he found the squeezable bottle of honey that was one of her favorite treats. Grinning, he held it up. "Want to play some more?"

Her eyes widened. "Husband, you are bad." An inviting look appeared on her face. "I love honey."

"So do I, *cher*. So do I." He'd never felt this carefree in his life. Flipping open the lid, he held the bottle upside down and started to draw meandering swirls of honey over her breasts, her stomach, lower.

She sighed when he put down the bottle and started to lick his way down her body, swirling his tongue, using his teeth to scrape, his fingers to smooth. Minutes later she began to tremble. He stroked his hands on her thighs as he bent over to lick her stomach. Her beautiful feminine muscles clenched under his attentions. He kept going, pulling her bottom closer to the edge to facilitate his taste of honey.

Her hands clenched in his hair as he tracked the last possible drop, lapping at her most sensitive flesh. Moans filled the kitchen as his wife climaxed, surrendering to the pleasure he lavished on her. Satisfied by her shudders, he rose and picked her up in his arms. Her legs wrapped around his waist.

"Where are you taking me, husband?"

"Do you care?"

"No. You may take me wherever you wish."

He narrowed his eyes at that double entendre, unsure whether it was just her grasp of English or deliberate provocation until he caught the hint of mischief in those tawny depths. "I'll remember that the next time I see you bent over the kitchen table."

Her laughter filled the night. When he sat down in a chair, with her spread over him, she slid her hand between their bodies and down. "Why is it that you are always clothed when I'm naked?"

"Bad timing?" He groaned as she slipped her hand under the elastic waistband of his briefs. Stroking him gently, she chuckled at his response.

A man could only take so much. Barely ten seconds later, he'd kicked off his only item of clothing and got himself covered in a much more pleasurable fashion. She slid onto him like hot silk. And then she rode him.

Given their newfound joy in each other, the plane trip to Zulheil the next day was markedly different from their first flight together. Marc had brought along papers to look over but didn't even take them out of his briefcase, too enchanted by his wife.

More at ease on this flight, she teased him to laughter and tangled her fingers with his, her eyes holding a look of pride. "You're a most magnificent man," she whispered, halfway through the flight.

He could feel a blush creeping up the back of his neck. "What brought that on?"

She winked at him and pressed a spontaneous kiss to his cheek. "Can a wife not simply compliment her husband?" Putting her head on his shoulder, she settled against him, warm and…loving?

He didn't dare think that he might've found his dreams, but he could almost imagine that he was seeing the real woman, with none of her customary masks.

Only one thing gave him pause—the way she still occasionally looked at him after a particularly saucy comment, as if anticipating a rebuke.

He knew that her reaction was rooted in the emotional abuse she'd witnessed in her home, scenes of a wife being humiliated by the very man who should've been her champion. He hated it, but he could forgive her that instinctive reaction. Yet so long as that look was in her eyes, he couldn't expect her full commitment to him as a man, as a husband. Before she took that chance, she'd have to accept that he'd die before turning into a man like her father. Unfortunately, there was nothing he could do to help her reach that point. In this shatteringly important moment, he was helpless.

"Have you ever been inside the royal palace?" Marc asked Hira on their second night in Zulheil, fiddling with his bow tie and hoping the evening would be cool.

She moved to him and took over the job. "Yes, of course. The royal palace is open to its citizens, aside from the private wings for the family. But you're one of the very few foreigners who has been allowed access."

He was aware of the privilege and the duty it carried. Trust in this desert land was given slowly but would hold fast unless he abused it. "Impressive, isn't it?" His eyes followed Hira as she moved away to pull on a top coat of the finest gossamer silk.

The sheer fabric was an almost metallic silver and was gathered under her breasts with a single tie. The rest of the coat fell to float just above the floor, splitting open over her legs to display an underskirt of thick silver satin. The long-sleeved silver top she wore underneath the gauze overlapped the top of the skirt and was heavily embroidered with tiny white pearls. The material seemed shot with shards of pure crystal.

"I may be a mere male but I like what I see." Marc was looking at her appreciatively when she turned.

In Hira's eyes, he was the gorgeous one, big, dark and very masculine. "It's a Jasmine Zamanat creation."

His eyes sharpened as he recognized the name of the sheik's wife, a well-known designer. "Clever little witch. Getting us brownie points with the palace, are you?"

She was pleased by the compliment in his eyes. "It will not hurt, though they won't be so easily swayed. But I truly like her designs so it's no hardship."

"You're definitely easy on the eyes. Let's go, princess. The drive from Abraz to Zulheina will take a while. Wouldn't want to be late for this meeting."

Though informal, the meeting with the sheik was important. If things went favorably, Marc would be allowed to sign an agreement with Zulheil to export a durable, flexible plastic discovered by its scientists.

"And aside from its other advantages," Marc said as they got out of their limo in front of the palace, after having been cleared by security, "it crunches down into small packages. So it's very portable and can be used for tents, et cetera."

"Which means it can have military applications as well as many other uses." Hira nodded. "Why hasn't it already been exported?"

"It hasn't been a priority for Zulheil with their gemstone business bringing in so much income. But the rest of the world could do with it."

Just then, a beautiful redhead dressed in a lovely sky-blue top and skirt in the way of Zulheil, walked through the palace doorway. "Welcome." She smiled and held out her hands to Hira. "I'm so delighted you could finally make it. I hear that you had to reschedule because of the welfare of a child."

"Jasmine al eha Sheik, it is an honor," Hira began, a little overcome at the easy welcome from the most powerful woman in the country, though it was well known that neither the sheik nor his wife stood much on pomp and ceremony.

Jasmine waved a hand. "Call me Jasmine. Ah...here he is." Letting go of Hira's hands, she looked over her shoulder at the man who'd appeared beside her. Her eyes held such deep and abiding love that the warmth of it was an almost physical touch.

Hira noticed the way Sheik Tariq's hand immediately settled on his wife's hip, the way the two shared a secret smile before he spoke.

"Dinner is served and the demon who is pretending to be our son is fast asleep. Welcome to our home." He shook Marc's hand and turned to lead them inside.

Almost immediately the men fell back behind the women, already beginning to talk business. Hira was a little irritated at being disregarded so easily.

"You're annoyed," said the woman by her side.

Hira glanced at Jasmine. "Lady..."

"Call me Jasmine and don't worry about it. He annoys me on occasion, too." Her smile was open.

Hira decided to be honest. "I don't like being sidelined when serious matters are being discussed."

"Neither do I. That's why we'll be talking about a different idea that I've cooked up with Tariq."

Hira's eyes widened. "Another proposal?"

"As you know, Zulheil likes to keep to itself. When we find someone we like, we try and squeeze our worth out of them. Tariq trusts your husband's integrity and acumen."

"And what about me?" She wasn't going to be ignored.

"Until this evening, though we've had dealings with Marc, you were an unknown commodity. Tariq knows you socially but I've only seen you once."

"I remember. In the gardens after your marriage." Aware that Jasmine must've been informed of the Dazirah family's attempts to make a match between her and the sheik, Hira had known that this lovely woman wouldn't appreciate her presence. So she'd tried to stay in the background, despite her parents having urged her to find someone else with royal connections, since many important visitors had been at the gathering.

Jasmine led them into a beautiful formal dining room. "Yes. My husband expects you to earn his respect. It's the same demand he makes of everyone."

Hira nodded, accepting the fairness of that.

"But," Jasmine continued, giving her a shrewd look. "I've made my decision. You're no pretty trophy. That husband of yours wouldn't look at you the way he does if you were."

"And how is that?"

"With the deepest pride. If he is as akin to the men of Zulheil as he appears, then that's a great thing indeed." Jasmine turned to take a seat beside her husband on the other side of the comfortably small table.

A little shaken by the power of that quiet statement, Hira took the chair Marc held out for her. There were no servants in the dining area tonight, because this was most definitely a meeting, despite the abundance of delicious dishes on the table. He touched her fleetingly on the shoulder before taking his seat.

It made her aware of how he *always* touched her, and had done so since shortly after she'd learned about the orphanage. A caress, a stolen kiss, a squeeze of the fingers, she'd become so used to being touched by Marc that she'd never questioned what it meant...until she'd seen the sheik touch his wife, and realized that for a strong man to show such open affection implied a great deal of feeling.

Smiling, she turned to him as he sat down and gently put her hand on his thigh, out of sight of the others. He looked startled but then favored her with that slow smile that always proved lethal to her composure. His hand drifted down to hers and their fingers intertwined.

"Let's begin with a toast." Tariq held up his glass and they followed. "To a long and happy partnership."

They all clinked glasses. The dinner took more than four hours, with all of them ending up in a small sitting room talking over several documents. Hira spent considerable time discussing an interesting idea regarding the tigereye prism with Jasmine. Marc didn't even check up on her once, and his trust that she'd look after their interests cemented her love for him as nothing else could've done.

Eleven

"**G**od, I'm exhausted." Dressed only in his dress pants, Marc fell back onto their bed. Rubbing his eyes with his hand, he smiled, looking very much like a satisfied hunting cat. "But it was worth it."

She nodded. Having already changed into a short nightdress with thin straps, she crawled onto the bed and knelt facing her husband, combing her hair. "This could build into a long-term business relationship."

Marc's eyes followed her strokes. "I intend it to. I like working with Tariq. He's got integrity as well as the negotiating skills of a shark."

"That's why he likes you also." She put the brush down on the nightstand and moved to undo his belt, using the excuse to stroke his firm abdomen. Under her hands, he was pure male strength, the seduction of his hunter's body enough to make her ache for his possession.

His smile as he watched her with blatant proprietariness made her stomach tighten in expectation. Marc had a particular look in his eye tonight, a look that said he intended to take his time with her.

She was proved right.

They'd both agreed to spend the next day with her family. Hira wished to see her mother and brothers but didn't particularly care about her father.

"It's only one day. You can stand the man for that long," Marc said when she made a sulky face.

Sighing, she nodded and got out of the car, waiting until Marc was beside her before heading up the steps to the place that had once been her gilded prison.

Her mother was overjoyed to see her. Even her brothers were happy, welcoming her with crushing hugs and small but thoughtful gifts that touched her. Perhaps they'd turn out all right after all. Her father grunted and shook Marc's hand, smile wide. Hira left him to Marc and went to spend time with her mother, the documents for the account she and Marc had opened in Amira's name safe in her purse.

Marc watched Hira go off with Amira Dazirah with mixed feelings. On the one hand he was glad she was happy to be in Zulheil, but surrounded by reminders, he couldn't help but remember the way he'd rushed her into marriage. Her father had provided the impetus, but the choice had been his. He couldn't deny that he hadn't tried very hard to change Kerim's mind. He'd wanted Hira, and he'd gone after her with every bit of his considerable will.

It hurt more than he could've imagined to know that

because of that single rash act, his wife would never view him with the kind of tenderness and love she'd told him she'd dreamed of. How could she possibly understand that when he'd seen her on that balcony, it hadn't been her beauty that had transfixed him?

No, it had been something far more ephemeral, something that had tugged at his soul, a *knowing* that she was his, a possessiveness that hadn't let him sleep until he'd made her his in reality. How could he explain that to her without ripping open his heart? He wasn't ready for that, not when she sometimes still looked at him with shadows in her brilliant eyes.

His wife had adjusted to him, but he needed far more than simple coexistence from her. He needed her heart and soul, her hope, her everything. He needed her to need him, because all of him, even the lost and lonely bayou boy he'd been, had become enthralled with her. It was an enchantment that demanded his soul. He couldn't fight it, couldn't go back to his lonely, untrusting existence…couldn't stop needing her so much that his hunger was a physical ache.

Late the next day Hira tried to talk to her husband about what had turned his gray eyes dark when she hadn't been looking. In the space of a few hours, he'd gone from teasing and laughing with her to almost complete silence.

"Nothing," he said, his tone curt.

When she pushed, he kept responding with monosyllabic replies that made her want to hit him over the head with a blunt object. Frustrated by his recalcitrance, she finally left him and went off to indulge herself with a bath, muttering under her breath about males in general and one male in particular.

He found her fifteen minutes later, while she was sitting on the edge of the huge square-shaped bath filled with cool flower-scented water. Because of her perch, the lapping water only covered her up to the thighs. Looking up, she saw familiar desire flare in his eyes as he gazed at her naked form. Ignoring the heat that uncurled luxuriously in her stomach, she stared back, feeling just a bit put-upon by his moodiness.

"What?" she finally said, when he remained silent.

"Nothing. I have to go out."

"Fine." She glared at him.

"Don't you care where I'm going?" His tone was jagged, torn, those eyes of liquid silver gone cloudy.

And she wanted to hit him, not soothe him. She'd had it! Absolutely and utterly! Letting out a stifled scream, she picked up the sponge she was using to smooth water over her body, and threw it at his chest.

He caught the sponge against his body. When he lifted it off, a wet patch marred his vivid blue shirt. Before he could speak, she said, "Why should I worry about a husband who turns cold on me when I've done nothing wrong? You and your black mood can both go to hell for all I care!"

That was when he stalked to her, all male arrogance and smoky eyes filled with some emotion she couldn't read. She sat in place, though it was difficult to be composed while her body was laid out for his perusal.

He was close enough to touch. "You just told me to go to hell." Holding her gaze, he dropped the sponge into the water, sending ripples chasing across her thighs.

"Why do you sound so surprised? After the way you've been acting today, I'm entitled to my temper."

To her complete and utter shock, he kicked off his shoes and sat down beside her, straddling the bath. One jean-covered leg went in the water, the other remained outside. He didn't even blink. "You don't have that look in your eyes anymore," he murmured. His hand began to play with a strand of her hair that had come undone from the knot on top of her head.

She slapped his hand away. "What look? And don't try to get back in my good graces. I want to enjoy my bath without my bad-tempered husband." Turning away, she scooped up water in her hands and let it run over her legs.

If he wanted to watch, that was fine. She refused to be hurried just because her body reacted like wildfire to his. She could control herself, she thought grimly. She would not give in to the urge to rip open his shirt and lick her way up to his lips. She would not! Why was he still sitting there? A woman only had so much self-control, even when she was using anger to fuel it.

"Aren't you wondering why I've been acting like I have?" Marc finally asked, scooping up water in one hand and dripping it over her thighs.

She sniffed to fight off a shiver at the intimate act, pressing her thighs together to still the ache in between her legs. It only intensified. "I don't know what it is that I did, but clearly, I've done something wrong. You're merely trying to reinstate your rights over me by showing me this coldness." She made a face at him. "I will not be treated so!"

At that instant her American did something she'd

never expected. Putting both hands on her shoulders, he pulled her toward him and planted a hard kiss on her startled lips. "To hell with my rights!" Wild hunger raged in his eyes, but this hunger was deeper than the body, so deep that she thought she could see his soul in the suddenly piercing quality of those always-well-guarded eyes.

"The reason I've been acting like a wounded bear is because I worship the ground you walk on. Being here reminds me too much of how we started this marriage, how I killed all hope of love between us with the way I claimed you without courtship. I love you, princess, and I can't stand it that you'll never love me back." He kissed her again, strong and swift. It felt like a brand on her heart.

"Heck, love doesn't begin to describe what I feel for you— This emotion's like a fire inside of me that refuses to go out. It's passion that stuns me when you smile and tenderness I didn't even know I could feel. It's not roses and moonlight, it's lightning and forever."

Hira was stunned speechless by Marc's defiant declaration. Her proud, inflexible husband had to know that by acknowledging his love, he was giving her a weapon over him, and surely he'd never give such a weapon to a woman like he'd once believed her to be, a mercenary beauty like that bitch Lydia. He wasn't finished, either.

"I love your smile and, yes, I love your face. How could I not, when I adore the woman you are? I love the way you talk to the boys and let each of them feel as if he could win your hand if he were old enough. I love the way you're so generous with your body and your affection."

His voice was raw; painfully, powerfully intimate. "I love the way you try to love the bayou because I love it. I love *you,* and I've had it with trying to hide what I feel."

Powerful and passionate, it was her first true glimpse of the intensity of her husband's feelings. His love would be wild, an inferno that would demand everything from her.

Trembling, she raised her hand to his cheek and leaned close. "Marc, husband, I c-can't…" Her voice was an emotion-choked whisper.

"Hush. I know." There was something bleak in his gaze. He'd given her his heart with no expectation that she'd reciprocate. How much strength did that take for a man who'd never been loved? How much courage? How much love?

Her heart felt so big in her chest, Hira didn't know how it remained inside her body. "Did you know my father has never once told my mother that he needs her? Not once. Yet he relies on her for so many things."

"I need you more than you'll ever know." It was a rough acceptance, another glimpse into his proud heart.

This hunter of hers had far more depths than she would've believed when they'd married. Dropping her hand, she moved closer and began to unbutton his shirt. "What about when I'm old? When I have wrinkles? Or lines from bearing children?"

"I want to grow old with you. I want to put laugh lines on your face, and I want the birth of our children to change your body. Imagine a lifetime of change, *cher.* A lifetime of learning each other anew." His eyes were liquid silver but shadows still hovered in the background, remnants of the neglected child, the final pieces of the vulnerability he hid so well. "What's the fun in remaining the same?"

His shirt was open under her hands. She pushed it off his shoulders and to the floor. Her hands went to his belt. A big male hand stopped her.

"No, sweetheart. You don't have to…give me anything. My love's free. And it's for always."

It was his tenderness that shattered any remaining doubts she might have harbored. He sounded so very careful, so very worried that she might feel obliged to him, so very concerned about *her,* when he was the one who'd taken the risk of stripping his soul bare.

Swallowing, she raised her head and looked into those ghost-gray eyes. "Marc, husband, I once told you I could tell lies very well."

"I'd rather have honest affection than a dishonest avowal of love," he said, mistaking her meaning. There was an intensity in his gaze that challenged her. This man would never settle for gilt when gold was his goal.

She bit her lip. "No, I mean to say that I once told you a lie. I didn't plan to, it just came out that way." She'd been panicked and afraid, and it had been the only thing she could think of to keep him at a distance.

His face hardened. "Oh?"

"I said I wouldn't have picked you if I'd had a real choice. I said that the only reason I married you was because there was no way for me to refuse my father's commands."

"Yeah." Marc had tried to get over that, but it continued to torment the bayou boy inside of him. The one who'd never been chosen for love. The one who was so madly in love with his wife that her lack of feeling for him hurt him with every breath. But he would never let her know that because as he'd said, honest laughter and affection were better than dishonest love.

"Did you know that my father had a marriage offer for me almost every week?" Hira confided softly.

He stared at her, his mind immediately beginning to holler questions.

"Marir was just one of many. I could've picked one of the others, because there were several with businesses that would've complemented my father's. And of course they had impeccable family links." She was talking really fast, as if trying to get something past him.

His mind and heart refused to let her off that easily. "Would Kerim have let you?"

"Oh, yes, for if I was an *unwilling* wife to you or any other man, it would've jeopardized his business. Far better to have me be a willing wife whom he could mold, even if that meant I was married to someone less influential.

"At the time that my father ordered me to marry you, I told myself I didn't put up a fight because I was hurting from Romaz's rejection, but that rejection had come many months previously. I'd had over eight offers for my hand since then. One was from a prince in another desert country, another from a British millionaire who is considered a very eligible bachelor."

Something hungry deep inside Marc, went very, very quiet. *"Eight?"*

She nodded and gave him a guilty look. "None of which I had trouble rebutting, though my father drove me crazy with his orders for me to agree. He kept threatening to throw me out on the street. Marir was his attempt at scaring me when I refused all the suitors after barely a single meeting. He would never have wasted me on a lecherous old friend. Don't be angry with me."

She was fiddling with the button on his jeans, even as she explained. Her lashes hid her eyes but he could tell she was giving him surreptitious peeks to see how he was taking the news.

He narrowed his eyes. "You made me feel like I was the best of a bad lot." His tone was light, his heart buoyant as he finally understood what his proud princess was confessing.

She'd preferred the scarred bayou beast over every other man who'd asked for her hand.

Looking up, she made a face at him, a smile flirting with her eyes when she saw that he wasn't angry. "You were. Except for you, every other male was bad. Then I saw you, and suddenly I had no resistance. I could no longer fight my father—all my will was gone, lost the moment you smiled at me. You were just the best. Compared with anyone. So, you see, I wished you for my husband. Only you."

Her unknowing echo of his thoughts only made her confession more poignant. He felt his throat lock as the power of what she was saying roared through him.

When he didn't answer straight away, she said, "Do you understand, Marc? You're the love I waited for all my life, though when you came, it took me a while to recognize you. You see, I didn't expect you to be so blatantly *male*." The teasing light in her eyes made him kiss her.

After he set her free, she continued to speak. "I feel so much for you, I don't know if I can find the words to tell you. In Zulheil, there is a saying—*Ul al eha makhin. Makhin al eha ul. Lael gha al aishann.*" Her voice was full of so much passion, he could almost see her love in the air.

"What does it mean?"

"You belong to me. I belong to you. Together we are complete." Her voice shook.

It was perfect, saying what he'd wanted to but hadn't been able to. "Princess, I promise you that that will never change. *Never.*"

"Until I loved you, I didn't know the whole of the woman I could be." Her eyes were huge and wet. "That woman's love will only grow stronger with time."

Leaning forward, he sealed their pact with a kiss. When she sighed and melted into him, he couldn't help but stroke that golden skin of hers, now almost dry. "You didn't finish your bath," he whispered against her lips.

"Ummmm." Giving him a sultry smile that was full of a joy he'd never before seen, she slipped out of his arms and into the water, beckoning him with her finger.

Grinning, he stood from his straddling position and went to work on his jeans. There was more than enough room in the huge marble bath for one crazy-in-love ex-thief. He could almost feel the tantalizing coolness of the water; it would be a sensual pleasure on its own after the unrelenting heat of the desert. But the most pleasurable aspect of the pool was currently looking at him with a distinctly feminine proprietariness in her tawny gaze.

Every male instinct in him was aroused and alert. This was his woman, and he was at once proud of her and ravenous. She was so sexy she was a fantasy and yet it was the very human softness of her that he found the most enticing. His ice princess had turned out to be a woman of hot blood, and he couldn't have been more pleased.

Holding that dark gaze, he undid the buttons on his jeans and stepped out of them and his underwear at the same time. Her throat quivered as she swallowed.

Aware of the ways his wife's body betrayed her arousal, he looked at her thighs. Beneath the water, they were pressed tight together. Her body was flushed with heat that hadn't been present a moment before, her lips parted as if waiting for him.

He walked into the bath, conscious that her eyes had dropped to his erection. He was huge with desire for her, and he was proud of his passion. This was something no other man had ever given her and no other man ever would. He reached her as that possessive thought crossed his mind. He could think of a hundred things he could do to his princess and she to him on this slow desert evening, but first he just wanted another kiss. A kiss that was given joyously by the woman who loved him.

"Marc," she murmured against his lips. "Husband mine."

He went to kiss her again, but, with a mischievous smile, she slipped away and into the water. He followed, stalking her into a corner. "Princess, come here."

"Why do you call me that?" she murmured, letting him trap her.

He winced. "At first it was because you made me so mad when you went all icy."

She chuckled and kissed him, telling him he was forgiven for those early taunts. "And now?"

"Now, I feel like the hero in some fairy tale who got

the girl." His hands began to slide over her body. "I beat the dragon and won the princess." The timbre of his voice dropped, becoming husky and intimate.

When Hira thought he would pull her into his lap and take her, he put strong hands around her waist and lifted her to the edge of the bathing pool. She gasped as cool marble met her bottom.

In front of her, he spread her legs to position her as it pleased him. Very aroused, she let him stroke her thighs apart, fingering her own hands through his hair. "Husband," she whispered. "Why do you do this?"

His laugh was hoarse. "Baby, you know I like the taste of you." Against her sensitive skin, his breath was a hot caress, a lover's kiss. Moving closer, he put her legs over his shoulders.

She gulped as his hands stroked her flanks, as if leading up to a taste of her. "But you wish to come inside me now. This isn't what you wish."

His grin seared her. "*Cher,* have you got a lot to learn about your husband. But don't worry, I have a lifetime in which to teach you the finer points." There was such sheer delight on his face that she found herself laughing with him. "Lesson number one—what I wish is for you to be screaming when I take you."

That was all the warning she got before he dipped his head. Hira shuddered and tried to keep her control, but it was futile. Before long she was clutching her fingers in his dark hair, moaning her desire and asking him for more. He gave her more, took more, demanded more. And at last she screamed.

When he finally pulled her down, the water lapped over her in a cool caress that soothed her sensitized flesh but did nothing to quench the boiling cauldron inside of her. She wrapped her legs around him and, with a sigh of exquisite relief, welcomed him into her body, even as their eyes locked in an even more intimate dance.

Her American hunter took her and she let herself be taken. It was far too late to fight, because at last she knew that she was conquered territory, marked with the stamp of this one man alone.

Perhaps it might've made a weaker woman angry to be considered as such, but Hira wasn't weak. Belonging to Marc allowed no half measures. But, she thought with a smile as the stars exploded around them, Marc wasn't a man who loved by half measures. He'd given her all his passion, all his strength, all his heart. If she'd been conquered, then her conqueror had surrendered into her loving arms.

"People treasure their dreams," Marc whispered into her ear, as they floated down from the pinnacle of pleasure. "Let me treasure you for the rest of my life."

It was the most romantic thing anyone had ever said to her. Contrary to his own beliefs, her hunter of a man knew exactly what words to give his wife. "We will treasure each other," she managed to whisper, holding her perfect prince of a man to her.

* * * * *

HIS WEDDING-NIGHT WAGER

by
Katherine Garbera

KATHERINE GARBERA

One brief trip to Las Vegas and Katherine Garbera was hooked with endless story ideas and a fascination with that playground known as Sin City. She's written more than twenty books and has been nominated for *Romantic Times BOOKclub's* career achievement awards in Series Fantasy and Series Adventure. Katherine recently moved to the Dallas area where she lives with her husband and their two children. The only thing she loves more than writing is talking to readers. Visit Katherine on the web at www.katherinegarbera.com.

This book is dedicated to Matt!
Thanks for a fabulous wedding night and all the
nights that have come after!

Acknowledegment

Special thanks to Chris Green who answered
all of my Vegas questions and gave me an
insider's perspective.

Thanks also to Natashya Wilson and
Debbie Matteucci for their editing insight!

One

Long legs, expensive silk hose and the kind of hips that he could sink his fingers into. She had it all. She always had. Hayden still couldn't believe Shelby Anne Paxton was here in his kingdom. He'd never thought to see her again.

Her calves were well formed, tapering down to trim ankles and a pair of stilettos that sent his libido into overdrive.

The Chimera Hotel and Casino was his life. The 24/7 world of Vegas had always been his home. He wouldn't do anything to jeopardize the success of the hotel and casino. He'd sacrificed to make it into one of the premier destinations on the Vegas Strip. And he owed it all to this woman who hadn't believed in him and to his father.

Hayden had made the Chimera the number-one casino in Vegas to prove that their lack of faith wasn't an obstacle in getting what he wanted from life.

His entire operation was first-class, right down to the hotel's own shopping wing, which housed only sophisticated retailers. Always expanding and changing, it was about to add Bêcheur d'Or, a high-end lingerie boutique.

Bêcheur d'Or was on the fast track to the top. It's owners, Paige Williams and Shelby, had been profiled in *Entrepreneur* magazine earlier this year. Apparently Shelby had made more of his money than he'd ever expected her to.

But it had been Paige with whom he'd spoken to cinch the deal, and Paige with whom he'd met to sign the contract. Funny that Shelby had shown up here and now, especially considering he'd never expected her back in Vegas after she'd left him standing at the altar.

A long, low wolf whistle jolted Hayden back to the present and the hallway outside the newest merchandise location at the Chimera. "Well, well, well. What have we here?"

Hayden turned to see the tall, lean, dark-haired form of his best friend stroll up. Pain tightened in his gut. He didn't want even Deacon Prescott to know who this woman was. He'd simply referred to her as the gold digger that one time he'd gotten drunk and talked to Deacon about his marriage.

Hayden glanced at Deacon and fought the surge of possessiveness swamping him. "You're a married man."

"Definitely. But that doesn't mean I'm dead. Besides, Kylie knows I'd never stray."

Deacon and Kylie had been married for almost two years now and things were going well. They were the exception to Hayden's golden rule that marriage was a business deal.

"No, you wouldn't," Hayden said more to himself than to Deacon. Deacon had found something that Hayden would never admit he'd once wanted. His friend had found forever love and happiness. As for Hayden...well, he'd learned his lesson long ago.

Still, Hayden didn't begrudge his friend. Deacon had come a long way from the man Hayden had first met several years ago. A long way from the mob enforcer who'd wanted to go straight, longing for a better life that he didn't know how to find. Now Deacon owned the Golden Dream, a very successful resort and casino that was second only to the Chimera in terms of success.

Deacon had also found love and seemed to buy into the whole illusion of it since his marriage. Hayden knew better then to try it himself.

He wished the ending for his own story had been as happy, but reality had a way of making sure the scales were kept firmly balanced. And to Hayden's way of thinking, if you grew up with every luxury money could buy but a father who couldn't seem to love you, then something had to give. For Hayden it had always been the softer things.

"Are you going to go inside or just stand in the doorway?" Deacon asked.

Normally he'd walk on by, but not today. "I'm waiting for the right moment."

"And that would be when?" Deacon asked.

"When you get the hell out of here."

"You didn't leave me alone when I went after Kylie."

"Hey, we had a bet. I had to keep tabs on you," Hayden said. He'd bet Deacon that Kylie wouldn't marry him. It was one of the few times that Hayden had lost when he'd gambled, but he hadn't minded the loss.

"Want to make another wager?" Deacon asked. "Only this time—"

"I'm not looking for Ms. Right like you were."

"Why aren't you, Mac?" Deacon asked. His friend always called him by that nickname. It was a holdover from when they'd first met and Deacon had needled Hayden about being the "Mac Daddy." The big guy with lots of cash.

"You know I already tried marriage and didn't find it to my liking," he said, playing off the incident as if it were nothing more than a minor inconvenience, instead of a life-defining moment.

"But you didn't make it to the finish line, so to speak," Deacon said.

"I got close enough," Hayden said. No woman was ever again going to get him to stand in front of a church full of his friends and family and wait for her. There were few feelings he could recall as clearly as the humiliation and anger that had simmered in his gut as he'd faced all of his guests and told them that the bride wasn't coming.

Was it getting closer to forty that was catching up with him or was it Deacon's happy union?

"That doesn't mean it won't work with another woman. This one looks fine."

"Deacon, stop staring at her ass or I'm going to send the surveillance video to Kylie."

Deacon put his hands up and backed away. "I thought you might want a little of the good life."

"I think I've already got it."

"Yeah, well, if you change your mind, I'm here and I've got good advice."

"On what?"

"Romance."

"I don't need advice from you, Prescott."

Deacon flipped him the finger and walked away. Hayden leaned against the wall opposite the glass storefront, continuing to watch the lady unpack her boxes. Damn it had been a long time since any woman had gotten to him like this. Why did it have to be Shelby?

He couldn't stand outside her shop forever, so he pushed away from the wall and entered.

She straightened and her auburn hair fell in waves down the middle of her back. She had a phone tucked between her shoulder and ear as she pulled items from the open box.

"I haven't seen him yet. I'll check in on Friday like we planned. Please don't call me again."

She disconnected the call, turned on her heel and froze. Her jaw dropped and he knew she'd spotted him. Her face went pale as she reached behind her and braced one hand on the countertop, on top of her cell phone.

He walked through the room with a long, easy stride that he strove to keep nonchalant. He schooled his features and forced himself to treat her the way he'd treat any other businessperson who'd leased space from him. He wasn't a first-rate gambler for nothing. He knew how to bluff with the best and how to keep his emotions under wraps.

But he couldn't resist slipping his hand deep into his left pocket and rubbing the top of his left thigh where he had a tiny tattoo of a medieval knight's fist wrapped around a bleeding heart. It was his constant reminder that he no longer allowed his emotions to be a part of his sexual relationships.

It took a lot of guts for Shelby to come back to Vegas after what she'd done. It took the kind of gall of someone who had nothing left to lose. And she'd not only come back to his home turf but taken up residence in his kingdom.

She was still the most beautiful woman he'd ever seen. But she'd changed. Before, she'd been kind of wild—more untamed. The kind of woman who'd made his dad crazy because she was obviously eye candy.

God, he'd been an ass when he was younger. He hoped like hell that Shelby hadn't been aware of that part of him. But he suspected she must've been. Otherwise why would she have taken the million dollars his dad offered and left him?

"What are you doing here?" he asked silkily.

"I own this place," she said.

God, her voice was still soft and sweet. Everything

he remembered about her was the same. She still looked twenty-two. It wasn't fair that time had been so kind to her. He'd be able to handle this reunion a lot better if she'd gained weight, had gray hair, something like that.

"I meant in Vegas," he said, leaning in closer and putting his hands on either side of her, caging her between his body and the counter. Ten years had passed, but right now it felt as if she'd just left him. That had been more than enough time to get rid of any lingering anger, but seeing her again had brought it all to the fore. He wasn't ready to let her go.

He'd never forgotten Shelby's voice. The way it sounded when she was happy. The way it deepened when she came in his arms. Or the way she'd sounded on the phone during that hurried conversation when she'd explained that she had to leave.

"I'm working," she said now.

"I remember a girl who used to say she'd never work a day in her life."

"I changed my mind. Money has a way of running out."

"Even the cool million you took from my dad?" he asked.

But when he saw the color leave her face and watched her pupils dilate, he didn't have the rush of adrenaline that he'd thought he'd feel. Instead he felt big and mean, like the bully his father had always been.

"Of course it did," she said. But inside, a part of her was aching. It had been easy to forget the implications of what she'd done while she'd lived on the East Coast. Distance had provided a kind of barrier for her.

Shelby Anne Paxton stared at the man she'd almost married for his money. She'd been looking for a rich boy to marry and Hayden had been looking for a nice-looking girl to annoy his dad. She couldn't explain it even now, but there'd been a connection between the two of them that she'd always thought went deeper than his money and her looks.

He'd changed in the last ten years but not nearly enough. He still had a thick head of dark hair that curled rakishly over one eye. He had bright blue eyes that had always been able to see past her defenses, and thick lips that made her remember how they'd felt on hers.

Damn, where had that come from?

"Did you know this was my hotel?" he asked.

"Yes, I did," she said softly. There was no way she was going to tell him that his father had flown to Atlanta and suggested she bid for this location. *Suggested* was really too nice a term for what he'd done. Alan MacKenzie had practically blackmailed her into coming back here. He'd threatened to leak the information about her gold-digging past to several magazines. Bêcheur d'Or was gaining an international reputation for class, and the last thing she needed was negative exposure. But Alan had also dangled a carrot—he'd offered her anything she wanted, within reason, if she agreed. Shelby knew he expected her to ask for money.

Yes, Alan had pushed her to come back, and she had.

But now that she was here, she wasn't sure she should have listened to him. The problem was, she still had an obsession with Hayden. He was the man she thought of late at night when she was alone.

"Then why are you here?"

"Um…" She couldn't tell him the truth. Would he believe a part of it—that she needed some closure and to pay him back for what he'd unknowingly given her by asking her to marry him? If he hadn't done that, Alan would never have paid her the money she'd needed to get started in business. Her exclusive line of boutiques turned a huge profit and were considered a value-added chain to many luxury resorts around the world. All of that was thanks to this man.

"I'm waiting, Shelby. Tell me why you're here. Are you hoping to strike it rich again in Vegas?"

In ways he'd never understand.

He stood before her, seething with anger. But she couldn't explain why she was back. Or that she couldn't stay away once Alan had approached her.

She'd forgotten about the anger. Maybe because of the way she'd left. Their last meeting had been a joyous one. The night before their wedding. She swallowed hard. She'd forgotten about her own emotions and how hard they could be to deal with.

"When you say it like that—"

"You sound like the gold digger you are," he finished for her.

"Not anymore, Hayden. I'm here because it's a smart business move." She'd left him at the altar. Called him from the airport with his father's check in her hand. How was he ever going to forgive that?

"Nice touch with the boutique name," he said after a few moments had passed.

A brief smile played at her lips. Naming the shop with the French word for "gold digger" had been her idea. After all, she'd always been unflinchingly honest when it came to what she was. She'd grown up too poor to pretend that money meant nothing to her. "At the time it seemed kind of tongue in cheek," she explained. "I mean, you know how I started out."

"With nothing," he said. She realized some of the anger had faded from his eyes and he was looking at her with something akin to lust.

Passion had never been the problem between them. She'd always been the biggest obstacle in their relationship. Only after a few years of therapy was she able to see that they probably wouldn't have lasted together even if she hadn't taken the payoff his father had offered. Hayden had been more interested in having the most attractive woman on his arm, and she'd been too interested in having financial security. Their relationship had been very shallow.

"And now you have this," he said.

His aftershave hadn't changed in all the years they'd been apart. Still a spicy, masculine scent that she knew he had custom blended in France.

"What do you want from me, Hayden?" she asked when she realized he was staring down at her.

He lifted one of his hands and stroked down the side

of her face. His touch was gentle. She stood still, fighting the urge to close her eyes and lean into that hand. Hayden had always been so gentle with her.

Something few other men ever had been.

He'd wanted a wife and she'd left him to deal with their friends. She'd always felt guilty about that. She doubted that Hayden wanted her back in his life. Though now that they were face to face, she was beginning to realize that was something *she* wanted.

"The wedding night we never had."

"Sex?"

He nodded.

Shocked, she didn't know what to say. The same sensual spell he'd always cast around her surrounded her now. She felt the force of his will and his desire. She closed her eyes and opened her mouth, leaning toward him before she realized what she was doing.

In Alan's words she was supposed to bring some closure to Hayden and get him ready to find a nice girl and settle down. Now that he was feeling his age, Alan wanted grandkids and for his son to be happy. But Shelby knew Alan didn't have her in mind.

She scooted away from Hayden but he reached out for her again. The years fell away and she was suddenly that trailer-park girl wanting the golden boy once again. And there was a part of her who still wanted that man.

Since leaving Hayden she'd had two other relationships—both with wealthy men—but things had never really heated up. Her fault. She was the first to admit she didn't trust her passionate side. Because the one time she had, she'd lost her heart.

"Are you really looking for sex?"

He cocked his head to the side. "Yeah."

"Is this only a revenge thing?" she asked. Because she realized she wanted to say yes. She'd like nothing better than to go to bed with Hayden, even with all the years and anger between them.

"I'm not sure."

"Thanks for not lying." But then Hayden never had. From the beginning he'd said he was the spoiled son of a wealthy man. He'd been kind of immature in those days but so had she. Hayden had also seemed like a knight in shining armor. Shelby had known that eventually he'd wake up and realize he'd made a mistake in marrying her.

"I'll save that for you."

This was more what she expected. She wrapped her arms around her waist and backed farther away from him. She bumped into one of the packing crates and almost lost her balance.

Hayden grabbed her arm and held her until she was steady on her feet. She swallowed hard and tried not to flinch from his touch. But there was nothing harsh in his touch. Just a gentle hold.

"Okay?" he asked in that low, raspy voice of his that never failed to send shivers down her spine.

"Yes. Thanks."

They said nothing for a few minutes. Shelby tried to marshal her thoughts. Tried to find her balance in a world that was suddenly out of whack. She glanced around her boutique, her gaze falling on the poster advertising Puccini's *Madame Butterfly* at the Met. Slowly she let the familiar world she'd created soothe her troubled soul.

She took a deep breath and stepped away from Hayden. As tempting as it was to fall into bed with the one man who'd made her feel really feminine, really alive, she knew she couldn't. She'd changed from the girl she was. No MacKenzie man was ever again going to make her feel embarrassed about who she'd been.

She'd been afraid of being like her mom and in the end that was exactly what she'd become. Someone who traded on her looks for money…for security. But she was a different woman now. She made her own way in the world. She was Hayden's equal in every way that mattered.

"We can't be together if you treat me, like…well, like I suppose you have a right to. I'm really not into that kind of pain."

"I don't want to hurt you, Shelby. I never wanted that."

She believed him. Despite his seemingly shallow playboy attitude back then, he'd always treated her like a lady. She couldn't really explain it to anyone who hadn't grown up the way she had, but when your mother dressed like a tramp and you had a rotating stable of "uncles" in and out of your life, people treated you like trash. But Hayden never had.

"It's been ten years, Hayden. Why do we both still feel like this?" she asked, realizing that Alan had done her a huge favor by sending her back here.

"Honestly, I don't know."

She tipped her head to the side and acknowledged that despite the years she'd never really forgotten him. "I came back because of you."

He tipped his head to the side, not saying a word, just watching her with that electric gaze of his.

She spoke again. "I can't...move on until I figure out what went wrong between us."

"Hell, Shelby, that's an easy one."

"Please, don't say it again. I wish I had the money to pay your dad back so that it wouldn't be an issue between us."

He narrowed his eyes and walked toward her. "So what do you say to some sort of compromise? You give me what I paid for."

"What your father paid for," she said.

"I paid for it in ways you can never understand."

But she did and it made her ache to realize it.

"A night of sex? I don't think I'm worth a million dollars."

"What about a week?" he asked.

"Sex and money. They were my mom's downfall. I—I couldn't do that. If we're going to try this again, I want it to be a real relationship."

He nodded. She saw understanding in his eyes and she realized that if she was going to find any kind of peace with him, it was going to be through bonds of friendship. She wasn't sure she could risk her emotions with him. He'd made her feel so vulnerable. And she didn't want to be that woman again.

"Have dinner with me, Shel. Let's figure this thing out."

"I…"

"It's just a meal."

"I have a lot of work to do here and a short time to do it. I need to hire staff, finish unpacking." The words sounded like an excuse to her and she knew they were. It was just that even though she'd planned to come back to resolve the past, now that the moment was at hand, she was afraid.

But her running days were over. And at the end of the day, Hayden MacKenzie was still just a man.

Yeah, right.

Hayden entered his office in the casino nearly an hour later. Kathy, his assistant, was gone for the day. The small desk lamp glowed at her workstation. She always left it on for him because she knew he kept late hours. There were two messages from his dad, and one from the star of his European-style revue, Roxy O'Malley.

He dialed the backstage number for the revue venue and got the director. "Roxy called me."

"She's onstage right now. Want me to have her call you back?"

"I'll stop by after the show. Let her know."

"I will."

"Any problems?"

"A few guys were hanging around after the first show but security took care of them."

"Keep me posted."

He hung up the phone, leaning back in his chair. His office had windows on two sides that showed the Strip out of one, and the Chimera's hotel building out of the other. One wall held a bank of security monitors and Hayden crossed to them.

He took the access remote and keyed in Shelby's store. The lights were on but the place was empty. Had she run? But then he saw her. Standing in the shadows staring at something in her hands that he couldn't make out.

He reached for his phone and dialed her shop. He saw her move from the shadows to the counter near the register and pick up the phone.

"Bêcheur d'Or."

"It's me."

"Hayden."

Just his name softly whispered. He saw her hand go to her throat and her eyes close. What was he doing?

"Are you okay?" he asked at long last. No matter what he wanted from her, no matter that he intended to find some closure from their relationship whatever the price to her, he really didn't want to hurt Shelby.

She put her hand on the counter and straightened up. "Yes, why do you ask?"

"I'm watching you."

"How?" she asked, pivoting to see if he was standing nearby.

"On video surveillance."

"I'd forgotten that part of Vegas. So, am I on closed circuit?"

"Why?"

"No reason. I just want to know who's watching."

He hit a switch and turned off access to her shop at every other monitor except his. "Just me."

"Why are you watching me?" she asked. Wrapping one arm around herself, she looked small, vulnerable. Not a bit like the schemer his dad had called her.

"I was debating something."

"What?"

"What would happen if I took what I want from you," he said.

"What is it you want, Hayden?"

"I thought I told you. Revenge."

He saw her bow her head. Even though he was several floors above her and in a different wing of the hotel, he felt the sadness that swamped her at his words. "I want to give you that."

He was surprised. "Masochism your new thing?"

"No, but reparation is."

"Shelby—"

"Don't say anything else, Hayden. Let's have dinner and talk terms."

Two

Shelby wasn't sure she could do it. She stood in the suite of rooms she'd been given in the Chimera to use until the shop was open. She was only here temporarily until the boutique opened in three weeks, and then she'd be returning to headquarters in Atlanta, where Paige was holding down the fort, until their next shop opened in the fall. Right now she wished she was back in her safe little condo in Buckhead, watching television and eating fat-free microwave popcorn. Safe but boring. Those words described her life and she had to admit she was ready for a change.

So, here she was in Sin City with the one man who'd never been safe or boring. And she was hesitating in front of her closet as if it was her first date. The last time her choices had been simpler. She'd set out to catch herself a wealthy husband. But this time she had no idea what role she was in.

She closed her eyes and tried to find the confident woman she'd been until she'd glanced up and seen Hayden MacKenzie staring straight back at her with anger, lust and pain in his eyes. She'd known then that the dreams that had been haunting her had led her back to this place to do one thing. To find a way to give this man peace in exchange for what he'd unwittingly given her.

She had a successful career and the life she'd always dreamed of. But did Hayden? Seeing how deeply her choice still affected him made her want—no, need—to make up for it in some way. If parts of her dream life weren't exactly perfect, well, that was a price she'd happily pay.

She pulled a brightly colored wraparound silk skirt from the hanger and shed her business skirt and thigh-high hose. The fabric was cool against her legs as she fastened it just below her waist. She shrugged out of her suit jacket and tossed it on the chair in the corner.

She had firm breasts so she scarcely ever bothered with a bra. Tonight was no exception. She paired the skirt with a soft white camisole. She took a quick glimpse of herself in the mirror. She looked the way she always did, cool and polished. She tried to fluff her hair up and then realized what she was doing.

Hayden wasn't really dating her. She closed her eyes, leaning her forehead against the mirror. Then she took a shuddering breath. She was strong, capable, and this was the only penance available to her.

Over the years she'd tried to pay Alan MacKenzie back the money she'd taken. Not in one lump sum, as she'd never had that much disposable cash on hand. But in chunks. And he'd always refused, saying that he didn't want her money; he only wanted his son to be happy.

She didn't doubt that. Alan and Hayden had a complex relationship that she'd never taken the time to understand until it had been too late. She'd realized that Hayden had only dated her to needle his father. But she'd been dating him for his money, so she hadn't quibbled.

She was exactly the wrong type of woman for a man with Hayden's future back then. Hayden would never know how right his father had been. Alan had made it clear that he'd tell Hayden every detail of the life she'd hidden from him if she hadn't taken the money he'd offered.

But now… A lot had changed in ten years. Now apparently Alan thought that she could help Hayden. And in order to pull this off she'd have to keep that secret from the man she'd betrayed.

She was dithering and that didn't fit with who she was, so she pushed away from the wall, put on her strappy gold sandals and left the room.

She didn't look back or hesitate. She'd made a conscious decision when she'd come to Vegas. Facing the past had never been an easy thing. She'd always looked forward because the past— She didn't want to go there. Not now.

She exited the elevator in the lobby and glanced

around for Hayden. She didn't see him at first but then found him standing off to one side talking with an extremely attractive blonde.

Shelby realized that for all she knew, Hayden was involved with another woman and really was just using her for revenge. It didn't matter that she'd said she was doing whatever it took to bring Hayden some peace; she knew in her heart she still wanted him.

Hayden had changed clothes as well, wearing a button-down shirt in midnight blue and a pair of faded jeans. On anyone else the outfit would have seemed casual, but the way he carried himself belied that impression.

He glanced up and caught her gaze, motioning her over. The woman he was talking to had the kind of beauty that made Shelby feel like an ugly duckling. Her long blond hair fell past her shoulders and her makeup, though a little heavy, accentuated her classic bone structure.

Hayden gestured for her to join them. The woman glanced over at her and smiled. It was a sweet, welcoming smile and Shelby felt warmed by it.

"Roxy, this is Shelby Paxton. She owns a boutique that's opening here in the Chimera in the next few weeks. Shelby, this is Roxy O'Malley, the star of the Chimera's top-rated revue."

"Nice to meet you," Shelby said.

"Same here. What kind of shop do you own?"

"Lingerie."

"My favorite kind. I'll have to check it out."

Shelby reached into her purse and pulled out an invitation to the grand-opening party. "We're having a little party to celebrate."

"I'll be there," Roxy said. She glanced over at Hayden.

"I'll look into that matter we discussed," Hayden said.

"I'd appreciate it, Hay. I know he could be harmless, but something about him made me leery."

"No problem, Roxy. I'll let you know what I find out."

When Roxy left them, he turned his attention to Shelby. She felt his hot gaze on her, taking in the length of her bare arms, lingering on the scooped curve of her neckline and then skimming down to her feet in the tiny sandals.

She crossed her arms around her waist but then realized she was projecting her vulnerability for him to see. And Hayden was intimately acquainted with some of her weaknesses. She didn't need for him to know that he rattled her.

"Thanks for joining me for dinner," he said. "Can you walk in those shoes?"

"Yes. They're surprisingly comfortable. What were you two discussing?"

"Jealous?"

She tipped her head to the side. "Yes, I think I am."

He laughed. "Don't be. It was only business."

"She didn't seem like just an employee."

"You're right, she's not."

"Is she your lover?" Shelby asked, though she hadn't gotten that intimate vibe from the two of them.

"No. More like a kid sister. I really try to make the Chimera like a family. So many people come here alone and..."

Hayden knew loneliness. It was one of the things they'd both had in common. Something Shelby hadn't had to lie about when they'd been dating long ago. Her mother had always been working, just like Hayden's dad. It had given them some unexpected common ground.

She tucked her hand under his elbow. "You're a nice man."

"Sometimes."

He escorted her out of the main lobby to the escalators that led to the mezzanine level. "Where are we going?" she asked.

"To the stars."

"We're going flying?" This was the man who'd swept her off her feet years ago. He'd offered her the fantasy of romance and she'd lapped it up without thinking of the consequences. Like those sunset airplane rides in his Cessna. He'd taken things that she'd never imagined she would do and made them happen.

"Not tonight. Last year I had a planetarium built. Well, Deacon and I did."

"Who's Deacon?"

"Deacon Prescott. He owns the Golden Dream. We work together on a lot of projects. I thought we'd have a drink under the stars before dinner."

"Isn't that going to be a little awkward with all your other guests?"

"No, Shel. I closed down one of the theaters. I'd rather my guests stay in the casino anyway."

"More money to be made that way, right?"

"You know that money makes the world go round."

"Yes, I do."

He slipped his hand under her elbow and led her through the mezzanine. He was stopped twice by his employees with questions that he had to take. Owning Bêcheur d'Or made her understand how demanding running any kind of business could be. She'd checked in with Paige early this morning and had a conference call scheduled for tomorrow at 9:00 a.m. with the builders of the next boutique in Washington, D.C.

Finally they entered a long corridor that was sparsely occupied. The piped-in music wasn't some generic Muzak but the sophisticated beauty of Wynton Marsalis playing the trumpet.

Shelby closed her eyes and wondered for a moment if this might have been her life had she made a different choice all those years ago.

"Vegas has changed in the last ten years," she said, though she suspected it was the changes inside herself that made the city seem so different.

"Yes, it has."

"Did you have anything to do with that?" she asked to fill the silence and keep her mind off the uncomfortable feeling that maybe she hadn't changed as much as she wished she had.

"What do you think?" he asked.

She paused and tilted her head to the side to study him. She knew without a doubt that he was on the image committee and the development committees for the Strip. Hayden wouldn't chance leaving any detail that could affect his business to someone else.

"Yes. I like how sophisticated your hotel is, but that doesn't change the fact that one block over, the area is still a little sleazy."

"Everyone is looking for something different in Vegas and we like to say we can accommodate any type of poison."

"What about me?" she asked, wondering what he thought about her was dangerous. *What you think of yourself is the only thing that matters*. But she'd never held herself in high regard.

"What about you?" he asked. He pulled her into a small alcove.

She felt secluded from the rest of the world with the wall at her back and Hayden blocking her front. He stared down at her with an unreadable expression and she shivered deep inside, realizing how much of life she'd been missing since she left this man.

Because she'd never been able to really trust a man enough to let him affect her the way Hayden always had. She swallowed against a dry throat and said, "What's my poison?"

"Only you can say. I suspect that it's a mix between the gritty reality of where you grew up and this." He gestured to the ornately decorated hallway.

"What about you?" she asked, not willing to dwell too much on how gritty her reality had been.

"I'm the center ring, master of ceremonies. Making sure that whatever reason—fantasy or desire—you brought with you gets fulfilled."

There was a husky sensuality in his voice. She looked

up at Hayden, into his deep blue eyes, and realized that he wasn't all show and both of them knew it.

Hayden liked the feel of Shelby's arm under his hand. The lobby of the planetarium was actually between his hotel and Deacon's Golden Dream. They'd funded a wing together last year that would enhance the experience for their guests. He also had a traveling Impressionists exhibit down the hall in the art museum.

Most people came to Vegas for a reason and Shelby's was probably just profit motivated, but his gut said there was more. He wanted to know more about those reasons.

Hayden had asked the head chef, Louis Patin, to send up champagne and strawberries for a predinner snack, and one of the hostesses handed a wicker basket to Hayden as they entered. He took Shelby up the back stairs into one of the VIP rooms.

"Give me a minute to get everything set up," he said.

"Can I help?" she asked.

"No. I've got it." He gestured toward the plush velvet covered seats positioned in front of the low wall. "Enjoy the show."

She sat down and Hayden watched her carefully cross her legs, then shift to find a more comfortable position on the chair. The slit in her skirt widened and he realized it was a wraparound type and that only one or two buttons were keeping that silky fabric in place.

He caught a glimpse of her thigh before she pulled the fabric over her leg, covering it up. He sighed and then turned to open their champagne.

She was watching him as he poured the liquid and handed her a glass. The material from her skirt slipped free of her fingers. It slid down her leg. The woman had great legs.

"Why are we playing these games, Hayden?" she asked, running her fingers along the length of exposed skin. The stars had begun to appear on the planetarium ceiling, and soft classical music began to play.

"I wasn't aware we were. We both like to flirt," he said, lightly touching his glass to hers then moving back to regard her. Her flesh looked so soft and tempting in the muted lighting in the room. His own fingers tingled with the need to caress her. He clenched them and sipped the bubbling drink.

"I thought you were the master of ceremonies. Flirting is where we both try to pretend that we're not still attracted to each other."

"Is that what you've been doing?" he asked. Already his blood was flowing heavy and every nerve in his body said screw talking and take her. She didn't want the niceties he put on when he was trying to be a gentleman instead of the gambler he essentially was.

"I've been trying. And not successfully I might add," she said, twisting her fingers together in a nervous gesture that made him realize that it might not be real desire that motivated Shelby. It was the waiting. Not knowing which way things were going to fall between them.

"Why?" he asked, needing to know more.

"I can't figure it out. There's always been something

about you that makes me feel…I don't know, like I'm about to jump off a cliff. I know that it's going to be an exhilarating ride but I'm not sure my parachute is going to open in time."

It was different for him. He'd spent the last ten years protecting his emotions from the women with whom he got involved. It hadn't even been conscious at first, but the last woman he'd broken up with had said that he was the coldest man she'd ever slept with. White-hot in bed but stone-cold out. And Hayden had realized the truth about himself. The truth that had probably been there the entire time. He couldn't do things by half measures.

"We agreed to dinner," he said.

"I know. But I got nervous when I saw you watching me."

"Wanting you," he said.

He closed the distance between them and bent down on one knee. Up close he could see the smooth, lightly tanned skin.

"Do you want me to want you that way?"

"Yes," she said. "Yes, because that gives me something real to cling to."

He shouldn't touch her. Not now. Yet he couldn't help himself. He reached out, scraping one nail along the edge of the material that covered her leg. She shivered, but didn't pull away.

Her hand fell to his shoulder, holding on to him while he touched her. Stroking her was addictive. Her skin was softer than anything he'd touched in a long time. Her muscles weren't hardened by hours in the gym, but softer. It was a very feminine thigh.

Taking the fabric in his hand, he drew it up over her leg and uncovered her. She dropped her hand to the top of her thigh, lightly resting it on top of his.

"Sit with me, Hayden. Let's talk."

He didn't ask why. He knew that she wanted that sweet feeling that had always been between them. The real reason he could never forgive Shelby wasn't so much because of the money she'd taken. It was because of the lesson she'd taught him.

He'd never been the kind of man who had let anyone inside him. Never let anyone see the real man behind the trappings of the spoiled rich-boy facade. But he'd been tempted to let her in and she'd walked away.

"Why'd you do it, Shel?"

She trembled and lifted her hand from his. She pushed away from the chair and walked a few steps from him, looking out over the railing up toward the stars that were playing across the wide ceiling.

He stood but kept the distance between them. When she spoke it was almost too soft for him to hear, but he could make out the words.

"I needed security."

"That's it?" he asked, sensing she was hiding something. He knew then that subterfuge was a big part of what was going on here and it had little to do with sex. It was all about who they both were and who they didn't want the other to see. "Lay it out for me, babe. Because that just sounds like a line."

"I left because I knew that you were twenty-four-carat solid gold and I was that spray-on stuff they use at fairs that wears off after a few days and leaves a green mark."

She turned her head away from him. "I wanted to leave before I left a mark on you that you'd have a hard time getting rid of."

Hayden led Shelby out of the planetarium to a very exclusive restaurant on the fifty-fifth floor of the Chimera. They were led to a private booth that faced the floor-to-ceiling plate-glass windows overlooking Las Vegas. The view was breathtaking. She slid onto the bench and straightened her skirt, looking casual and at ease.

But Hayden wasn't. Tension rode him like a gambler trying to find a winning streak.

Knowing it tightened the knot in his gut. Why did this woman still have a hold on him? And would revenge be enough to loosen her hold?

His mind warned that logic didn't play a part in his actions here and now, but he wasn't really listening with his mind.

The curve of her neck was looking fragile and vulnerable, and he realized that talking about her past was one of her weak points. They'd never really talked about where she'd come from. Perhaps he'd been too shallow to care or too arrogant to think any of that mattered. But now, with the years between them, he realized that her past very much shaped the kind of relationship they'd had.

"Thanks for showing me the stars tonight," she said.

"You're welcome. Would you like some more wine?" he asked.

She shook her head. "Let's get down to business. I believe you said you want to get what you paid for, right?"

When she said it like that he sounded like a bastard. It didn't matter that they both had been acting true to form in those days. He had been a spoiled young man who'd picked a pretty, shy girl who needed him. He'd liked the way she'd clung to his arm, let him pay for everything and make all the decisions. That wasn't politically correct but he wasn't really a PC kind of guy. Despite the money he'd always had, sophistication had always eluded him.

"Yes. That's what I want."

He saw in her eyes that she knew it as well. Knew that she was sitting across from a man who wasn't quite the gentleman he pretended to be.

"You make me feel very feminine when you look at me that way. And I'm not at all used to it. Most men I date are intimidated by me."

"Why?"

"Who knows," she said, but bit her bottom lip.

She knew. Shelby always knew why people acted the way they did. She made it her business to pay attention to those details. "Just guess."

"Because I'm driven to make my company a success. I made too many mistakes when I was young."

"Like you're old now?" he asked.

"You know what I mean. Sometimes I'm amazed at how immature I was when we were together."

He leaned back, resting his arm on the seat behind her. He wanted to pull her closer to him, to cradle her against his body and protect her. But Shelby didn't need him to do that. He imagined that was what she'd been talking about. That men realized that Shelby was an independent woman who made her own way. It was a bit intimidating.

"You've done really well. I read an article about your company in *Entrepreneur.* The reporter said you were one of the savviest business minds he'd ever encountered."

She shrugged the comment aside. "I think he was just being nice."

"Reporters are never nice. He respected what you'd done." Hayden realized he did, too. She'd taken the hand that life had dealt her and rolled with it.

"Well…" She shrugged. It was clear to him that Shelby wasn't there yet. She didn't really respect herself. Had he played any part in that?

"Let's get back to us. I think your dad paid me off so—"

"No, Shelby. I paid that money to you." He hadn't meant to say it but it was best she knew the facts. He wasn't playing around this game—the stakes were high and he wanted to be damn sure Shelby realized it.

"What?"

"Old Alan wanted to make sure I never forgot the lesson he was teaching. He gave you the money, then made me pay him back every cent." His father had always been real fond of that kind of demonstration—one where the lesson was reinforced by humiliation. It didn't help that Hayden had played on his father's biggest weakness: a woman with big soul-filled eyes and an empty bank account.

"Hayden… I had no idea. I'm so sorry. I took the money…well, I didn't mind taking it from your dad because I knew it was how he kept score."

He said nothing. She'd pegged his father easily. It was how Alan kept score and he'd paid off three wives of his own, so Shelby knew that it didn't bother him. Hayden didn't say anything else but he knew that he'd paid for Shelby with more than just money. He'd paid for her with his soul and now he wanted hers.

Shelby couldn't have been more shocked. She'd never imagined that Hayden had ultimately paid for her giving up their relationship. But then she'd allowed Alan to push a wedge between them. Let him threaten her with revealing the secret she'd kept from Hayden. The one she still didn't really want him to know. She wished there were some way to escape the intimacy that he'd created around them. She didn't want to be sitting so close to him while hashing out the past.

In her mind it was easy to pretend that she was noble and wanted to pay him back—whatever the cost—so that he could find some peace from the past. But the reality was, it hurt. She didn't want to flirt with the only man with whom she'd ever really been honest emotionally.

She didn't want to open up herself and him to the kind of hurt that would undoubtedly come. Because she knew that she wasn't going to be able to just give him a week of sex and then watch him walk away.

Hayden put his arm around her and pulled her against his side. She closed her eyes and pretended that this was something else. Something that she'd done without for a long time. Comfort was easy to take from Hayden. He had big shoulders and a solid chest, and he was more than capable of carrying any burdens.

But that didn't mean that eventually the burdens wouldn't be too heavy for him. She turned in his embrace, put her arms around his waist and rested her head over his heart. His hands moved up and down her back, before settling on her hips, holding her close.

His breathing changed, grew heavier. She felt his body changing under hers as well. There was no getting around the fact that sexually they were like kindling and flame. But was that the kind of fire that could be tamed or would it once again consume them?

He brought one hand up under her chin, tipping her head back. "What are you thinking?"

She struggled against telling him the truth. He already saw more of her than anyone else except Paige. Most people she met were content to see only the surface of who she was—a driven, competent businesswoman. But Hayden...he'd known the vulnerable woman underneath. The one who still wasn't sure of her place in the world.

"I'm thinking this is a mess that I made and it's past time I cleaned it up."

"I think we can both carry the blame," he said, stroking her cheek with a gentleness that made her heart beat a little faster.

"Do you ever feel like life is really a great tragedy? Like the ones in operas?"

He didn't say anything, only continued stroking her back. Shelby wondered if she'd said too much. Her life had never been ideal, but comparing it to a tragedy... She wasn't some scared little miss. She needed to stop acting like one.

"I think that in some ways much of our lives is like opera, how operas show the intense emotions that sometimes influence our decisions. Why?"

This was the man who'd convinced her to take a chance and marry him. This soft poet's soul that she'd scarcely glimpsed since her return to Vegas.

"I thought maybe we were caught at the end of the second act. You know, where all seems doomed."

"And that maybe it was time to move on to the third act?"

She couldn't answer. In one of her favorite operas, *Tristan und Isolde,* the third act had them both dying. But for a love that was so true and right that it captured both of their souls, uniting them even in death. Maybe that was the trailer-park girl deep inside her, but she wanted a man to love her that much.

"What do you want from me?" he asked.

That was the million-dollar question. Alan wanted his son happy and expected her to fix whatever she'd broken when she left. Hayden wanted closure and revenge. But what did she want? Shelby had never really figured that out and it was time to. "I guess a chance to make this real."

Hayden could tempt her into believing that if she showed him her soul he'd reward her with his heart. But she suspected if she did that, he'd take the revenge he so richly deserved. She felt the Sword of Damocles hanging over her. Knew that at any minute the hair might snap.

"How could it not be?" he asked in that deep voice of his.

He was right. There was nothing subtle about the man holding her and nothing tentative in him. He was going to pursue her for his own reasons and she had to decide what she was going to do. She knew with bone-deep certainty that she wasn't going to resist him. He was her secret longing and she'd never forgotten him. So now she had to decide. Was she really going to meekly let him take charge of this? Or was she going to meet him on a level playing field?

"I want you, too, Hayden. And I have an offer for you."

"I'm listening." He traced the line of her spine up her back. His finger circled her neck and toyed with the strap of her camisole.

"Let's make this real. Let's say what this really is. I want a chance to get to know each other the way we never did before."

He pulled the strap of her camisole toward her shoulder and then lowered his head, blowing on the exposed skin. As shivers moved down her arm and back, she undulated in his arms, holding more tightly to his waist.

"Okay," he said.

"Okay?"

She couldn't think when he was this close to her. When he surrounded her with his heat, his touch and his scent. She just wanted to close her eyes and pretend that they didn't have the past between them. Close her eyes and imagine that Hayden MacKenzie really could want Shelby Paxton just for who she was.

"I'll let you try to make me fall in love with you. But honestly, Shelby, I don't have a heart."

"Yes, you do. And I'm just the woman to find it." She promised herself she would. There was no problem she couldn't solve once she put her mind to it. She'd figure Hayden out—find out what made him tick—and slowly work her way into his heart, because she knew from hearing him speak of her betrayed that he still had one.

"You might be right. After all, you were the last one to see it."

She shivered and this time it wasn't from his touch. It was from the coolness beneath his words. She realized this time she may have risked more than she'd anticipated.

"Double or nothing," she murmured, realizing that was exactly the bet she'd made. Both of their hearts united and at peace or once again broken.

"That's the kind of gamble I make every day in business, but this…"

"I'm in if you are, Hayden," she said, unable to keep the challenge from her voice.

"Oh, I'm in."

Three

"The only way to do this is to live together," Hayden said while they were eating dessert.

Shelby choked on a bite of her tiramisu. "What?"

He patted her back and handed her a glass of water. He liked the thought of it now. Her living in his home. Shelby there when he woke up and there when he went to sleep. She said she wanted a chance to know him, to seduce him this time. Living together made the most sense.

"You okay?" he asked.

"Yeah. No. I can't think this late at night. I've had too much rich food."

He smiled at the way she said it, but he knew the truth. She wasn't ready to make a decision. Once she saw his home, though, she'd capitulate.

"Come up to my place and just see it."

She shook her head.

He frowned. In the past, Shelby had never denied him anything. But of course, this wasn't the past. And she was a different woman.

"Why not?"

"Because unlike you I need more than four hours of sleep every night. I need a solid eight and I'm tired."

She had a point. His cell had been vibrating with new messages and he saw Raul, his general manager, hanging around the hostess stand waiting for him. Hayden's reality involved work for almost a solid eighteen hours a day. But that didn't mean he was letting this go. "Are you free for breakfast?"

"Just coffee. It takes a lot of work to open a store in three weeks, plus I have a conference call with Paige and the developers for our D.C. project at 9:00 a.m."

He pulled his BlackBerry phone/PDA from his pocket and checked his calendar for tomorrow. He had an 8:00 a.m. meeting with the gaming commission. Followed by a meeting with his roulette-table staff. And he needed to talk to his head of security about the man who'd been sitting in the front row at each of Roxy's performances for the last three weeks.

"What time?" he asked. He'd move some stuff around if he had to. But his schedule was already tight. Why was he doing this? He didn't question his motives, only knew that if Shelby was willing to work toward something solid, hell, he was, too. It felt right, having her here with him.

She shook her head, her thick hair slipping over her shoulder and down her chest to curl over her breast. "I don't know...seven?"

He remembered how her neck tasted, how soft her skin had felt under his touch, and everything in him went on alert. He wanted this woman. Wanted her naked in his bed. He could see her against his gray sheets. A splash of color in his black-and-white bedroom.

She stared at him.

"What is it? Seven isn't good for coffee?"

He shook himself, but he couldn't push away the image of her lying on his bed with a couple of pillows shoved under her hips. Those lush long legs open, inviting.

"No, that's perfect. I'll have a key card sent to your room. Just come up when you're ready." He was ready now. He didn't know if he could wait. If he could let her set the pace for this reunion of theirs. He wanted to take the lead. Get her into bed and push away the past in the most elemental way. To reassert his dominance over her by making her his.

"Hayden..."

"Yes?" he said. He signed the check and slid out of the booth.

"I'm supposed to be seducing you," she said, joining him.

"Do you think Tristan really waited for Isolde?" he asked, reminding her of the opera she loved, the one that he'd let her talk endlessly about when they'd dated long ago.

She smiled. It was all that was sexy and sweet. Much

like the woman herself. "I'm sure he didn't, but he was a warrior."

"Maybe I am, too," he said, putting his arm around her and leading her out of the restaurant. He'd learned some hard lessons when she'd left him. He'd become a different man because of her. He had realized he was no longer the golden boy who had everything handed to him. Instead, he knew, in his heart, he was a man who'd fight for what he wanted.

"I thought you were a gambler," she said.

"Can't a man be both?" he asked, leading her to the bank of elevators. He didn't really want to dwell on his own shortcomings.

"You tell me," she said.

"I already did."

"Where are we going?"

"I'm escorting you back to your room."

"That's so sweet," she said.

He bit the inside of his mouth to keep from smiling. "I'm a sweet guy."

"Ha. Don't think you can put the moves on me and I'll invite you in."

"Put the moves on you? Give me a break. I'm a little more suave than that."

They got in the elevator car. There was another couple already in there who got off on the thirtieth floor. Shelby's suite was on the thirty-fifth. She pulled her key card from her purse when the elevator stopped on her floor.

"Good night," she said, stepping out.

He followed her into the hall. "Yes, it has been."

"Don't, Hayden. This isn't easy for me."

"I'm not pushing, baby. I'm just seeing you home. Something we never did before."

She flushed a little bit. He wondered at the secrets she hid. Her background wasn't like his, and he hadn't pushed her to talk about it. Maybe that had been part of the problem. He'd easily accepted the personal boundaries she'd set because they'd allowed him to make her into what he wanted her to be.

"About that…"

"Don't say anything more. This is double or nothing. The stakes are high, and as you said, you need some sleep. We'll start again in the morning."

He took her key card from her hand and unlocked her door for her, pushing it open. She paused in the entryway, the glow from a lamp backlighting her.

She looked ethereal, with her thick wavy hair falling around her shoulders. Her skin was soft and pink, and that little white top skimmed her curves.

He bent down to brush his lips to hers. Just a sweet salute to the agreement they'd made. But once his lips touched hers, all that fled and he needed more.

She parted her lips and he tasted her sweet mouth. He touched his tongue to hers as he braced one hand on the doorjamb and buried the other in her hair, holding her head still.

He lifted his head slowly. Her eyes were heavy lidded and he saw the first flush of desire on her face. If he pushed now he could have what he wanted tonight, but he knew that he'd lose ground when tomorrow morning came.

He rubbed his thumb over her lower lip before dropping his hand to his side. He passed her key back to her. "Now it's a good night."

He waited for her to step inside her room and close the door and then he walked away. He wasn't really sure what was going to happen with Shelby. He didn't believe in love. Which might be why he'd overlooked the fact that Shelby had obviously kept a lot of her life from him. But for the first time since he'd opened his casino, he felt really alive.

Shelby had set her alarm for six o'clock but didn't need the buzzing to wake her up. Her sleep had been plagued by fevered dreams of Hayden. He'd always been her guilty, erotic, secret dream man. The one she visited late at night when no one else could know.

His kisses had refueled a fire that had never been extinguished. She was restless and edgy when the alarm finally rang. She hurried through her shower and dressed in record time.

Everything with Hayden was exactly the way she'd always dreamed it could be. But in the back of her mind the thought that Alan had sent her here weighed heavily. She didn't know how to bring up Alan without alienating Hayden once more.

Anxious to see him again, she deliberately hesitated in her suite. She didn't want him to know how much she craved him. She wanted to have a little of the control she'd ceded so easily to him last time, some sort of equality. But she wasn't sure how to find it.

The key card for his penthouse apartment had been delivered to her last night, just twenty minutes after he'd left. She held it in her hand. It was the key to something she'd always wanted. Something she hadn't believed in enough to stick around for the last time. But now…

The phone rang before she could complete the thought. She picked it up reluctantly. Only two people would call her here. Paige, her business partner, or Alan.

"This is Shelby."

"How's our plan going?"

Alan's voice was deeper, scratchier than his son's, thanks no doubt to years of smoking. She hated that he never identified himself. She suspected he did it to prove that everyone remembered him.

"You still there?"

"Yes, I'm here. I…it doesn't feel right. I'm here but that's got to be the end of it, Alan. I don't want to be talking with you behind his back."

"Do you really think that my son is going to accept your past? Do you really think that you can make him overlook the fact that we MacKenzies can trace our ancestors back to the first westward migration and you don't even know who your father is?"

His words hurt and made a wave of shame roll over her. Yes, she did think that. Hayden was no snob, and it was more Shelby's business image and sense of personal privacy that would suffer from the exposure. But she knew she had her work cut out for her in changing Hayden's opinion of her anyway. "I'll do whatever I have to." With those words she hung up on him.

Her phone started ringing again but she didn't answer it. The last time she'd listened to Alan, she'd ended up hurting Hayden. Not this time.

It was exactly seven o'clock when she stepped off the elevator and arrived at Hayden's door. She hesitated a minute and knocked. Despite the key, she didn't feel that she should just let herself in.

He opened the door a few seconds later. He wore a pair of dress pants, a blue shirt that highlighted his eyes and a discreetly colored tie and had a phone cradled between his neck and shoulder. He gestured for her to come in.

"Sounds good," Hayden said into the phone. "Call my assistant and set up a meeting for tomorrow."

He disconnected the call. "Right on time. I was hoping you'd come early."

She didn't know how to respond to that. She'd been so needy before that she was afraid to let him see how much she still needed from him. Still wanted from him.

"I had them set up a light breakfast out on the terrace. I'll give you a tour later, if we have time."

She followed him across the hardwood floors through the living room. There was no video equipment or expensive television, which seemed odd to her for a bachelor. The leather sofa and love seat were situated to face a seascape scene on the wall.

Floor-to-ceiling windows lined one wall and there was a bar along another wall and a small poker table set in front of it. The room was definitely masculine in its decor but so comfortable that she immediately felt at home.

"I like this," she said, stopping to take it all in.

"Good. You can change anything you want when you move in except for my poker area. I host a quarterly poker weekend for some of my friends."

"Tell me about them," she said. She wanted to know more about Hayden. She'd been afraid to meet his friends when they'd been together before. Afraid that they'd make Hayden realize how different she was from his set, how she didn't really belong with the golden boy he'd been.

"Well, I've mentioned Deacon. He's a trusted friend as well as a business partner. Then there's Max Williams—we went to the same prep school. And Scott Rivers—I met him when I was bumming around Europe."

She raised her eyebrows. Former child star Scott Rivers was still an A-list celebrity. She hadn't known he and Hayden were friends.

"When'd you do that?"

"After you left."

"Why?" she asked. She remembered what he'd said about having paid the million dollars she'd taken from Alan. She'd never thought about how he'd earned the money.

"I was trying to make the old man give in and release my trust fund."

"Did it work?" But she knew it hadn't. Alan was a stubborn man and he'd been intent on teaching Hayden a lesson. Unfortunately it had worked better than Alan had anticipated.

"No. It didn't. Finally I ended up on the Côte d'A-zur—with no money. I stayed with Scott for a while and then one morning I woke up hungover and out of cash and realized that I couldn't keep living that way. The old man wasn't going to give in. So I went to the first casino I came to and asked for a job."

"Why a casino?"

"I had this idea of showing the old man up."

"Did it work?"

"I don't know if I showed him up, but it gave me an understanding of where he was coming from and eventually it enabled us to have something to talk about."

He led her outside to a wrought-iron table that was set with a carafe of coffee and two plates. "I remembered you liked croissants but I couldn't remember anything else."

"A croissant is fine," she said when they were both seated.

There were also eggs, bacon, sausage and home fries. But she wasn't hungry. She couldn't think about food when Hayden was nearby. She just...wanted him.

"What do you think of the view?"

She glanced out at Vegas. This was the vantage point she'd always wanted to see it from. And knowing that, understanding that she was still that trailer-park girl wanting desperately to escape, she hesitated to say anything else. Because she didn't really know if she wanted to say yes to Hayden because of the view or because of the man.

* * *

Hayden's PDA beeped, reminding him he had to be downstairs in five minutes for his eight o'clock meeting. But he wasn't ready to leave yet.

"What was that?" Shelby asked.

"I've got to go to a meeting in a few minutes," he said. For the first time in recent memory he wasn't ready to go to work. Shelby was more exciting than business.

She pushed to her feet, dropping the napkin on the table. "I need to get to work, too. Thanks for inviting me up for breakfast."

He captured her wrist in his hand, holding her by his side. Her bones felt delicate under his big hand, but he knew that she held all the power. He wanted her. And he'd do whatever he had to do to have her. "I invited you to move in with me."

"I know, but if I do that we'll be in bed together and...I'm not ready yet. I don't want to make the same mistakes we did last time."

"What mistakes are those?" he asked. He'd always figured last time his only mistake was not showering her with presents. But he knew now he'd done other things wrong, too. Frankly, he wasn't sure he'd do them right this time. He wanted Shelby—she was the only woman he'd never forgotten—but he wasn't sure he had forever left in him. His world changed with the roll of the dice or the flip of a card.

"The mistake," Shelby said, "was and would be letting great sex cloud the fact that we don't know each other."

Back then, they'd spent most of their time together naked. He knew he'd been Shelby's first lover and to be honest it had seemed as if they'd been made for each other. He still got hard thinking of the chemistry between them in those days.

"Great sex?" he asked. Maybe he wouldn't have to work so hard to convince her to move in with him after all.

She pulled away from him and wrapped her arms around her waist. That was the second time he'd seen her do that. Why did she? "Trust you to fixate on that."

"It was the only good thing you said." And it was. The sex between them had been great. It had been easy to let sex and lust take the place of friendship and genuine affection. This time he knew she wanted more— but he wasn't exactly sure he would allow it.

"Are you free later on?" he asked.

"For what?"

"A flight over the desert. I recall you liked flying at sunset." She'd never been in a plane before he'd taken her up in his little Cessna. Hayden loved to fly. His plane collection was more extensive now.

She bit her lower lip. "You remember a lot about me."

"Too much sometimes," he said, more to himself.

"I'm embarrassed to say I don't remember the details like you do."

"Why embarrassed?" he asked.

"Because…I was so shallow back then. I was…"

"What?" he asked.

"Fixated on not becoming my mother." She said it so quietly he knew that she didn't want to admit it.

"Are you still?" he asked.

"I think the fear is so deeply embedded in me that I'll never escape it."

He'd never really asked about her family. He'd known that she hadn't had a lot of money—that had been part of her initial attraction for his younger, rebellious self—and that her family wasn't very close, but beyond that he knew nothing.

"What do you like?" she asked at last.

"Pleasing you," he said smoothly. He hoped she didn't realize he was using the same lines and practiced moves on her that he did with all the women he dated. But he knew no other way.

"I don't think so. If we're going to do this...if I'm ever going to move in here, Hayden, we have to have honesty between us."

He rubbed the back of his neck. He was unable to believe she'd called him on his behavior, especially since she had at least as many secrets as he did. "That works both ways."

She swallowed and her face lost color. "Okay, what do you want to know?"

"What did my dad say to make you leave?"

She shivered. He saw her and almost reached for her, but he knew that he used sex as a substitute for real emotions and forced himself to keep his hands by his sides.

"I...um..."

"Just say it. Nothing is that bad. Was it about your mom?"

"Yes. My mom is a stripper."

"Okay. What else?"

"Nothing, just that I don't know who my father is. Mom isn't even sure."

He reached for her then, pulled her into his arms and just held her. She felt small and fragile, and Hayden wanted to take this burden from her. But he knew his dad made a huge issue of ancestry. "I don't care."

She tipped her head back, glancing up at him with those wide eyes of hers. "I do."

He rubbed his hands down her back, not sure what to say. After a few minutes she pulled back.

"Now, what do you really like to do? I want tonight to be to you what flying at sunset used to be to me."

He let her change the subject, lighten the mood because he sensed she needed some distance. "Anything I can gamble on—poker, basketball, skydiving, a fast ride on a desert highway on the back of my Harley, hot sex."

She tipped her head to the side, studying him again. "Wow, that's some list. Let me see what I can come up with. I should be finished in my shop by eight."

Hayden didn't want to relinquish control of her. He knew it was because he'd been burned the one time he'd trusted her. He knew he should let the past go but he couldn't.

She framed his face with her cold hands. Leaning up, she kissed him. There was a lot of emotion, past and present, in her kiss. Her mouth moved over his in a way that was more enthusiastic than practiced. He slipped his arms around her waist and tugged her closer to him.

She lifted her mouth from his and looked into his

eyes for a long moment. What was she looking for in his eyes?

"Let me do this. I want to know the man you've become and show you the woman I am today."

He dropped his arms and turned away, taking two deep breaths to try to get the scent of her out of his nose. But he couldn't. He was inundated with Shelby. Her taste was on his tongue, the feel of her soft skin under his fingers….

His phone rang and he cursed, pulling it out. "I have to go."

"I won't keep you, but what about tonight?"

"I…"

"Hayden, I know that I lost your trust, but let me do this. It's important to me."

He stared at her. "Okay."

She smiled up at him and he felt like a hero. Something he hadn't felt in a long time. But he also felt a little bad that such a simple thing could make her so happy.

"What should I plan for?"

"I'm not sure yet. I'll call your assistant during the day and leave the details."

She turned to leave and then stopped. "You won't interfere, will you?"

"How?"

"By watching me on the security camera or monitoring the calls I make?"

He shrugged. "I can't really monitor your calls."

"And the security camera?"

"I like watching you, Shel."

She blushed then. "I like watching you, too."

"Say the word and we could move you in today."

"Not yet. I want you to ask me after you get to know me."

"I know the important stuff."

"Like what?"

"That we both like great sex," he said.

She laughed and they walked to the elevator. The doors closed and he watched her leave but knew he'd made progress in getting her back in his bed.

Four

Shelby's day passed too quickly. She had no idea what to do for Hayden. But she wasn't giving up. She hadn't come from a trailer park to where she was by being easily swayed from her goal. She wracked her brain as she worked, trying to think of a date that Hayden wouldn't expect but would love.

It was harder than she expected. Why couldn't Hayden be like other men? The men she'd dated since she'd left him at the altar all those years ago. A man who was…not important to her, she realized.

Despite the fact that Alan was responsible for her being in Vegas at this time, she wanted Hayden for herself. She wanted him with her for the rest of her life. The thought scared her because it made every action she took more important.

And though she hated to do it, she called Alan for some suggestions. The fact of the matter was, Alan knew Hayden better than she did. Shelby vowed that would change. Alan gave her the number to the marina on Lake Mead where Hayden kept his yacht and said he'd call in the morning for an update.

Shelby made a mental note to turn her cell phone off before Alan called. She longed for a time when she could be with Hayden and just be herself. The first time she'd been too young and too afraid he'd see what she really was. Where she'd really come from.

Ultimately that had led to her leaving him. This time...well, this time she was balancing between keeping him from finding out that Alan had sent her here and just falling for him.

She thought it was telling that Hayden hadn't mentioned his yacht. She wondered if she'd stumbled on to a private thing he liked to keep secret. From running her business she knew how demanding a career like Hayden's could be. Was the yacht his escape valve? His one place where no one could find him?

She hated the out-of-control feeling. But she couldn't figure out how to be herself and keep Hayden. It wasn't that she didn't think she deserved a man like him. It was just that being back in Vegas reminded her sharply of the girl she'd been. And that girl had too many insecurities.

The phone rang and she finished fastening the leather bustier to the headless mannequin before going to an-

swer it. The scarlet garment had a matching thong and
was one of Bêcheur d'Or's top sellers.

"I approve of the outfit," Hayden said, his voice low
and husky. She smiled to herself.

"Voyeur. I'm wearing jeans and a T-shirt."

"So I like to watch. That's not a sin."

But his voice sounded like one, a carnal sin. This
morning he'd been low-key, a man biding his time, but
not any longer. Shelby felt restless inside and knew that
Hayden had to feel it, too.

She ran her hands down the sides of her thighs. She'd
changed into jeans and a T-shirt in one of the dressing
rooms earlier. Unpacking boxes was sweaty, dirty work.
But she liked seeing the store come together.

"Would you bend over a little and run your hands
down your backside?" he asked.

"Is that what you want?" she asked, surprised at how
easily his voice and words got to her.

"Baby, you know it is."

She knew that she was playing a dangerous game
with Hayden. On a sexual level she'd never been adven-
turous, never taken any risks. Ha, who was she kidding,
she didn't take any risks with her life.

But now, in Vegas this time, she scarcely knew herself anymore but she couldn't help it. She wanted to be
his fantasy. Leaning forward, she ran her hands down
the back of her legs, then tossed her hair and glanced
around to where she thought the camera was located.

"How's that?" she asked, deliberately dropping her
voice an octave.

He groaned. "Perfect. Now go slip into that leather number and do exactly the same thing."

The phone was cordless so she moved over to the mannequin and picked up the red leather bustier from the open box. "Have you ever worn leather undergarments?"

He laughed. "No."

"You'd have to make it worth my while," she said, fingering the supple cloth. In truth she liked wearing leather. It made her feel extremely sexy.

"Uncomfortable?"

"Not really, but they don't hide any imperfections."

"What imperfections?" he asked in such a way that she knew he didn't think she had any.

She shrugged. She knew she had them. She spent the majority of her time sitting in an office working. Though she tried to make it to the gym, most days she didn't.

Her thighs were soft, and no matter how many sit-ups or ab crunches she did, she'd always have a slight swell of a belly. Still, she was happy in her body, it was who she was. She just didn't like to see herself in bright light. Didn't like letting anyone see her looking anything but perfect.

"Don't make me say it out loud," she said carefully. Looks had always been important. Her mother had drilled that into her through Shelby's childhood. "Looks are all a woman has when she's poor," Terri Paxton would say. But Shelby had found that brains were better than looks.

"Okay, I won't. Did you make plans for us tonight?" he asked.

Yes, but she was playing her cards close to her chest on this one. "I'm still trying to come up with something you'll like."

He was quiet for a long minute and she could hear only the sound of his exhalation over the open line. "I like being with you, Shel. I always have."

She hugged one arm around her waist and tried not to let the words settle around her heart but they did. She felt a welling of emotion that she hadn't felt in a long time. "You know the right things to say to make a woman buy leather undergarments."

He laughed again and she smiled to herself, pushing aside the deep feelings his comment had evoked. She had to keep her balance here.

"That was my plan," he said.

"I don't know you well enough," she replied slowly.

"I'll show you. Want to spend the night in the casino?"

"I'm not a big gambler. I like to have something to show for my money after I've spent it."

"Like what?"

"Shoes," she said.

"Shoes? An evening in the casino is better than shoes."

She took a deep breath. "Well, maybe one thing is better than shoes."

"Sex?"

"With you," she said, hanging up the phone. She winked at the camera and put the bustier and matching thong in a gold Bêcheur d'Or's gift bag and placed it on the counter next to her purse.

* * *

Hayden spent the day making arrangements for the World Champion Celebrity Poker Showdown. The televised competition would air next month and the producer and her two production assistants were in Vegas for twenty-four hours to get the layout.

Scott Rivers was one of the best poker players in the world and had been a child star of movies and a television show that had run for fifteen years. He'd grown up on TV and Scott liked to say everyone thought they knew him.

But few did. Even after all this time, Hayden still suspected there was a part of Scott that was kept hidden. Growing up in the spotlight had made Scott something of a chameleon. In fact, Hayden had never seen his friend in a situation that he wasn't at home in.

Scott was one of the few people who'd seen him at his lowest. And that had forged a relationship in which both men felt comfortable with each other. Scott was one of his closest friends and Hayden was glad he would be visiting soon. Also, talking with the television people was a distraction. Seeing Shelby this morning, flirting with her on the phone and watching her like some lust-crazed man…well, it wasn't conducive to work.

His cell phone rang as he entered his private elevator. "MacKenzie."

"Hey, Mac Daddy. You up for poker tonight?" Deacon asked.

"Can't. Maybe next month when Scott is here."

"Next month? How about tomorrow night?"

"I'm busy."

"With whom?"

"Why do you suddenly need something to do in the evenings?"

"Ah, let's just say that it's better if Kylie thinks I'm busy."

"Lying to your wife?"

"No. What are you doing? Dating that redhead in the lingerie store?"

Hayden wished sometimes that he and Deacon weren't such close friends, but the truth of the matter was, Deacon was one of the few people Hayden allowed himself to care about. "Maybe."

"Great. Bring her over. We can all have dinner."

"Can't. We have plans."

"Please?"

"What does Kylie have you doing tonight?"

"Dinner with the Vegas Preservation League. A bunch of wealthy do-gooders."

Hayden felt for his friend. Deacon had grown up on the Vegas streets being looked down on by the very people Kylie had invited into his home. "Sorry, I can't help you."

"Page me at eight-thirty."

Hayden laughed. He knew Deacon might want to leave but wouldn't. He wanted to be with his wife. He was besotted with the woman and wouldn't leave her side in spite of the VPL.

"Later, Deac."

"Later."

Hayden rubbed the back of his neck as he stepped off the elevator. God, he hoped he was never so wrapped up in a woman that he was willing to sit through something like that dinner.

Shelby was waiting for him by his penthouse door.

"Are you okay?" she asked.

He dropped his hands, walking toward her. "I am now."

He leaned down to claim the kiss he'd been craving all day. She stood on tiptoe, leaning into his body. He cradled her to him, cupping her face in both hands and angling her head for deeper penetration.

His entire body tightened in anticipation. God, he wanted her. This wasn't a lust thing that could be satisfied with any other woman. He craved her taste on his tongue. Her soft skin under his hands. Her soft curvy body against his muscular frame.

He whispered her name against her skin, skimming his mouth down the line of her neck and nibbling on the pulse beating so strongly at the base. She said his name in a throaty voice.

He bit her gently and she arched closer to him. He licked the spot and then suckled her there. He wanted to brand her as his. To make sure that any other man who saw her knew she was taken. That she already had a man.

She sighed, tunneling her hands into his hair and pulling back from him.

He raised both eyebrows at her. "Please say we're staying in."

"Not quite," she said. Her face was flushed and her lips were wet and swollen. She looked as if he'd done so much more than kiss her. He skimmed his gaze down her neck and was pleased to see the mark of his possession there.

"I figured out something for us to do, but I couldn't catch you before you left your office."

She wore a pair of khaki-colored capri pants and a black tank top. Her hair was twisted up and tendrils curled softly around her face. Her eyes were wide and questioning. Clearly she was unsure if she'd made the right choice.

"Great. What'd you decide? Do you want to take me to a private gentleman's club?"

"Has any woman ever suggested such a thing?" she asked in that haughty way of hers. This was part of the new Shelby. The old Shelby was very pliable. She'd done whatever he said and never stood up to him. But this new woman had a backbone and too much sass.

"I've seen it happen in movies," he said with a grin. She made him happy deep inside where he'd been alone for too long.

"What kind of movies?"

He tipped his head to the side. "Come to think of it, not the kind of movie you'd watch."

"Sex movies?"

"Uh, I'm pleading the Fifth on this one," he said, taking her hand and leading her into his home.

Her deal with Alan had some pluses to it. Shelby had made arrangements to have Hayden's yacht readied for them. Lake Mead was located just east of Vegas and

Shelby had gotten driving directions from the bell stand earlier before going to get Hayden.

Shelby felt a little bit of dread at the thought of someday having to reveal to Hayden that his father was once again behind the scenes manipulating things. She made the decision right then to stop talking to Alan. She wanted to learn about Hayden on her own, not through his father's scrutiny.

She shook off those fears for tonight. The sun was setting and a warm breeze blew through the open windows of her SUV. Hayden had a slight smile on his face.

"Where are we going?" he asked.

"It's a surprise."

"Baby, I've lived here my entire life. I'm not going to be easily fooled."

"I'm prepared for that." She'd spent most of her childhood in Vegas and there was still so much she didn't know about her hometown. Of course, she'd frequented places that Hayden would never have gone to. Places that were saved for the poor and addicted.

"How?" he asked.

She shook off the feelings evoked by her childhood memories and focused instead on Hayden. Focused on the fact that after all this time she was determined to make a relationship work with the man she'd promised herself she'd marry.

She signaled and pulled off the interstate onto the shoulder. The interstate was busy with traffic and she was pleased that Hayden looked a little unsure. She rarely got the upper hand with him.

"This is it?" he asked, glancing at the guardrail and the expanse of desert stretching out toward the mountains. "What could we be doing here?"

To keep from smiling she bit the inside of her mouth as she took the black silk mask from her purse and held it up.

He fingered the silk and when his eyes met hers she saw the heat in them. And shivered. She had the impression that Hayden thought this was the prelude to some exciting sexual adventure.

"Kinky sex on the side of the road. How'd you guess?"

Before she could caution him, he ran the tip of one finger down the side of her neck, his thumb rubbing on the mark he'd left earlier.

"Got anything else in your bag, like a pair of satin lined handcuffs?"

"Maybe. How do you feel about being tied up?" she asked, leaning forward to slip the mask on him.

His pupils dilated, he cupped the back of her head and held her close to him. His minty breath brushed against her. "I'd rather tie you up."

She knew that. He was the kind of man who'd have to be in charge. Her lips were suddenly dry and she licked them.

He leaned forward and traced the line she'd just left with his tongue. Arousal whipped through her body. Her breasts felt full, her nipples tight, and she was so aware that all she had to do was lean forward the tiniest bit and her breasts would brush his chest.

She was shocked at how quickly he'd turned the tables on her. She was the one blindfolding him but she sensed he held all the power. He held her in his thrall and she was helpless.

She bit his lower lip, sucking it into her mouth for a brief second before pushing back into her seat.

"I'm just teasing you. This mask is all I want you to put on for now."

"Ah, baby, if I do this, you're going to owe me."

"Really? What will I owe you?" she asked.

"A dance."

"A dance?"

"Yeah, a nice sexy dance with you in that red leather outfit. Deal?"

She tipped her head to the side to study him, but his words and that sexy tone of voice made her want to do it. "Deal."

He took the black silk mask that she'd brought from Bêcheur d'Or. He slipped it on and leaned back in the leather seat.

The Lincoln Navigator was the same model that Shelby drove at home in Atlanta, so she was very comfortable behind the wheel. Her cell phone rang before she could pull back onto the highway. She glanced at the caller display. It was Paige, and for the first time since she and Paige had opened Bêcheur d'Or, she hesitated, not wanting to think about business tonight.

"I have to get this. Sit tight."

"My pleasure."

She answered it. "Hey, Paige. What's up?"

"Nothing, just touching base to get your take on how the D.C. conference call went this morning."

"I thought it went well. Can I phone you tomorrow to discuss it?"

"Why?"

"I'm kind of on a date."

"A date? With Hayden?"

"Yes."

"Okay, call me in the morning. I want details, and I don't mean about D.C."

She smiled to herself. "Will do."

She hung up the phone and shifted the car into gear.

"Who was that?"

"My partner, Paige. You met her, right?"

"Yes. I like her. You chose well, Shelby."

"Thanks," she said.

He reached over and settled his hand high on her thigh. His fingers traced a random pattern that made her center tighten. She wanted him more than she'd wanted any other man.

"Give me a hint," Hayden said once they were moving again.

"About what?" she asked.

His fingers moved, slipping between her legs and coming teasingly close to her core. She tightened her legs to prevent him from moving any higher.

"Stop, Hayden."

"No. Every time you tease me, I'll reciprocate."

"It's something you like to do."

She shifted her thighs apart, and his touch retreated

but not far enough. She was so aware of his hand on her inner thigh she could hardly concentrate on driving.

"Is gambling involved?"

"No," she said, reaching down with one hand to capture his wrist and move his hand back to the top of her thigh.

"Pretty confident of your answer," he said, turning his hand under hers and lacing their fingers together.

"Yes, plus your sense of fair play."

He leaned his head back. "Don't count on that, Shelby. I'm not always a nice guy. There's a reason I'm a gambler."

"You are so much more than a gambler, Hayden. Don't doubt that."

"Don't let me hurt you, Shel. I'm trying here, but to be honest I don't know how to hold on to something I want."

"Do you want me?" she asked, aware that he wasn't acting at all vulnerable with the mask on.

"Yes, I do."

Her hands shook and she was incredibly grateful that he wore the mask so he couldn't see how deeply his words affected her.

"Then let's make sure we don't hurt each other again."

Five

The soothing scent of the water was the first thing he noticed. Shelby had insisted that he keep the mask on and led him through the parking lot. He felt the wooden planks under his feet and stopped.

How had she known? This was one of his most closely guarded secrets.

"We're at the lake," he said, wondering how she knew about his recent obsession with boating. Not even his assistant knew about the boat he kept at Lake Mead. It was the one thing he'd kept to himself, kept *for* himself and shared with no one. But Shelby knew about it.

She paused next to him. "Are you surprised?"

"Yes. How did you know about this?"

"I can't reveal my source. But it took a lot of time and energy to figure this out."

He pushed the mask up and off, pocketing it for later. He was touched she'd dug deep enough to find this out. "Did you rent a boat?"

"Uh, my source said you had one."

"I do. Follow me."

He noticed she held a picnic basket loosely in her left hand and that large leather bag she called a purse was slung over her shoulder.

He led her to the *Lady Luck,* his thirty-foot yacht. She smiled as she read the name. "Has luck been a lady?"

"More times than not. I always treat her right," he said.

"You do have a way with the ladies."

He helped her on board. Her words echoed in his mind. His way with women had served him well. There had never been a lady he'd wanted that he hadn't been able to date. But the women never stayed. What did that say about his way?

The only constant in his life was the Chimera. He'd spent his life betting on the roll of the dice or taking risks, but that meant that life was constantly changing.

He piloted them out of the marina toward the middle of the lake. The evening was nice and warm and a breeze stirred the short hair at the back of his neck. He glanced over at Shelby, still amazed that she'd taken the time to really find something that he liked to do this evening.

It hadn't been a test for her. But if it had, she'd have passed. That scared him because there was so much he'd forgotten about Shelby. She made the world brighter and more exciting. Even when they were younger, it had been the same. She made him want to take bigger risks—and that was dangerous.

"Ever piloted a boat before?" he asked her. He needed her in his arms, closer to him.

"No. One time Paige and I catered a party for some suppliers that was on the lake."

"Tell me about your business. To be honest, I was surprised when I realized you owned such a successful chain of lingerie stores."

She bit her lower lip. He glimpsed a hint of sadness in her eyes before she turned away.

He scanned the area in front of them. No other sailors. He reached for her, pulling her around to face him. "I didn't mean that as an insult. You just never seemed interested in anything like that when I knew you."

"I know. I was only interested in you and having fun."

"I think it's safe to say we both shared those interests."

She hugged her arms around her waist and stared up at him. "When I left with the money…I thought all my problems were solved. I couldn't believe I had a million dollars. You can't understand this, Hayden, but I never imagined I would see that much money. It felt almost unreal."

"Just because I've always had money doesn't mean I can't understand that. What'd you do with the money?"

"I went on a shopping spree. Then about two days later I realized that everything I'd purchased would be gone eventually and I'd be back in the same boat and…"

He stopped the engine on the boat and dropped

anchor. He couldn't concentrate on Shelby and the boat simultaneously.

"What?"

"I couldn't do that again, Hayden. Whatever else you believe about me, please know that leaving you was one of the hardest things I've ever done."

He traced her jawline with his finger, realizing that in some ways, this strong independent woman was worlds too soft for him. Too innocent. Despite the fact that she'd left him, he knew that he and his father were to blame. When he'd started dating her to get at his father, he'd put her right in the middle of the power struggle they'd always engaged in.

"I know," he said softly. "Tell me how you started your store."

"Well, first I decided to go to college. Since I wasn't going to be using my looks to make money, I figured I'd better use my brains."

"It doesn't have to be one or the other."

"I know that now. But I was only twenty-two. You know, at the time I thought I was very mature. I mean, I knew things about life that other people didn't. But there was still so much I didn't know."

Hayden nodded, realized what she was talking about. He, too, had felt he knew it all as a young man, and in retrospect he realized how little knowledge of life he'd really had.

She walked to the railing, glancing out at the deepening twilight. "I met Paige in college and we were both working in a chain lingerie store at the mall. We had this idea that kind of grew from that. Something more exclusive, more high end. Paige said we needed a French-sounding name because the French know everything about sex."

Hayden laughed at that. Shelby did, too. "Paige is crazy sometimes with the things she says, but she was right. Since we'd both come into our money in unorthodox ways, I suggested calling the shop Bêcheur d'Or. Most consumers recognize the French word for gold and it gave us our brand. Those little gold bags set us apart from other shops, and the rest is history."

"How did Paige come up with her share of the investment money?"

Shelby paused, eyeing him. "She was a wealthy man's mistress for about a year. I don't know the details."

She stared as if she expected a cutting comment, but Hayden had heard it all, living in Vegas.

Hayden was impressed with what she'd made of her life. He was also a little leery of getting involved with Shelby again because she had vulnerabilities that he'd never really explored before. And he didn't want to hurt her again.

Shelby hadn't meant for the evening to get so serious. This night was supposed to be about him not her. They'd had a light dinner and now were sitting on the bow of the boat. She'd removed her shoes, dangling her feet over the water.

"What did you do today?" she asked.

"Meetings and the like."

"Just casino business all day?" she asked, because it sounded as if he was hedging.

"No. I also went to a children's facility that Deacon and I set up."

"What kind of facility? Something for sick kids?"

"No. It's for kids whose parents work in casinos. A place for them to hang out and be safe. Kind of like day care, but for older kids."

"What do you do there?"

"Usually I spend my time climbing on the rock wall. We have a scoreboard that tracks times up and down. A lot of the regular kids like to challenge me."

"Do you let them win?"

"Hell, no. What kind of lesson does that send to kids if you let them win?"

He had a point. "You like it."

He tipped his head and looked her straight in the eye. "I didn't expect to. But yeah, I do."

She'd learned more about Hayden in the forty minutes they'd spent on the water than she had in the weeks she'd spent with him before he'd asked her to marry him. He was a deeply complex man, and a part of her worried she'd never be able to fulfill all his needs.

But she was willing to try. She was falling in love with him all over again. Only this time she knew it was the real thing. Not just a chimera shimmering in the distance. But something real and substantial. An emotion that would last for all time.

Hayden leaned back on his elbows, like some potentate. He was too sexy for his own good. She was still hot and restless from his hands on her in the car. It amazed her how easily he turned everything into something sensual.

"Were there film people in the casino today?"

He arched one eyebrow at her. "Your source is very well connected."

She had to be careful about revealing the things Alan had told her. She wasn't cut out for the kind of intrigue that this type of deception entailed.

"That was the buzz in the buffet," she said, hoping she didn't sound as defensive as she felt.

"I was joking with you. Not accusing you of anything. They weren't film people. The Celebrity Poker Showdown is coming to film here next month."

"Sounds exciting."

"Do you watch it?" he asked.

She didn't really spend much time at home. She was a workaholic who took time for the occasional opera performance and that was about it. "No, I'm really not much on TV. You?"

He shrugged, pushing himself up. "Not too much. I try to watch when I know Scott will be on."

She shook her head at this second reminder of the differences in their lifestyles. "I can't believe you know Scott Rivers personally."

"Should I worry about that? I don't really think of him as anything other than my friend who's very good at bluffing." There was complete honesty in Hayden at that moment and she knew that he didn't view Scott Rivers any differently than he did her. Well, perhaps a *little* differently.

In Hayden's voice she heard the affection he had for the man. She knew from the past and from what she was learning about the man he was today that he had few friends. He was nice to many people but he let few know him.

"Why do you like coming out on the lake?" she asked. He was so at home in Vegas that seeing him out here was almost jarring.

"I don't know. It's just the only time I'm alone. I can kick back and not worry about any of the details I'd have to when I'm at the casino. Sometimes I fish, other times I just drift like we're doing tonight."

"What's it like running the Chimera?"

"Exhilarating, frustrating, fun, a pain in the ass. It's a million things at once but in the end I wouldn't trade it for anything."

"I feel the same about my shops."

He smiled at her. "Are we going to talk business all night? I thought you were supposed to do some wicked seducing."

"Did I agree to that? I think that's your fantasy."

"Let's not quibble about the details."

"Well, I wish I'd planned better. I think swimming in the moonlight with you could be a lot of fun."

"What didn't you plan for?"

"No swimsuits."

"We don't need them."

Skinny-dipping. Despite the fact that she was thirty-two, the thought of it was still forbidden...naughty somehow. And Shelby had spent her entire life following the rules in a game that had always seemed weighted against her.

She pushed to her feet and Hayden stood up next to her. "Did I shock you?"

"Did you want to?"

"Yes. You seem so self-contained, so...untouchable, sometimes I want to shake you up."

He had no idea how much he did. She watched him carefully, her fingers going to the hem of her black shirt. "Will this count instead of the sexy dance?"

"You want to bargain now?"

"Yes."

He scratched his chin. "I'm not giving up my dance, so we'll have to bet on something else."

"What? There's nothing out here but the two of us."

He studied her carefully, gliding forward until no space remained between them. He put his hands on her hips and pulled her fully against his rock-hard body. Each breath he took caused his chest to brush against her breasts, rubbing over her already sensitized nipples.

She struggled to keep him from noticing her reaction. But she could tell by the look in his eyes that he knew she wanted him. He knew she was his for the taking. She pushed against his chest.

He was too used to the power, too used to being in control. Shelby needed to be in charge. Just this once, she thought.

"Last one in is a rotten egg," she said. She kicked off her sandals while tossing her shirt on the deck.

Hayden was a competitor who liked to win so he stripped out of his clothing as fast as he could. Watching Shelby's curvy body emerge from under her clothing slowed him down, however. He knew the moment she realized that he was watching her.

She tipped her head to the side and ran her hands over her breasts and down the center of her stomach. Her fingers toyed with the button at her waistband. "Are you giving me a head start?"

Her voice was deeper than normal, husky almost, brushing over his aroused senses like the whisper of a win in a gambler's ear. The lure was totally irresistible and all he could do was helplessly watch her long legs.

Winking at him, she pivoted away from him and bent at the waist to push her pants off. The thin strip of her black thong pulled tight against the crease in her backside. He clenched his hands at his sides as she straightened.

She glanced over her shoulder at him and pulled her hair free. Shaking her head, she let her hair fall in a cascade down her back. He saw red. A haze came over him and he stepped toward her, but his pants caught at his knees and he almost stumbled.

"I'm going to win," she said, taunting him as she daintily folded each bit of clothing she'd removed. Then she took a leap off the edge of the boat.

Hayden's pants caught on his feet and he kicked them off just before he tumbled over the side, splashing down a scant second before she did. As the water closed over his head, he heard the sound of her laughter filling the air.

Lazily he pushed to the surface, coming up behind her. Reaching for her, he skimmed his hand down her spine. She trembled under his touch.

"I won," he said.

She glanced back at him. "Don't get all arrogant about your victory."

"Why not?" he asked, pulling her closer while he treaded water to keep them both above the surface. The action forced his legs between hers.

"Because there was no skill involved," she said, undulating against him so that her entire body caressed his.

"Then you know that resistance is futile," he murmured against her skin.

She pulled away from him. "Did you say 'resistance is futile'? Isn't that from *Star Trek*?"

"I thought you said you didn't watch TV."

"*Star Trek* is more than TV. But it doesn't seem your cup of tea."

"I went to that exhibit over at the Hilton a few years ago, to see about doing something similar at the Chimera."

"Did the hotel benefit from that trip? Because apparently your legendary charm didn't."

"I beat you once, Shel. Don't make me do it again."

"You can try," she said, and dived. He followed her easily, making out the shape of her white legs under the water.

He caught her ankle and pulled her to him, using a powerful scissor kick to bring them both to the surface.

His skin was too tight and he felt as if he was going to explode if he didn't get inside her soon. But he loved the sensual way she moved. He snaked one arm around her waist and fondled her belly button before cupping her breast in his hand.

"I don't need skill. I have raw talent."

"You've got raw something all right, but I don't think it's talent."

"I'll prove it," he said. It had been too long. Still, he knew he had to take this slow, because despite her teasing, Shelby was still feeling her way in this new relationship with him. And the last time, sex had clouded everything else.

She pushed away from him and dived under the water once more.

Shelby still hadn't surfaced when he felt her hand on his knee, skimming up the inside of his thigh. She cupped him in her hands.

He forgot to tread water and started to go under. Shelby surfaced a few inches from him. "Still going to prove something to me?"

He laughed. This was what had been missing from his life. This element of sexy teasing had been absent in all of his relationships until now. He stroked over to her, capturing her from behind.

She turned in his arms and kissed the base of his neck, nibbling at him and then soothing the ache with her tongue. He tightened his hands on her soft body. He wanted to toss her up on the deck of the boat and bury himself hilt deep inside her. He wanted to bind them so close to each other that they'd never really be separate again.

She lifted her head, her eyes sparkling up at him. "Don't try to tempt me with that smooth voice. I remember it well."

He closed his eyes, inhaling the scent of Shelby, letting the feel of her in his arms totally overwhelm him. He needed her like the air that he breathed and he followed that desire the way he'd always allowed all his cravings to rule his life.

Her wet hair snaked over her shoulders, falling onto his. He liked that feeling, and pulled her closer. He wanted them so deeply intertwined, she'd forget everything except being with him.

Grasping her waist, he lifted her slightly and lowered his mouth to her breast. He traced her nipple with his tongue, lapping at it gently until her nails dug into his shoulders. Carefully he scraped his teeth over her and heard her cry his name. They both sank beneath the water and he realized they needed to get out of the lake right now.

He needed more. He needed it now. And so did she. Holding her carefully with one arm, he swam them both back to the boat and lifted her up onto the platform at the back.

When she would have stood, he stopped her with a hand on her thigh. "Not yet."

Six

Hayden pushed himself out of the water using only his arms. His erection was large and fierce looking.

He scooped her up and stepped over the railing onto the deck of the boat. The remains of their dinner and their clothing still lay where they'd been left.

Shelby was a little embarrassed at her abandon, but there was a sense of rightness about being in his arms that made her realize that they belonged together. A kind of confirmation that she'd made the right decision to come to Vegas to resolve the past and cement the future. She and Hayden weren't finished. Their story was still continuing and she was glad about that.

She wrapped her arms around his neck and shoulders as he strode across the deck of his yacht. His heart beat strongly under her cheek and she closed her eyes, pretending that it beat just for her.

He set her on her feet next to the king-size bed in the stateroom. She was dripping on the carpet but she knew that Hayden didn't mind. He watched her with eyes that seemed to be on fire for her.

"Don't move."

He liked to give orders and she wasn't about to fall into the trap that had plagued their first whirlwind relationship. She followed him into the bathroom area. He bent over to retrieve two thick navy blue towels.

Shelby pinched his backside, then ran her fingers down to cup him.

He glanced up at her. "I thought I told you to stay put."

"I don't take orders well," she said. But she realized that she needed this to be about something more than power. She needed to not get swept away in Hayden but to have both of them get swept away in each other.

"We'll see about that," he said, pushing to his feet.

"Yes, we will see."

She took one of the towels from him. "Stand up and I'll dry you off."

He rose, towering over her. There was a look in his eyes that she scarcely trusted. "I like that idea."

She reached out with the towel but he stopped her with an iron grip on her wrist. "Use your tongue."

She swallowed. Hayden was a dominant lover and she freely admitted that he appealed to her as no other man did. Two could play at this game. He liked to give orders but she knew he wasn't immune to her.

"Close your eyes," she said, softly tracing her finger down the line of hair at the center of his body. The hair tapered down to his erection. She caressed him, coming closer and closer to his erection but making sure she did nothing more than brush it.

She licked the drops of water that still clung to his chest, while he dried her with long, languid strokes of the other towel. She dropped to her knees in front of him, following the trail of water down his strong thighs.

She really wanted to push him beyond boundaries, to push herself further than she'd ever gone before. She lowered her head, letting her breath wash over his erection first. His hands came to her head, rubbing her hair but not holding her or pulling her closer.

She tipped her head back and looked up at him. His skin was flushed with arousal. His breaths were rapid and his pupils dilated.

"Hayden, can I...?"

"Only if you want to."

She definitely wanted to. He felt like satin under her fingers. She lowered her head and ran her tongue up and down his length. Taking her time, she tasted him and discovered the different nuances of him. Reaching between his legs, she cupped his sac, massaging it in the palm of her hand as she took him fully into her mouth.

She sucked him deeper in her mouth, felt his body tighten as she worked up and down his length.

She tasted a salty bit of his essence before he pulled her away and lifted her to her feet.

He carried her into the bedroom, cradled in his big

arms, then slowly lowered her to her feet. She loved the feel of his solid frame against her. He wrapped his arms around her, anchoring her to him with his hands on her back.

He lowered his head slowly and she was consumed by the fire that he effortlessly brought to life inside her. She rose on tiptoe to meet his mouth. She loved the way he kissed her, as if he had all day and wouldn't stop until he'd explored every one of her secrets. She wanted to know him the same way. Reaching up, she took his jaw in her hands and held him still.

She traced the seam of his lips with her tongue, tasting him with small delicate darts. His hands on her back tightened but she didn't hurry. He always seemed so in control. What would it take to rattle him? she wondered.

Slipping her tongue past his lips, she ran it over his. She stroked her way into his mouth before retreating and coming back again.

He groaned and his erection pulsed between them. She felt him growing even harder against her belly and reached between them to enfold him in her grasp.

Not about to be outdone, Hayden placed her on the center of the bed. His hands made long strokes down the center of her body, lingering over her full breasts. He circled her nipples with the tip of his finger. She arched her shoulders, wanting to feel his mouth on her.

"Hayden, kiss me there."

"Yes, baby." He lowered his head and took her nipple in his mouth, suckling at her strongly as she cupped the back of his head, holding him to her.

He rubbed small circles around her belly button before delving lower. His fingers separated her. As he slipped one finger into her creamy warmth, her legs moved restlessly on the bed.

He slid a second finger inside her and brought his thumb down to rub her with a small up-and-down movement that made her want to scream; it felt so good. His fingers thrust in and out of her body and she was arching into him, needing more.

Everything in her body focused on his hand between her thighs and his mouth on her breast. He thrust slowly, driving her up toward a pitch until everything in her body tightened and she knew she was going to come.

Suddenly her entire body clenched and she called out his name long and low. She smiled up at him and she felt a sense of rightness. She wrapped her arms around his head and held him to her.

Hayden waited until Shelby's body stilled before he pushed himself up on his elbows to stare down at her. She smiled at him. Her lips were swollen and still wet from his kisses. Her nipples poked into his chest and though he'd satisfied her, he knew she wanted more.

He needed more as well. Once was never enough for Shelby and him. He freely admitted that only when he was lying between her legs, buried deep inside her body, did he really feel as though he was seeing the real woman. She had no chance to put up barriers then.

He set about arousing her again. Sweeping his hands

down her body. Using his mouth to trace the same path. Slowly building her once again to fever pitch.

She didn't lie passively under him but caressed his back and buttocks. Skimmed her hands over him and then scraped her nails in patterns everywhere she could reach. When he could wait no longer, he kissed his way up her body, lingering at the base of her neck. He sucked against her sweet flesh and bit softly until she was moaning his name.

"Open your legs."

His voice was gruff, guttural even. She'd pushed him past his boundaries. When she did as he asked, he settled his weight over her. Taking her hands in his, he stretched them up over her head, forcing her fingers to curl under the headboard mounted on the wall.

"Don't let go."

She nodded.

He lifted her legs and paused at the entrance of her body. The tip of him slipped inside her. She was so wet and so ready. Her body tightened around him as he entered her. He cursed and pulled out. "Are you on the Pill?"

She shook her head. He didn't want to use a condom; he knew he was free of any diseases and wanted to feel her wrapped around his erection, but he couldn't chance pregnancy.

He pushed off the bed and went into the head and found the box of condoms he kept in the medicine cabinet. He grabbed one, sheathed himself before returning to the stateroom.

Shelby hadn't moved. Her arms were still above her

head, holding the headboard. She was so beautiful to him in that moment, caught up in the feelings he'd brought to her, that he paused to watch her.

"Baby," he said between clenched teeth. He dropped to his knees near the bed. Starting at her neck, he nibbled his way down her body. Lingering over her pretty breasts, he circled the plump globes and left her nipples untouched.

She shifted her shoulders to try to move her nipple to his mouth. He allowed her to get closer, licking the tip before turning his head to her other breast and slowly exploring it.

He slid his hand down her body. Her earlier orgasm had left her body flushed and sensitive to his fingers. She was wet and creamy and he used her juice to coat his fingers, bringing them up to her nipples and rubbing her own moisture on them.

She craned her neck to watch him. He, too, was helplessly fascinated by the sight of his large fingers sliding between her thighs and entering her body.

"Hayden, I can't wait much longer."

"Yes, you can," he said, levering himself on the bed and over her.

He settled between her open legs, taking his erection in his hand and rubbing it up and down her center. He pressed it to her little bud until she tightened her thighs around him and her hips jerked upward.

"Not yet, Shelby. Hold on, baby. Wait for me."

She closed her eyes, breathing deeply, and he knew he'd pushed further than he'd intended to tonight. Putting his arms under her thighs, he lifted her legs, opened her fully to him and entered her. Slowly he filled her until he was seated hilt deep.

Her brilliant eyes opened and she watched him take her. For a moment he remembered the first time he'd taken Shelby. He'd been her first and it had been a surprise. She'd been as openly candid about her appreciation of him and his body then as she was tonight.

Her muscles tightened around him as he pulled back for a second thrust. Her hands gripped the headboard so tightly that he knew she was close. He wanted them to come together this time.

His own orgasm was almost on him. He hurried his pace, thrusting deeper and deeper into her. Finally he felt that telltale tingling at the base of his spine.

"Now, baby."

She came at once, her body tightening around him like a wet, hot glove. He emptied himself into the condom, wishing he'd been able to empty himself into her womb. He wanted to claim her. To stake his claim and make sure that no one—man or woman—ever doubted that Shelby belonged to him.

He collapsed on top of her, spent from the powerful climax. He nestled closer to her breast, idly sucking on one nipple. Her arms wrapped around him and he shifted his weight to the side so that he didn't crush her.

He felt as if he'd found his home. That disturbed him deep inside because he hadn't realized that he'd been searching for one until this very moment.

* * *

Shelby didn't want to wake up. She saw the sun shining across the bed, but the feel of Hayden's arms around her was too good to give up. Even to the reality of morning. How many times had she dreamed of him holding her this way only to wake alone once again?

But she wasn't one to hide from reality. And she knew this morning he was real, not a figment of her hungry soul. But this time she had to deal with her own guilty conscience. Deal with the fact that she had gone behind his back to seduce him with the things he loved.

Her thighs and breasts were pleasantly sore from last night. She was a little scared at the intensity of their lovemaking.

She'd enjoyed herself, no doubt about that, but he'd made her feel vulnerable. She didn't like that. She was a business owner—not exactly an occupation for wimps. She was used to dealing with her fears head-on and would deal the same way with this one, too.

Rolling over and opening one eye, she found herself nose-to-nose with Hayden. His eyes were wide open and the most arrogant male grin split his face.

"What are you smiling about?"

"You, here with me," he said. Leaning down, he kissed her.

It was the slow kind of kiss that didn't put any pressures or demands for more. She felt precious to him. It made her realize how vulnerable she was once again to Hayden. Before, she hadn't really loved him, but this time he was so much more to her than a wealthy man.

Now she was starting to know him, to know that he was constantly going. A moving ball of energy. And that he liked to bet on anything and everything.

She tunneled her fingers through his chest hair, caressing his warm, bare skin. She wanted to snuggle closer. To sink into him until they were just one person and then didn't have to face the day apart.

He lifted his head. "We have to get back. I can't believe I left the casino this long without checking in."

He propped himself up on the headboard and she blushed as she remembered how he'd made her hold on to it until she came in his arms.

He saw her color and shook his head, tugging her into his arms. "Thank you."

"For…?"

"Last night. It was…incredible, Shel. I wish our first time had been like that."

"I don't."

"Really? I've always regretted that I took you too quickly that first time."

"I don't. You were perfect, Hayden. And I don't think we could have handled last night before. We were both…"

"Both what?"

"I can't speak for you but I was pretending to be someone else. Hoping you wouldn't notice."

"Why?"

"Why what?"

"Why were you pretending?"

"Because I wanted a rich boy to marry me and normally you wouldn't have looked twice at the real me."

"Yes, I would have," he said.

"You might have looked but you wouldn't have proposed. I know that firsthand."

"Because of your mom?"

"Yeah. She's never been married."

"Where is she now?"

"Arizona."

"Do you keep in touch?"

"No."

"Why not?"

"She's part of what I was running from when I left, Hayden."

"Aren't you ready to stop running?" he asked.

She couldn't answer that. She thought about her mom a lot. Her mother wrote her a letter once a month and Shelby never wrote her back, but she read those letters over and over and regretted that she'd been so ashamed of herself and the woman who raised her that…sometimes she didn't like herself very much.

Hayden was right, but Shelby didn't know how to bridge the gap she'd forced between herself and her mom. He hugged her closer, his hand coming to rest over hers. He twined their fingers together and then brought her hand to his lips and kissed her.

"Yes, it is time to stop running," she answered finally. "That's part of why I came back here."

"I know you didn't come back because of money."

"Well, I kind of did. The Chimera location is going to make Bêcheur d'Or a lot of money."

"That's business."

"Yes, it is."

The covers slipped lower on his hips. God, she could stare at him all day. She noticed a tattoo on the top of his left thigh. "What's this?"

He covered the tattoo with his hand. "Nothing."

"No secrets, remember?"

He sighed and she realized that though she thought she was coming to know Hayden, he was still a mystery.

He slid his hand away. She bent closer looking at his tattoo. It was a knight's fist, gripping a bloody heart.

Instantly she knew that he'd gotten it after she'd left. She realized that she'd made a huge mistake. But she couldn't decide if sleeping with Hayden last night had been a bigger one than leaving him all those years ago.

Seven

Hayden strode through the main casino two nights later feeling like a gambler riding a streak of luck that just wouldn't quit. Shelby had shown up at the children's facility yesterday afternoon and had given him a run for his money on the rock wall. They'd had a lot of fun and she'd gotten the girls together to compete against the boys.

Last night he'd taken her up in his old Cessna, the same one he'd had when they were dating. They'd flown out over Hoover Dam and Shelby had mentioned that she'd been thinking about going to Arizona to see her mom. Hayden felt as if this time he was really getting to know Shelby.

The sounds of the bells and whistles of the slots and

the rolling of the roulette wheel always excited him, but seeing Shelby standing at a blackjack table, holding one of those small Bêcheur d'Or gold bags, excited him even more.

She still wouldn't move into his penthouse but he contented himself with the fact that she denied him little else. Like tonight. He wanted to show her his world. Wanted her to experience what life was like in the casino and though she said she wasn't much on gambling, here she was. Waiting for him.

She glanced up as he approached, smiling sweetly at him, and it was the sweetness that wrapped around him, stopping him in his tracks mentally. This thing with Shelby was the kind of risk he never took outside of gambling. But he couldn't stop it.

He approached the table and noticed that Rodney, one of his best dealers and longest employees, was the dealer. "Evening, Rodney. You treating my lady nicely?"

"I am, sir, but the cards…not so much."

Shelby laughed a tinkling sound that lit the dark places of his soul and made him want to keep her happy always. "I am the worst player ever. Isn't that right, Rodney?"

He shook his head. "I've seen worse."

"I think he's just being nice."

"Maybe you need some expert help," Hayden said. He took some chips from his pocket and placed them on the table in front of Shelby. She sat perched on the high stool but was still shorter than his six-two frame. Two other players joined the game, but Hayden scarcely noticed them.

He wrapped his arms around Shelby and looked over her shoulder as she picked up her cards. She had the queen of diamonds and a two of spades.

Hayden signaled Rodney for one card, which he dealt faceup. The card was a nine of diamonds. Shelby won.

She squealed and turned in his arms to kiss him. She won the following three hands, still with Hayden standing behind her. "Thank you. I think you're my good-luck charm."

"Ready to try it on your own?" he asked. He wanted to be more than her good-luck charm. He wanted her to move into his house. To sleep with her every night in his bed and wake up with her every morning. He doubted winning a few hands of blackjack was going to sway her.

"Yes. I think I've got it now."

Hayden grabbed an empty stool from a nearby table and joined the play. Shelby lost the first and second hands. Finally she tossed her cards on the table and picked up her winnings.

"Giving up?"

"I don't want to lose all your money," she said, handing the chips back to him.

"They're just chips."

"No, they aren't. I know that you're going to think— I just can't take money from you." She picked up her big leather bag and the small gold lingerie shopping bag.

Hayden pocketed the chips and nodded goodbye to Rodney. This wasn't what he'd planned. He wasn't the most sensitive guy in the world, but he knew that Shelby was telling him something that had to do with more than gambling.

Suddenly all the pieces came together. He realized that while he was dealing with the fact that she'd taken the money and left, she was dealing with the fact that his money, any of it, represented paying her off again.

"Come on." He took her hand and led her out of the casino.

"Where are we going?"

"I wanted to take you to see Roxy's show tonight. We never do anything that's really Vegas."

"Everything with you is Vegas, Hayden."

He tucked his hand under her arm and led her to the theater where Roxy performed. Hayden had a private box where they sat and watched the show. Shelby seemed to really enjoy it, but afterward she was still quiet and he knew that money was still an issue between them. That he'd been insensitive earlier. He still had no idea how to fix it.

"What's next?" she asked.

He had nothing else planned. But he knew that he had to get her away from the casino and taking her back to his penthouse didn't seem right. He needed to get her out of here, to find a way to take that melancholy from her. Somehow he was responsible for it and didn't really know why.

"Let's go someplace a little quieter so we can talk."

"About what?" she asked, but stood and grabbed her shoulder bag once again. He handed her the small gold lingerie bag, not willing to let her leave that behind.

"Luck and Vegas."

"Well, I think we've established I'm not lucky."

"Not at cards," he said, draping his arm around her waist and pulling her into the curve of his body. He shortened his stride to match her shorter one and used his body to protect her from the throng rushing to get to shows or casinos.

He led her out of the casino into the night. The pool and waterfalls were off to the left, but to the right was a small box-hedge maze, and nestled in the far back corner was a padded bench and gazebo.

"Where are we going?" she asked. Her eyes were weary and he knew he didn't want to stare into them anymore.

"It's a surprise," he said, taking from his pocket the black silk mask she'd used on him days earlier. He'd been carrying that damn thing around, tormenting himself with the different ways he wanted to use it with her.

She laughed as he slid the mask over her eyes, fastening it in the back. Leaning down, he brushed his lips over hers. She sighed and opened her mouth for him. She snaked her arms around his waist and laid her head on his chest right over his heart. And he could do nothing but hold her. To make this moment an oasis in two lives that had seen too much chaos and hurt.

The sensation of being blindfolded was difficult to adjust to. Shelby already felt vulnerable from realizing that she was losing Hayden's money in the casino. Sure, she knew it wasn't a lot of money, but still it was the principle of the matter. She'd vowed before she left Atlanta that this time she wasn't taking any money from Hayden. She meant to keep her word—even if it was only given to herself.

After trading herself so cheaply to Alan MacKenzie, Shelby had taken a hard look at herself and her life and she'd promised to never be in that position again. To never be vulnerable to any man. So how exactly had she ended up here—blindfolded with only Hayden's warm hand in hers to guide her through an unfamiliar world?

Panic raced through her. She heard people moving around her and felt as if she was ten again at Meredith Nelson's birthday party. Meredith and the other girls had all disappeared when Shelby had donned the pin-the-tail-on-the-donkey mask. When she'd pulled it off, she'd been left all alone. Standing there in the secondhand dress her mother had purchased on the way to the party. Tears burning her eyes, secure in the knowledge that she wasn't like other kids and would never fit in.

She felt that way again. Being back in Vegas brought all the old insecurities to the surface. It had to be the money thing. Money always triggered that same gut reaction. The blindfold was too much. She reached for the mask.

He caught her fingers, holding both of her hands easily in his grip. "Shh, baby. Don't panic. I'm right here."

"I know I did this to you, but I don't think I like it," she said.

He leaned down and whispered into her ear, "You look so sweet and sexy. I like the fact that I'm responsible for you. I have to protect you. Will you let me do this?"

"I'm a grown woman, Hayden. I don't need a man to protect me."

"Do this for me, please."

He never said please. She nodded her head. She'd try for him, because he'd done it for her without any complaints. But then she doubted he'd ever been in any situation where he wasn't comfortable.

"Are you still upset from the blackjack table earlier?"

She had no response to that. No idea how to respond and still preserve what she now knew was her own illusion that she'd fooled him. The show had been nice but all she felt while she'd been sitting there in the dark was that once again she was in the land of make-believe. Surrounded by people who were pretending their real lives didn't exist.

She felt the warmth of his fingers feathering up her arm, rubbing gently against her skin, wanting her to relax.

"What is going on tonight?" he asked, murmuring his words against the top of her head.

"I don't want you to think I'm after your money," she said, blurting out the words. Then she groaned. She'd never meant to say that.

"Honey…"

"Don't. Let me continue. I'm never going to have as much money as you do. And we'll never really be social equals. But—"

He stopped the wild flow of words with his mouth. His lips moved over hers with surety and strength, making her feel as if everything was irrelevant except him touching her.

He lifted his head but dropped several small nibbling kisses on her neck before taking her hand in his again. "Follow me."

She bit her lip and let him tug her along. She realized that her panic with the mask wasn't only due to the insecurity she'd felt earlier but also had to do with trust. She didn't trust herself. Didn't trust that the woman she'd become was real. Didn't trust that she'd really left behind the young girl she'd been.

Did she trust Hayden? She hadn't when she'd been twenty. But now...? She'd trusted him with her body; she'd set up her shop here based on the success of his casino. Obviously she was leaning that way, but to have the choice taken from her... To have to trust him to protect her while she couldn't see wasn't something she'd been prepared to do.

He stopped walking. She heard him pushing some buttons and then the release of a gate. She was surrounded by the scent of roses and night-blooming jasmine. Hayden wrapped his arms around her waist and pulled her back so that she was sitting on his lap. He nibbled at her neck and she surrendered to the feelings he always aroused in her.

"What's in that little bag?" he asked.

"What little bag?" she asked, turning on his lap so that she rested her head on his shoulder. His aftershave was strong at his neck. She scraped her teeth across the nerve-rich area and felt him stir under her hips.

"You know very well which bag I'm referring to," he said.

His hands roamed up her torso, settling over her breasts. He palmed both of them and she felt them swell and grow heavy under his touch. She reached for the buttons on his shirt, finding them and releasing the top three until she could slip her hand under the cloth and feel his strong, warm pecs. She scraped her fingernail in a random pattern over him and felt his muscle flex under her.

"Stop distracting me. I want to know what's in that bag. I never did get to see you in the red leather."

His thumbs were tracing her distended nipples through the material of her blouse. It felt so good that she couldn't speak for a minute.

"I know. I figured since you were so big on competition, I'd provide you with your own leather."

He groaned. "Damn, woman, I'm not wearing leather underwear."

"Come on. I'll make it worth your while."

"Like you did with the stripping contest?" he asked. His hand was on her waist and then she felt him pulling her shirt slowly up.

She panicked, gripping his wrists. "Hayden, we're in a public place, aren't we?"

He stopped though she knew he was stronger than her and could have pushed her shirt up despite her protests.

"It's time to decide if you trust me or not."

She felt a million things at once—nervous, excited, aroused and a little bit upset that she was so aroused. She shifted on his lap, pressing her thighs together and wondering if she could pretend this was just about sex.

But she knew it wasn't. Hayden wanted her trust and if they had any chance of moving forward, she had to give it to him.

With a sigh, she dropped her hands, knowing that Hayden would always keep her safe. It was him trusting her that had always been the issue. She acknowledged she'd never given him a chance to really trust her because she'd been lying to him. But this time Shelby realized she needed to learn to trust herself and stop lying about what she'd been running from.

Hayden knew they were completely secluded here. The garden was his private place to escape from the busy casino. He'd deactivated the cameras to this section and opened the security gate earlier. They were now in a private section of the maze. She was perfectly safe.

He knew he was pushing her, but couldn't help himself. He wanted—no, needed—to stake his claim on her and he wasn't going to wait any longer. Making love to her two nights ago had made the fact that she didn't trust him into a sharp ache. He knew he'd done little in the past to earn her trust, but this time...this time he was determined to do things right.

She let go of his wrists and he slipped his hands under her shirt. Her stomach clenched as he moved his hand over her. She turned to straddle him, draping her thighs over his, and held him with a fierceness that felt right in his soul.

Slowly, inch by inch, he peeled her shirt up and over

her head. He let his hands trace down the center of her body, stopping to free the front clasp of her bra as they went. She wore a pale pink bra with lacy demi-cups.

"I love your underwear."

She smiled at him and he couldn't resist kissing her one more time. With the mask on, her skirt up around her thighs, her shirt gone and that bra open, she looked like a fantasy come to life.

"Offer your breasts to me," he said.

She ran her hands up her stomach, slowly caressing her own skin, and he realized that Shelby was becoming more comfortable. She covered both of her breasts with her hands, then slowly peeled back the lace to reveal her pink nipples. She cupped her breasts, lifting them toward him. Her hand encircled the bottom and sides but left a small gap between each finger.

With his tongue he traced the gap and felt her hands tighten as he got closer to her nipple. He teased her by outlining the areola first then laved her entire nipple.

He attended to her other breast with the same care. He couldn't stop touching her, needed to caress more of her skin. He loved the way she felt as arousal spread throughout her body. Her hips shifted on the bench. Her hands moved restlessly over her own body, reaching out to hold his head to her as he scraped his teeth down her side.

"Lift your skirt for me," he said, his hands busy at her breasts.

The fabric of her skirt was gossamer light, as he'd noticed when they'd walked through the casino earlier. Ever since then he'd obsessed about it.

Slowly she brought her skirt upward to reveal her thighs and then the matching pink lace panties. Her tight auburn curls were visible under the light material.

He leaned back to study her. Awed that she was his. And she was his no matter how stubborn she was about living with him. Shelby belonged to him. A red haze settled over him and he was determined to prove it to her.

He set about arousing her using every bit of knowledge that he had but couldn't remember where he'd gained it. All other women dropped away. The experiences he'd had with them were only to enhance what he had with Shelby now.

He tugged on her panties, and she obliged by removing them. When she came to him again, he parted her with his thumbs before lifting her to taste the engorged bud he'd uncovered. He suckled her gently, her hips bucking, her hands fluttering to his head to hold him closer.

He brought her to the edge then backed off. He wanted to build a fury within her so that she'd feel the way he did. Out of control.

He kissed her stomach and dipped his tongue into her belly button. He skimmed his hands over her breasts, rubbing them in a circular motion.

Her hips lifted into his chest and he felt her moisture there, realizing he couldn't wait any longer.

"Hayden?"

"Yes, baby?" he asked. Lowering his hands between their bodies, he unzipped his pants and released himself. He slipped on the condom he'd put in his pocket before joining Shelby earlier.

He pulled her forward so that her hips were fitted to his. Now her back was arched and her skirt was still between them.

He grasped her waist and lifted her up. "Hold on to me."

She wrapped her arms around his shoulders, her legs around his waist. Hayden loved the feel of her soft skirt against his stomach and erection. He reached between them, parted her with one hand and guided himself to her entrance with the other.

He thrust upward, going as deep as he could. Shelby's nails scored his shoulders. Her breasts rubbed against his chest. Nothing had ever felt better than the wet heat of her wrapped around him.

She rocked against him again and again and Hayden leaned down, wanting to demand answers from her. But he couldn't. Emotions swamped him as he felt the telltale tingling at the base of his spine signaling that his release was imminent. He slowed his pace.

"Faster. I'm so close," she whispered in his ear.

He put his hands on her hips and thrust up into her as he ground her down against him. He heard her breath catch once and then twice and then a long, low moan as her orgasm washed over her.

He came a second later. He cradled her close to his body, very aware that even if it wasn't wise he was falling for Shelby Paxton, again.

Eight

Shelby spent the next few days in her store readying it for the grand opening tonight. She tried to ignore that more than sex had happened between her and Hayden. They were both busy with work but Hayden made time for her in his schedule. He'd shown up unexpectedly one afternoon after one of her staffers had to go home for a family emergency and helped her unbox the merchandise.

He'd also taken her for a ride on his prized custom West Coast Chopper. He was everything she wanted in a man and more, and she knew she was falling hard for him. Every day revealed another facet of the man and she had yet to see anything she didn't like.

But she remembered Alan and what had brought her to Vegas and worried over that. Not to mention what she'd been forced to realize about herself that night in the private garden. That Hayden already owned her heart and soul. She could try to pretend she hadn't completely given him her heart but she knew that wasn't true.

A part of her rejoiced. After all, she'd returned to Vegas with just that goal in mind. But the other part of her worried. Alan had been out of touch since the night she and Hayden had spent on his yacht, and Shelby worried that Alan was going to show up before she had a chance to talk to Hayden.

She'd tried several times with Hayden to bring up the subject of her return to Vegas. Tried to find the words to make him understand that she hadn't realized how much he'd changed, how much she had. But last night a letter from her mom had arrived and she'd been unable to deal with anything but that.

Hayden had taken her up to his penthouse and they'd sat on his balcony and talked until two in the morning. Talked about their single parents. She'd learned more about Alan than she'd expected to. Realized that once Hayden's mom died when Hayden was quite young, Alan had focused on Hayden, making his son's success the purpose of his life outside the casino.

When Shelby had talked about her own mother, she'd realized that it wasn't her mother she was ashamed of. It was the way other people had always looked at them. She told Hayden about how her mother loved to crank up old Elvis Presley albums after dinner and they'd danced and sung while they'd cleaned the dishes.

She'd forgotten how much she'd loved her mom until that moment. She'd made the decision to call her and set up a time to visit only to have to leave a message on the answering machine when she followed through.

Shelby felt as if all the loose ends in her life were finally being straightened out. She was thirty-two and just starting to get it together.

Last night Hayden had pushed her hard to move in with him, even going so far as inviting his friends Kylie and Deacon Prescott to his penthouse for dinner. Shelby had enjoyed meeting the couple. But more than that she'd enjoyed the feeling that she and Hayden were a couple. A real couple. A happily-ever-after couple.

And that scared her.

She glanced at her watch. 8:50 a.m. She had ten minutes until she'd be addressing her staff. Paige was due in this afternoon and they were having a soft opening by invitation only for the other casino owners in the area and VIPs from each of the surrounding resorts.

A soft opening was a pre-grand opening that was a test run for business owners. Shelby was always nervous at this stage. But as she stood in her office and glanced into the showroom at the gilded shelves filled with unique, sexy lingerie, she felt her confidence return. After all, this was the twentieth store she'd opened.

Her staff had been handpicked and Shelby knew they'd do a fabulous job. She'd decided that tonight, after the formal grand opening, she'd tell Hayden she'd move in with him. And she vowed to talk to him about his dad. To let him know that Alan had blackmailed her into coming back.

She had chosen her clothing for the day carefully, donning the red leather bustier and thong under a long-camel colored suede skirt with a black silk shirt. She'd pulled her hair up into a loose chignon and left several tendrils of curls hanging around her face.

She wore a pair of black heels, and a small gold choker as her only jewelry aside from her watch. Her clothes looked good on her and gave her an added boost of confidence as she exited her office and entered the shop.

Her small staff was already assembled, talking quietly among themselves. Shelby's cell phone rang.

She glanced at the number and saw that it was Hayden. "Hey."

"Hey, yourself. Will you have time before the opening for a drink with me?"

The day was jam-packed with activities and last-minute details. "Sorry, I don't think so. I'll probably be going over something with Paige."

"How about if I come to you?" he asked.

Nothing would make her happier. She liked that Hayden had made sure his schedule was always available to her so that she could find him whenever she wanted him. "Sure. In fact, I have a little surprise for you."

"Yeah? Is it something I've been waiting for?"

She thought about it. Thought about how long they'd both been together and apart. Thought about their lives and how they'd both used work as a substitute for relationships. And thought about how this time she wasn't leaving. "Oh, yeah."

"Dammit, I'm on my way to a meeting but I want to

come to you. Take you away from all this and just make love to you."

"Stop it. We both have work to do."

"I know. I'll be by around five."

She hung up quietly and turned to her staff. After giving them a pep talk, she walked outside the shop to observe the store, to see it from beyond the gilded gold leaf–inset doors. The window displays looked erotic and sophisticated.

"Nice job."

Shelby froze. Slowly she turned to face an older, more jaded-looking version of Hayden. "What are you doing here?"

"Checking on my investment," Alan MacKenzie said, putting his hand under her elbow and leading her out of the path of the foot traffic.

Shelby took a deep breath and tried to tamp down the sense of panic she felt. Everything was starting to go so well for her and Hayden. "This really isn't a good time. You know this entire casino is wired with security cameras that record everything. I don't want Hayden to get the wrong idea."

"I don't trust you to carry out our plan," he said.

"It's not our plan," she said, pulling her arm away. "Not anymore. I'm not sure I can do what you wanted me to. Please, Alan, just leave this to me."

Shelby turned away determined to leave Alan standing there. She ran into a solid chest and glanced up with a sense of dread in the pit of her stomach.

"Hayden—"

"Leave her alone, Dad," Hayden said, putting his arm around her shoulder and anchoring her to his side. "She's here because of business, not to be bullied by you."

Shelby was shaking and she knew that this moment was going to end badly. She should have told Hayden about his dad's proposition before now. Why hadn't she?

Because she'd wanted to make sure he really liked her before she dropped her bomb. Because she'd always understood that they had to have more than a great sexual bond between them. Because she knew that she needed Hayden's love and wasn't sure she'd had enough time to convince him that what they had would last.

"I'm not bothering her, Hay. I was congratulating her on her store. She's come a long way from the girl we both knew."

"Don't say it like that, Dad. We never gave her a chance."

Hearing Hayden defend her convinced Shelby without a doubt that she couldn't put off the truth any longer. She had to tell him. But she didn't want to spoil this moment. In her entire life, she'd never had anyone defend her the way Hayden was now.

Emotion choked her and she turned her face into his chest, hugging him tightly, trying to tell him without words just what that meant to her.

Hayden was glad he'd gotten down to Bêcheur d'Or as quickly as he had. He'd been in the middle of a meeting when Deacon had called him to say that he'd spotted Alan in the casino. Alan usually visited only twice a year and always caused some sort of trouble with the staff. Last fall Alan had handed out demerit cards to half of Hayden's blackjack dealers for minor infractions, causing distress before Hayden could explain that his father had no power over casino employees.

As soon as his dad disappeared around the corner, Shelby took a few steps away from Hayden. She was pale. He'd never seen her look like this.

"Are you okay?" he asked, lifting her face toward his. There were tears in her eyes, and no matter what she said, he knew his dad had been bullying her.

She blinked and her vulnerability slowly disappeared. "It really wasn't bad. I just know what your father thinks of me. And he makes me feel like…like I'm still a gold digger."

He lowered his head for a kiss, tenderly tasting her mouth, showing without words what she meant to him. He pulled back before he wanted to because he knew she had a busy day. "Well, I know how my old man can be."

Hayden rubbed the back of his neck, not sure how to explain to her about the man he'd become after she'd left. "He blames you for a lot of things, Shelby."

"What does he blame me for?" she asked. She'd put a foot of space between them and had her arms wrapped around her waist.

"Not having grandkids."

"I doubt you've been celibate since I've been gone. There was opportunity, right?"

"I'm not much on settling down. This business is my life. Could you imagine raising a kid here? I mean you've seen the kids at the center. What kind of life is that?" he asked, not sure he wanted her to say no.

"The one you had. You turned out okay."

"I'm a workaholic adrenaline junkie."

"Thought about this a lot?"

"Nah, one of the women I dated called me that."

"She was probably jealous."

"Of what?"

"Of this casino. She probably had just figured out that no woman could come between you and the Chimera. Anyway, your dad raised you here. And you two are still on speaking terms, so it can't have been that bad."

Normally he'd never have left his steering-committee meeting like he had, but here he was several floors away from some very highly paid men and women who were waiting for him. Especially since the dressing rooms of the revue venue had been broken into last night and a nasty note had been left for his star performer.

"No, it wasn't. We get along okay when he minds his own damn business. He thinks he can stroll into my operation whenever he wants and give me tips. The old man still thinks casinos should be run…old school."

Shelby laughed like he wanted her to. He reached out to toy with one of the loose waves hanging around her face. "He has the belief that he's always right, too. He can't believe that people can change."

"People or you?"

"Me," she said, sounding forlorn.

No matter what he said or did, their past would always be between them like an unacknowledged wound.

The past hadn't been healed by years of separation nor was the relationship they were building enough to wipe away the past hurt. He really stunk at relationships and had no idea how to make this right.

The only time he really felt in control around Shelby was when she was in his arms. He walked around behind her and surrounded her with his body, pulling her back against him, wrapping his arms around her waist and bending his head to whisper in her ear. "Don't worry, baby. I'll run interference for you."

And he meant it. The last time, he'd left Shelby on her own to deal with his dad, but now he realized he should have protected her better.

Why hadn't he been able to see that she needed him? He hadn't wanted to acknowledge that they were dependent on each other.

Her hands crept up over his wrists, holding him as he held her. She tipped her head back and looked up at him. He could tell she was searching for something in his gaze and he hoped she'd find it. Frankly, he knew that taking her to bed would go a long way to making him feel better.

"I don't need protecting. I'm a grown woman."

He waggled his eyebrows at her, trying to lighten the tension that lingered in the air like a streak of bad luck at a slot machine. "I've noticed."

"Trust you to turn this back to sex."

"Did I?"

She raised both eyebrows and gave him a very prim look. "You know you did."

He winked at her. "Can't help myself around you."

She sighed and then moved away. "Thanks for coming to the rescue, but I need to get back to work."

"You're welcome. What were you doing out here?"

"Checking out the store from the outside."

"You've checked it out before," he said.

She walked toward her lingerie store and stood out of the foot traffic, watching the action inside. "Sometimes it's hard to believe it's really mine. That this is my life."

"You've worked hard for your success. You deserve it."

"I don't know about deserving all this."

She gestured to her clothing and the shop and him. "I mean, I'm wearing a pair of shoes that cost three hundred dollars. When I was in Vegas before, I bought my shoes from the final-markdown rack."

"I never knew that," he said.

"I would have died if you had. I tried very hard to hide that part of my life from you. The house you picked me up at wasn't really mine—it was the Jenkinses'. I worked there as an after-school maid. Their daughter was two years older than me and Mrs. Jenkins used to give me her old clothes."

He saw now how little he'd known of her real life. Shelby had always looked like a million bucks. He remembered how careful she was of her clothing and shoes. He'd taken it for vanity and appreciated it because she'd made him look good. But now he was beginning to realize that she may have spent all her money on looking good for him. And he'd never noticed.

He told himself he was noticing now, but in his gut he hoped it wasn't too little too late.

Paige closed the door and locked it after the last employee left. Paige was tall, almost six feet, and she wore her jet-black hair in a classic bob. She was reed thin and could have made a fortune as a model in New York if she'd wanted to. Shelby finished cleaning up and stacked champagne glasses on the counter for the catering service.

"I think Vegas likes us," Shelby said. Her entire body was humming with energy. Excitement from the opening warred with sexual anticipation.

"Someone in Vegas certainly likes you," Paige said, pointing to the very large arrangement of exotic flowers that had arrived in the middle of the afternoon.

"I hope so," she said. Paige knew her like no one else, but there were still parts of her life that she'd never shared with her friend.

"I like Hayden, too. I'm glad you decided to come back here and face him."

"Me, too. But I still haven't told him about Alan."

"When are you going to?"

"Tonight."

"Good. You deserve some happiness. Where are you going to stay now that the shop is open?"

"Depends on how things go with Hayden. I'll definitely be at the hotel for the next few weeks."

"Are you moving out here permanently?" she asked. "What about D.C.? You know I don't do openings."

"Chill out. I want to think about telecommuting. I want to give this relationship with Hayden a real chance at working. I'll still do the openings and the traveling."

Paige wrapped her arm around Shelby's waist, hugging her close. "I hate change."

"I know. But nothing is really changing."

"Yes, it is."

"I don't have to stay."

"This is the man you always bring up when we talk seriously about life. I think you better stay. Maybe we can relocate headquarters out here. There's nothing holding us to Atlanta."

"What about Palmer?" Paige's current lover was in the process of getting a divorce.

"He's going back to his wife."

"Oh, Paige. I thought they were over."

"Apparently you and I were the only ones who believed that."

"If you'd seriously consider relocating the business, I think I'd like to be here even if things with Hayden don't work out. You know, since most of our shops are back East, maybe we need a few more out West. I've been thinking of scouting Arizona."

"Like maybe Phoenix?"

"Yes, and the surrounding area," Shelby said, careful not to say more. She'd kept her mom private from Paige, never mentioning Terri Paxton to her partner and best friend.

"We'd have to research the demographics, but why not?"

"Thanks, Paige."

"For what?"

"For making me go into business with you." Shelby hugged her friend.

Paige laughed in that loud way she had. "Hey, I didn't do that. I merely pointed out that the smart thing to do was to work with me."

But they both knew that she had. Shelby pulled away from her friend and started shutting off the lights. "What are your plans for tonight?"

"Uh, hello, it's after midnight, I'm going to bed."

"But you're in Vegas. The city never sleeps."

"Maybe, but I'm a small-town girl and I need some rest. What about you?"

"I'm meeting Hayden in the casino."

They set the alarm and left the shop. Despite the fact that all the stores in the retail section closed at midnight, there was still some foot traffic, but it was lighter than it had been earlier. When they left the shopping wing and entered the main casino floor, Paige said goodnight and went up to her room.

Shelby hesitated, glancing through the crowded casino trying to find Hayden. People stood two and three deep at the slot machines and there wasn't an empty seat at the blackjack tables. Rodney the dealer smiled at her as she walked past his table.

"Have you seen Hayden?"

"There was an emergency at the revue. Some kind of security issue," Rodney said.

Shelby headed that way, feeling like she was in a

maze. No matter which direction she turned there were more people and she was starting to feel closed in.

She retreated to a quiet corner of the casino, near one of the exits. She wasn't going to find him in this throng. She'd go back to his penthouse and wait for him.

That idea appealed to her. As she walked to the elevator, the scenario she wanted to create formed in her mind. Hayden had given her so much today. More than he could ever understand. She'd felt accepted and it had been a really long time—maybe her entire life—since that had happened.

Sure, Paige accepted her but that was more from an I-know-your-dirt-and-you-know-mine aspect. Hayden accepted her on a personal level, in a way that made her feel as if she was special to him.

An arm snaked around her waist and she glanced up to meet Hayden's intense gaze. "Hey, baby. How was the opening? I'm sorry I couldn't stay, but we had a major emergency."

"What happened?" she asked. Hayden was tense.

"Roxy was attacked."

"What? By whom?"

"Some crazed fan. He cut her in several places, some deep. They took her to the emergency room and she's having surgery now. Police have the man in custody."

"Oh my God. What can I do?"

"I've got to head back to the hospital."

"I'll go with you."

"You don't have to."

"Hayden, this is what being together is about."

"Thanks," he said.

"No problem."

Ten minutes later they were seated in the hospital waiting room. About five other cast members were there as well. After an hour had passed, they decided to go to the cafeteria to get coffee. Shelby sat next to Hayden, unsure how to help him. She knew that he thought of the Chimera staff as his family and he was taking this hard.

He rubbed the bridge of his nose. "Talk to me, Shel. Tell me about your opening."

She sipped the cafeteria coffee, trying to remember the opening. It seemed as if it was years ago instead of just hours. "It went really well. I can't believe how many people showed up."

"Did Deacon come?"

"Yes, with Kylie. She invited me to have lunch with her."

"Good. I like Kylie."

"Me, too," Shelby said. And it was the truth, though she knew she had little in common with Kylie who had confessed that she'd grown up with her nose stuck in a book. Still, she'd been open and friendly and had said she was glad to see Hayden dating someone with an IQ bigger than her bra size.

Kylie had given Shelby a glimpse of what Hayden's life had become. She'd promised to tell Shelby over lunch all about the infamous bet that Hayden and Deacon had made about Kylie.

Hayden's friendship with the Prescotts was obviously a strong one. Deacon had worked the room and Kylie had hung back, quietly confessing that she wasn't the outgoing person her husband was. She'd also told Shelby not to let being a casino owner's wife intimidate her. But Shelby knew whatever happened in Vegas, Hayden wouldn't ask her to marry him again.

The man in question spoke again, snapping her out of her thoughts. "Did you check out of my hotel?"

"Yes, earlier. I...well, darn, I was hoping to keep that a secret from you."

"Why? Did my dad bother you again? I told him to back off."

"No, nothing like that. I kind of had a surprise for you. But it doesn't seem right to bring it up now."

He put his arm around her and hugged her to his side. "We can have your surprise tomorrow. Tonight I need you to stay with me, baby. I'm trying to go slow and not pressure you, but...will you stay, please?"

Tears burned the back of her eyes and any doubts that she had about staying in Vegas totally disappeared. There was something between her and Hayden that couldn't be denied. And they both knew it.

Reaching up, she cupped his jaw in her hands. "That was my surprise. I'm not leaving your hotel. I'm just moving out of my room and up to your place."

His eyes narrowed. "For tonight?"

"And longer. If you still want me."

He pulled her to him, his mouth finding hers. His hands roamed up and down her back, forcing her more fully against him.

She clutched his shoulders, letting him support her

entire body. Someone at an adjacent table cleared his throat and Hayden lifted his head. But he didn't glance away from her.

She fingered her mouth where her lips still throbbed from his kiss. "I guess that means yes?"

Nine

Hayden couldn't believe the way everything was falling together. Shelby was moving in with him and now Roxy's doctor was giving him a positive report. Roxy had come through her surgery and was resting comfortably. She'd be able to return home in a few days.

Hayden knew Roxy had no family. He'd met her when she was sixteen. A runaway who was out of options wherever she'd come from; he'd never asked. He'd given her a job in one of the restaurants and a place to sleep. The rest, as they say, was history.

He talked to Roxy's doctor and to some of the other cast members of the revue who had agreed to stay with her overnight.

Hayden walked down the brightly lit hospital hallway to see Shelby standing there waiting for him. It seemed almost too easy that she was moving into his penthouse now. God knew that convincing Shelby had been harder than he'd expected.

But there was something right about it happening now. Something right about having her back with him after all this time. Something in his soul said that this hand was playing out accordingly and he should just keep playing the winning cards dealt him.

She slipped her arm around his waist. "Is she okay?"

He nodded. "Let's get out of here."

They were back at the hotel a few minutes later. The lobby was still a beehive of activity even though it was almost three in the morning. Hayden wanted to go up to his penthouse with Shelby but he had to make one more swing through the casino and check in with security.

"Babe."

She arched one eyebrow at him. "Yes?"

"I've got about thirty minutes' worth of work left tonight."

She nodded toward a comfortable-looking chair. "I'll wait over there for you."

Hayden conducted his meetings as quickly as possible and returned to Shelby.

"Where's your luggage?" he asked.

"I brought it up to your place earlier. Was that okay?"

She kept asking him as if she was afraid he'd changed his mind. "Of course. I gave you a key the first night you came back into my life."

She shrugged. "There's a part of me that's afraid to trust this, Hayden. The last time things moved so quickly."

"And they are again. But you have to face the fact that you and I live life at this speed. You wouldn't be able to wait months for me. Any more than I can wait that long for you."

She nibbled on her lower lip as they waited for the elevator and he tightened his arm around her waist. He wanted to stake his claim for the world to see. Yet at the same time he knew he wanted to take his time with her. To make sure that she understood how her action this night had impacted him.

He needed her in ways she couldn't understand. This wasn't the first time one of his employees had been injured on the job. But tonight with Shelby by his side... she soothed him. She gave him someone to share his burden with and he wanted to say thank-you to her without having to actually utter the words.

He shivered a little at the thought. She was the only woman he'd ever let in to his soul. He'd never been able to keep her out—then or now.

The elevator doors opened and they stepped onto the public car. There were two other couples and Shelby chatted to them as they rode to the fifth floor where they'd change cars. When they exited, she wished them both luck and slipped her hand into Hayden's.

"You'll make a good casino owner's wife," he said.

The words slipped out without intent.

"Hayden—"

He bent, taking her mouth with his. He didn't want

her to think or explain. He knew it was too soon, but knowing didn't stop him from wanting. And he wanted Shelby. She was what he craved deep in his soul, and he knew he was going to do whatever it took to make her agree to marry him.

He lifted his head. "Let's go home so I can make love to you."

She nodded and was quiet until they reached his front door. Then she stopped, grasping his wrists and holding each one in one of her small delicate hands. Her hands didn't even wrap completely around his wrist.

"Are you sure about this?"

"About what?" he asked, his mind already on the way she'd feel under his body. To finally make love to her in his bed was a fantasy he'd been entertaining for too long now.

"Me and you," she said.

He brought her hand to his body, where he was already hardening, readying to take this one woman who had always been so elusive. "This answer your question?"

She shook her head. "Not that. About me living with you. There's still so much about me you don't know." She *had* to talk to him about Alan. But…not now.

"I know the important stuff."

"This?" she asked, her fingers caressing him.

"Well, yeah, but more than that. I know that you grew up without any luxuries and that you don't like to take money or gifts from others. That you work hard to make your dreams come true but never at the expense of others."

He swept her up in his arms, bending to unlock the door and open it. He entered his apartment, then kicked the door closed behind him.

"I know that I need you in a way I never wanted to need any woman. That when I kiss you, you go up like fire in my arms."

He walked straight through the public rooms of his home, past the poker table and the doors leading to the balcony where he'd had breakfast with her. He entered his bedroom. One entire wall was floor-to-ceiling windows that looked out on his kingdom. His world. Vegas. The 24/7 lifestyle he'd always thrived on.

It paled in comparison with the lovely woman in his arms. He hugged her closer to him, buried his face in the curls at her nape. He inhaled her scent deep into him. Deep into his soul.

"I know that I want you here always. I want to keep you in my bed waiting for me. Ready to make love to every second of every day."

She lifted her head from his shoulders, her hands encircling his neck and her mouth finding his. She kissed him deeply and every part of his being responded. His erection strained against his pants. His chest swelled, his blood flowing heavier in his veins.

"I want that, too. But I couldn't bear it if you had regrets," she said softly.

He let her slide down his body, his hands settling on her hips when she would have moved away. "How could I regret the biggest win of my lifetime?"

* * *

Shelby knew in this moment she'd made the right choice. That all the pain of the past was fading away as she stood next to Hayden in his bedroom. Hayden was a good man with a deep well of caring inside him.

"I'm not good at taking chances," she said. "I worried about your reaction to my moving in here. But no more. Sit on the bed." The bed, she noticed now, was huge, the prominent feature in the dark-walled room appointed sparsely with sleek Danish furniture.

He raised one eyebrow at her. "I don't want to wait."

"Yes, you do. Trust me."

He settled onto the bed, leaning back on his elbows and watching her through narrowed eyes. "Okay."

Even in supposedly ceding control to her, power still radiated from him.

Once he was there watching her, nerves assailed her.

"Shelby, come here."

When she crossed to him, Hayden sat up, widening his legs and drawing her between them. "What's going on in that head of yours?"

She hated that she'd messed this up. "I wanted to give you your fantasy."

"You already have."

"No, something sexy but…"

He raised both eyebrows and brought his hands to the buttons on her shirt. Slowly he opened them, revealing the curves of her breasts where they swelled over the top of a bustier.

He leaned down and kissed the pale white globes.

Her breasts felt fuller under his lips. Holding the sides of her blouse in either hand, he drew the fabric across her skin, rubbing all over her but keeping that layer of material between her and his hands.

The torture was exquisite and she arched her back, tried to move his touch where she needed it. But he controlled her carefully, finally removing her blouse and tossing it on the floor.

He didn't take his eyes from her breasts, and watching him gave her the confidence she'd been lacking. She straightened her shoulders and ran her hands up her thighs to her waist, cinched in by the bustier.

He leaned back on his elbows and watched her. She took a half step away from him, to give herself some more room. She twirled around, feeling the suede skirt slide around her legs.

All day she'd been hyperaware of what she wore under her clothes. Aware that Hayden's eyes would glaze, just as they were doing now, when he realized what she wore. At this moment she knew she'd never been more perfect. More the perfect woman for Hayden, the perfect mate for him. The perfect person she'd always been so afraid of being.

Remembering what Hayden had said when he'd first seen her dressing the mannequin, she unfastened the skirt and partially unzipped it, letting it fall to her hips. She swayed them in time to the music that had been playing in the casino earlier. The slow steady beat of the Marsalis jazz that Hayden loved.

She danced around the room for him. Lost all track

of her body and the imagined flaws she didn't want him to see. Lost complete track of her fears that Alan would somehow ruin what she'd found with Hayden. Lost all of her inhibitions. She offered her body up to Hayden in a slow, sensual dance.

Hayden pushed to his feet. Slowly he unbuttoned his shirt, moving his body in the same rhythm as hers. He danced behind her, his hands coming to her hips and pushing the zipper the rest of the way down. He pulled her back against his erection as he moved with her, each undulation of their bodies inflaming them both a little more.

Her skirt fell farther, stopping just above her knees. She spread her legs, rubbed her backside against Hayden.

He groaned low in his throat, his hands afire on her body as he swept them up and down her torso. He cupped her breasts and pressed hot, wet kisses to her neck and shoulder blades.

Still the music burned inside of her, building to a crescendo in time with the desire flowing through her body. She turned in his arms, pushing his shirt to the floor, fumbling with his belt buckle, finally freeing it. He caught her up in his arms, carrying her the few short feet to the bed.

Tossing her onto the surface, he followed her down, one knee between her legs to keep them open. His hands on either side of her shoulders, he braced himself above her and slowly lowered his chest to hers. His mouth teased hers as his fingers and hands tormented her breasts. He found the pull-away cups on the bustier and ripped them off. He bent to her, suckling her into his mouth with deep, strong tugs of his lips.

Shelby shifted her hips on the bed. Needing more. Needing it now. Not it, him. She needed him deep inside her. She wanted to share with him this feeling that swamped her and made her want to be what he'd said earlier. Want to be worthy of his love.

He pushed her skirt and thong down her legs and freed himself. He fumbled in the nightstand for a box of condoms. She took it from him and opened it carefully.

She took his length in her hand, sliding up and down a few times before she placed the condom on its tip and smoothed it down his erection.

Groaning, he gripped her hips, pushing one pillow and then a second under them, angling her up for his penetration. He held her hips in his hands and stared into her eyes. She met his gaze as he brought himself to the entrance of her body.

"You're mine," he said, thrusting deep inside her.

He set a pace that drove them quickly toward the pinnacle. "Say it, baby. Say that you're mine."

She gasped for breath, felt everything shimmering so close to her. Her orgasm hovered just out of reach. She met his gaze and realized what she'd been waiting for.

"I'm yours, Hayden. Only yours."

They both tumbled over the edge. Hayden's voice echoed in the room as he shouted her name. Shelby clutched him close, realizing that something had changed in the foundation of their relationship and that there was no going back.

* * *

Hayden woke up twice in the night, assured himself that Shelby was still in his bed and made love to her. He was ravenous for her body. He couldn't get enough of the way she reacted to his every touch.

He rolled to his side, propped himself up on his elbow and stared down at the woman who'd haunted him since he'd first met her. Back then he'd been way too young to appreciate her, but there'd always been something about Shelby that quieted his soul and gave him the peace he longed for.

The sheet was bunched around her waist. She lay on her side with her arms curved under her breasts. His morning erection swelled. God, he'd never been this insatiable before.

The alarm buzzed before he could touch her. He shut it off. She smiled sleepily up at him and he felt a sense of rightness with his world that he'd seldom experienced before. Leaning down, he kissed her. She pulled back.

"I'm sore," she said softly, blushing.

He ran his hands down her body, hoping to soothe her aches. "I'm sorry."

"Don't be. I just can't this morning," she said, leaning up to kiss his whiskered jaw. She rubbed her hands over his face and down his chest. "I missed you."

"When?" He hadn't left her side the entire night.

"When I left."

He knew she was referring to their time together ten years ago. "I was so angry."

"I know. That's why I waited until I was at the airport to call."

"Why'd you do it?"

"The money."

"And no trust in me to provide it."

He rolled to his side. He hadn't meant to rehash the past but it seemed inevitable. Neither of them had ever really had their say.

He felt her move behind him, the bed dipping slightly beneath her weight as her arm snaked around his waist. She held him to her, her face buried between his shoulder blades. She brushed a soft kiss on his back.

"I…I needed the money. I'd spent my entire life believing that money would solve my problems. Remember how I told you I didn't grow up in that house you picked me up at?"

Her hand fluttered on his stomach, not caressing but gesturing nervously, trying to explain without saying the necessary words.

He realized anew how much he cared for this woman, and how little he'd known of her before. He rolled over, needing to face her. To see what she was feeling as she spoke. She wouldn't look at him. She dipped her head, tucking her face between his neck and shoulder. "Where did you live?"

She took a deep breath; he felt the warmth of her exhalation against his skin. His body stirred despite the fact that now wasn't the time. He closed his eyes and fought for control.

"In that dumpy trailer park four miles from town, the Silver Horseshoe."

He shuddered. He knew the place. Full of degenerates, drug dealers, prostitutes and other unsavory characters. How could Shelby have grown up there? She was worlds too soft for that kind of life.

"You know it?" she asked when he didn't respond.

"Yeah, baby, I do." Rubbing his hands down her back, he wanted to pull her completely into his body. To vow to protect her from everything, even the dark memories of her past.

He held her, rocking her gently to give her some comfort. He sensed she wasn't really here with him but had traveled back to that place she'd grown up in.

"When your dad offered me a million, I just couldn't take a chance that it might never come again. I couldn't go back to that place. Plus, he threatened to tell you about where I came from. And I knew he was going to cut you off and once you knew I'd lied about who I was... Well, I'm not the gambler you are. I had to take the sure thing."

He heard the conviction in her voice and understood for the first time what it must have taken for her to leave him. To be honest, every time she'd broached the subject of how they'd live without his dad's money, he'd put her off. He knew that he had funds the old man couldn't touch but he'd never shared that knowledge with her. And now he saw that he should have. That maybe he hadn't trusted her the way she'd needed him to.

"God, baby. I'm sorry." He bent his head and rested

his chin on her shoulder. The silky length of her hair fell on his shoulders and he just held her in his arms. She was all that was delicate and feminine. She had always had to protect herself, even once he'd come into her life. He wished he could go back in time and kick his own ass for never seeing beyond her body.

She lifted her face and there were tears pooling in her eyes, but she blinked to keep them from falling. "Don't be. I used you. I knew you had money from the first time you asked me out. I had to pay Christy Jenkins to take me to the country club with her. I was looking for a rich guy and I found you."

He was a little angry to hear her say so bluntly what she'd done. But he'd picked her for precisely the same reason. Because his dad wouldn't like her. He knew that he could screw this up again. That the last piece of the puzzle that was Shelby had yet to be revealed. But he also knew that this woman belonged to him. And if it took a lifetime to figure her out, that was fine by him. He fought to find the right things to say. And knew he'd fail miserably.

"I was just a bonus?" he asked, attempting some levity where there was none. He hated that she made him vulnerable but she did. Because even back then her loss had hurt him more deeply than he'd ever admitted to himself.

He waited for her to answer, wishing he'd kept his mouth shut or just gotten out of bed before their conversation had come to this point.

"No. You were more. I can't explain it but from the beginning I knew you'd break my heart."

Ten

The next week flew by. Hayden and Shelby visited Roxy in the hospital. But the showgirl wasn't always up for company. They went every day anyway. Shelby reminded Hayden a bit of Roxy. Both women had come from nothing to make great successes of their lives.

Each day Shelby's life and his become more seamlessly wrapped together. It didn't matter that Hayden's schedule was hectic. He made time for her in between meetings with the incoming television-poker people, visits to the kids' facility and other casino details.

Shelby, too, was busy with training a manager for her store and phone meetings with the developers of the D.C. project.

Tonight was one of their rare free nights, and they'd

chosen to spend it with the Prescotts, at the penthouse, for dinner and a game of poker.

Shelby sat across the small card table from him. Deacon and Kylie were on either side of them. The room smelled of cigars and fajitas. He had a hard time even calling this a real poker game. The women, having not spent the last fifteen years of their lives living in a casino, didn't have the same experience at the game that he and Deacon did.

By unspoken agreement the men were playing to the women's level.

He glanced up at Shelby and caught her staring at him. She flushed, so he knew the direction of her thoughts. He raised one eyebrow.

Deacon cleared his throat. "I believe it's your turn, Mac."

Damn. How had this happened? He had been determined to claim Shelby again—not to be captured by her. She had always been a fire in his soul and now that she was here and his, it was worse. Some nights he woke and stared down at her sleeping face just to make sure she was really here.

And that pissed him off. He was a cool player. A man of confidence. Not a person easily shook. But she shook him.

He glanced at his hand and tossed two cards on the table. "I'll take two."

Deacon gave him two cards. Hayden picked them up, realizing he had a full house. A pair of aces and three tens. A full house… That echoed in his mind. He'd been a loner for so long, but now he was living with someone. Not just anyone. Shelby.

Could he ever stand at the end of the aisle waiting for her again? He wanted her to stay with him.

She'd rounded out his life, showed him things that had been missing before. She loved every aspect of his life, even gambling, which she was horrible at. He'd never met a person with worse luck at cards than she had.

Kylie's green eyes twinkled as she took one card. Shelby grimaced at her hand. "How many do I have to keep?"

"Two," Hayden said.

She tossed three cards on the table. Deacon gave her three new ones. Deacon sorted his hand out and they all played to see Hayden's hand. Shelby should have folded.

"Baby, you don't have to stay in when your hand is that bad."

"I was bluffing."

Kylie laughed kindly, and brushed back her long brown hair. "Not very well. I'm not good at this either. Deacon has been giving me tips."

Hayden glanced over at his friend and saw him shrug. "What can I say? She thinks I'm an expert at everything."

Kylie scoffed. "Hardly. But you have potential."

"Can you believe the way she treats me? Not married two years and already she's seeing the tarnish on my armor."

Kylie smiled at her husband, reached across the table to take his hand. He rubbed the back of her knuckles with his thumb. "You're still my hero," she said, smiling into his eyes.

Shelby glanced at Hayden and then pushed her chair back. "I think I'll clean up these plates."

Hayden grabbed a couple of plates and followed her into the kitchen.

"I like your friends," she said.

"Yeah?"

"Yeah. They seem so…perfect for each other. How'd they meet?"

"Deacon saw her on a security monitor and said she was the one for him. I bet him he couldn't convince her to marry him, so he went down and found her and asked her out."

She punched his arm. "What were you thinking?"

He rubbed his arm. "Hey, it worked out okay."

"I guess. But why would you do that?"

"Relationships don't make sense to me. Gambling always does. I knew that Deacon wanted her but I wasn't sure he'd really go after her."

"So you gave him a nudge."

He shrugged, and crossing to the sink, he dropped the plates into the sink. Shelby moved around him, cleaning up the remains of their dinner dishes and putting them all in the dishwasher.

Hayden leaned against the countertop and watched her. There was something right about this and he wished there was some way he could not screw this up. But he'd spoken the truth to Shelby. He didn't understand relationships.

The kitchen door opened and Deacon and Kylie

poked their heads in. "We're going to take off. Thanks for the game and dinner."

"You're welcome," Hayden said. Shelby dried her hands and came to stand next to him. He slipped his arm around her waist and together they walked Kylie and Deacon out of the penthouse.

Hayden didn't hear anything they said as they left. He wasn't aware of anything but the feel of Shelby under his arm. When the door closed, he backed her up against it.

He swallowed her gasp of surprise with his mouth. She wrapped her arms around his shoulders and held on to him, let him control the kiss and the embrace. He slid his leg between hers and bent his knee.

He swept his hands down her body, cupping her rump and pulling her lower body into his. She straddled his leg, her hands clinging to his shoulders.

She pulled back to breathe. "What was that for?"

"For being you."

He swept her up in his arms and carried her into the bedroom and made love to her through the night. He hoped it would be enough of a bond to hold her to him for all time.

Shelby sank back into her leather office chair. Everything she'd ever wanted was within her grasp. The new store was more successful than she'd dreamed possible. But then Shelby had remembered the Vegas of her youth, not this new vibrant scene with too much money and elegance.

Hayden was gone for the day, flying some high rollers who had been staying at his hotel every year since he'd opened out over the Grand Canyon in Deacon's helicopter. Shelby had gone to Roxy's house earlier to drop off some flowers for her.

It made no sense in the factual world but Shelby swore she could feel that Hayden wasn't in the hotel and she missed him.

"Ms. Paxton, there's a guy out front asking for you," said one of her staffers, sticking her head into Shelby's office.

"Thanks. Tell him I'll be right there."

Shelby stood and straightened her suit. She'd had five different men seek her out and ask her to personally select an intimate wardrobe for their wives, girlfriends or mistresses. The service was one that Paige and she had offered from the beginning, but usually it wasn't that popular.

She smiled as she exited her office, but froze when she saw that it was Alan MacKenzie. God knew he wasn't here for her professional help.

Her staff was helping a guest near the fitting rooms and Stan, their stock-boy-turned-salesperson, was flirting with a couple of women in their early twenties.

"How can I help you?" she asked Alan. Hayden looked a lot like his father, except in the eyes.

"We didn't get to finish our conversation the other day."

"Come into my office," she said, pivoting on her heel and leading the way. She knew she needed to resolve this. If she'd told Hayden the truth weeks ago, this wouldn't be a problem now.

Alan followed her into her office and took a seat in one of the guest chairs. Shelby went around behind the desk and seated herself. She knew it was petty but she liked sitting behind her big expensive executive's desk. Because in the back of her mind every time she saw Alan she remembered how cold, small and cheap she'd felt when she'd taken that check from him.

"I'm not your enemy here."

But he always had been. From the first time they'd been introduced, he'd always looked at her as if she wasn't good enough for his son. Even when he'd come to her in Atlanta, she'd sensed his distaste for her. Just once she wanted…what?

She knew it was impossible but she'd love to find a way to be accepted by everyone. To find that seemingly easy way that Hayden had of being everyone's equal, be it the croupier, the first-time gambler, his celebrity friends or her.

"I think we both know you never liked me," she said carefully.

"Yes, but my son always has. Why else would I be doing this?"

"I honestly don't know. Thank you for telling me about the shopping wing and suggesting that Bêcheur d'Or bid on the lease here. But that's all this is."

"I think we both know I forced you to come back."

"I would do anything for my company."

He leaned deeper into his chair, crossing his legs and staring at her. She felt the way she imagined a stripper did at that last moment when she was finally naked in front of a crowd. Shelby rubbed her hands up and down her arms.

"You came back for more than this shop and we both know it."

"No, Alan, I didn't. There's nothing more to my being here."

"I thought you were past lying like this."

Shelby flinched. "I'm not a liar."

He narrowed his eyes and Shelby wished she'd never asked him back here.

"Aren't you living with my son?" he asked.

"Yes, but—"

"Are you sleeping with him?"

She nodded. There was no way Hayden was ever going to believe she hadn't been manipulating him. No way. She heard in Alan's voice the same emotionless tone that Hayden sometimes used when he was angry.

"Mr. MacKenzie, please leave."

He pushed to his feet. "Why?"

"Because you are never going to believe I care for your son."

"Do you?"

She bit her lower lip and nodded. He'd never understand how deeply she cared for Hayden. She was sure she did. But she knew there was no way she was going to allow his father to hurt him through her again.

"That's all I needed to know."

"I'm…I'm not sure how to tell Hayden about you and me," she said. Being around Hayden had shown her the value in asking for help…asking for others' opinions. He leaned on his friends when he needed to. Right now she needed to figure out how to fix things with Hayden. And his dad…well, his dad seemed like the only one she could turn to.

"I'll handle that."

He walked out of her office and she sat there feeling shell-shocked. What was Alan going to do? Time was running out for her and Hayden. She had to tell him the truth.

Her phone rang and she hesitated to answer it. She'd been hopeful that she'd left behind that little trailer-park girl, but no matter how far she ran or how much she changed, that girl was still deep inside her.

Finally picking it up and clearing her throat, she said, "Bêcheur d'Or, where your every fantasy is made reality."

"I like the sound of that," Hayden said. His deep voice brushed over her bruised soul like a soothing balm.

"Hayden."

"What's up, baby? You okay?"

"Yes. Just having a busy day," she said. The day was going to get worse, she knew, because she had to talk to him. Not on the phone but in person. And she had to be prepared that he would see the facts and not the feelings behind her actions. "I have to fly to D.C. next week."

"How long will you be gone?"

"Three days."

"You're coming back?"

"Yes. Of course."

"Good, I'm on my way back. Meet me up front and I'll take you away from your mundane life and give you the fantasy one you deserve."

She smiled at that. Hayden was more than a fantasy.

He always knew the right things to say to make her feel better. "Okay."

When she hung up the phone, she took a deep breath. The truth was never easy, but Shelby was determined to set everything straight. Tonight.

The casino floor was buzzing with activity. Hayden was greeted by many people as he moved toward the roulette tables. Shelby's small hand was tucked into his and she followed him quietly.

There was a sadness in her eyes that he couldn't banish. Trying to prove to himself that he could be the man she needed by not taking her to bed was harder than he thought. His gut said to make love to her and get rid of the shadows that way. In bed there was no confusion or doubts between them. Just the kind of white-hot heat that burned away everything and left the two of them with their souls bared.

"The casino is busy tonight," Shelby said.

"Yeah, it is. Damn."

"What is it?"

"Someone is in the casino who shouldn't be."

"Who?"

"A grifter," Hayden said. It didn't matter that he'd known Bart since they were both four years old. Bart's family had lost everything in the early eighties and he felt that the world owed him something because of it.

"Grifter? What is that? Someone like a whale?" she asked.

Hayden didn't really want the grimier side of the casino business to touch her. He pulled her out of the foot traffic behind a row of slot machines.

"No. He's a con man. Can I leave you alone for a minute?"

"Yes, I'll be fine. I'm going to try to figure out roulette."

"Don't bet any money until I get back," he said. He felt bad taking her money. He didn't mind it when others lost in the casino, but seeing Shelby lose anything bothered him.

"Why not?" she asked, teasing him. He was glad to see her smile.

"Because I don't want your money."

"I might win."

"I doubt it!"

He kissed her quickly and walked away. He felt her watching him as he moved through the casino floor. The con man he'd seen noticed Hayden moving toward him. Bart was a regular in Vegas. A grifter who had been in and out of jail more times than anyone wanted to acknowledge.

Bart's family had lived next to Hayden's in Henderson before Hayden's mother had died. And there was a part of Hayden that wanted to help out the kid he'd known back then.

Bart gave him a salute and turned and sprinted through the crowd toward the exit. Hayden keyed his two-way phone and alerted security. He also sent a quick e-mail to the other owners, alerting them that Bart was back in town and looking for action.

He rejoined Shelby but kept scanning the crowd. "Are you ready to play?"

"I'm not sure I understand the game."

Hayden pulled her back against his body, just because he missed holding her. "Everyone is given a different colored chip to buy in so that they don't get confused. Then they place their colored chip on the number they think the ball will land on."

"This isn't very scientific, is it?" she asked after a few minutes.

From what she'd said and what he'd observed, she liked everything to fall neatly into a slot. And gambling wasn't going to do that. In fact, much of Hayden's life wasn't going to do that.

"Not at all. Every roulette player is hoping that Lady Luck will be at his side when he puts his chip on a number. In the U.S. we play with thirty-eight slots. In Europe they play on thirty-seven."

"What's the difference?"

"We have an extra zero spot."

They watched while the eight players placed their bets and the wheel spun. Hayden felt Shelby hold her breath as the ball bounced and then finally stopped.

"Oh, look, there was a winner," she said, though it wasn't she.

"Yes, and several losers."

"That's good for you."

"Yes, it is."

She was quiet again then turned in his arms, looking up at him with those big eyes of hers, their depths fathomless, guarding the secrets of her soul. "I'm not sure I'll ever understand this game well enough to play it."

"That's okay."

"No, it's not. This is your life, Hayden. I want to be a part of it."

"I don't understand everything that you do."

She wrinkled her forehead. "But you do. It's business. And you definitely understand the corporate world."

"So do you."

Hugging her closer to him for a minute, he bent his head and nibbled on her neck. "You fit right here, Shel, and that's all that matters to me."

"I'm just afraid this won't last. That after the bells and whistles fade, we won't have anything solid."

He raised both eye brows at her. "I can't do the relationship discussion thing, Shel. It's not my strong suit. Suffice it to say, we have the important things in common."

"What? And don't say sex."

"Well, we do have that," he said. He led her through the casino and then down the short hallway until they were outside. The night air was warm, wrapping around them. Hayden led her down the path toward the pool bar. "We also have business in common, and similar taste in music. And you make me laugh."

He ordered them both drinks, a sweet Bellini for Shelby and a scotch neat for him. As she perched on the bar stool, he knew there was only one thing to do. Reaching into his pocket, he fingered the ring she'd sent back to him via his father more than ten years ago.

Oh, man, was he really going to do this?

She stared out over the pool. He threw back his scotch and signaled the bartender for another one.

"Hey, Shel. I have something to ask you."

She turned to look up at him, and for a moment everything in his life felt perfect.

Eleven

Shelby took a deep breath, suddenly unsure of what was going on. She'd planned her big confession but now he wanted to ask her something. Apparently after he tipped back his second scotch in just a few minutes.

"What?" she asked. This wasn't like him. She was worried. Had his father already told him? Once again was she a pawn in the power struggle between these two MacKenzie men?

She took a sip of her favorite, sweet peach-flavored wine. It never failed to amaze her that he remembered little details about her.

"Nothing. Don't worry. Let's walk."

She'd barely tasted her drink but she left it behind. She didn't understand Hayden when he was this way.

He always moved through the world as if he owned it. To be honest, that was one of the things that drew her to him. He was always in charge, but tonight he seemed…nervous.

He tucked her under his arm, pulled her up against his body as they walked around the grounds. The moon was full and the night air warm. The scents of the flowers and night-blooming plants filled the air. The distant sounds of voices raised in revelry and assorted casino noises provided just the right background music.

Vegas was alive and the rhythm of it beat through her body in time with her heart. This was Hayden's world and she wanted to become a part of it so that they'd always be together.

"When I built this place I was full of anger, you know. I just wanted to prove to my dad and in part to you that you'd both been wrong about me."

There was no emotion in his words, just a calm telling of what had happened. As if she hadn't ripped his heart out and then coldly left him behind. For a moment, she wanted to go back in time and slap the young girl she'd been. Rationally she knew she couldn't have stayed. Knew that if she'd attempted to, their marriage would have ended in divorce. But she wished she'd found the courage to talk to him. To really show him who she'd been.

"Oh, Hayden, I'm so sorry. It was never that I doubted you." The words sounded almost too pat. They weren't enough. They didn't really explain what had been going on in her mind at the time.

"I know that now," he said, stopping under a large

magnolia tree. He pulled her into his arms, held her gently against him.

She loved the way he did that. Held her like she was precious to him. Like it mattered to him if something hurt her. She couldn't explain, but it made her feel as if she'd finally found a person with whom she could share everything.

"The Chimera is a first-rate hotel and casino." She was filled with pride every time she saw it. She remembered the run-down old hotel that had stood here before. Hayden had taken something that would have made many men bitter and turned it into not only a profitable business but also a community enhancement. He'd given back to Vegas despite the fact that the city hadn't brought him the jackpot he'd been searching for when she'd left him at the altar.

"That's right. But it's not enough anymore. For a while I've been searching for something more but I've done it all. Brought in exhibits many said no one would visit. With Deacon we've upgraded everything you can imagine, from shopping to shows to casino floors. There's nothing left for me to achieve."

He pulled away from her, rubbing the back of his neck. In the moonlight his features were stark, harsh with the emotions she knew he didn't want to reveal.

"I don't know how to say this," he said at last.

She swallowed hard and realized that the idyllic time they'd been indulging in the last few weeks was over. Hayden was a man of action and he couldn't just keep moving along without a plan.

"Say what? Do you want me to leave? Am I making you remember the anger that drove you to build this place?" she asked, wrapping her arms around herself. God, she hated feeling this way. Just once she wanted to be enough for someone. No, not anyone but Hayden. She wanted to be worthy of the kind of kingdom he'd built.

"No," he said. "Dammit, I want you to stay. Not just for a few weeks or months but forever. I want to have you in bed every night. I want to be able to call you during the day and just hear your sweet, sexy voice. I want to spend my nights laughing and loving you."

She took a deep breath. "I want that, too. More than anything. I never expected to fall in love with you again, but somehow I have."

He reached for her, pulled her to him, bending to her and kissing her fiercely. His mouth moved down her neck, pushing her shirt out of his way. He nibbled and suckled against her skin. She knew he was leaving behind a small mark, as he'd done continually since her return to Vegas, and she relished the brand.

He lifted his head and she met his gaze. There was something hot and possessive in his eyes. "Am I branded as yours?"

"Yes. But it's not enough. I want a permanent symbol of our life together. A permanent reminder to both of us that you belong to me."

"Will you have one, too?" she asked. "I don't want to be your possession."

"Yes. I…I want you to marry me, Shelby. But I can't go through the big wedding we planned last time."

She swallowed, realizing what she'd taken away from Hayden when she'd left him as she had. She hated herself for that. She bit her lip and hugged him close to her, burying her face against his chest. Not wanting him to see her own self-loathing.

"So?"

"Of course I'll marry you. There's no one I'd rather share my life with than you."

But she knew she couldn't go to a chapel one more time with secrets between them. She allowed herself this one last night of peace between them. In the morning she'd tell him the truth. Tell him about his father and the deal she'd accepted to return to Vegas and to him.

Arousal flooded his body and he had to claim her. Why the hell had he picked such a public place for this? The ring still sat in his pocket and he knew he wanted to see it on her finger.

This time it meant more than it had the last time. When he'd originally purchased the ring, he'd done so because it was the most expensive one at the jeweler's. Over the years that ring had become his talisman, his way of thumbing his nose at his father and the rest of the world.

Now it would be on her hand again and he couldn't help but feel that Shelby was his good-luck charm. That maybe she had been from the beginning.

"Let's get out of here. I want to make love to you," he said.

She nodded, slipping her small hand in his. He led

them quickly through the casino and to his private elevator. As soon as the doors closed behind them, he took her in his arms, backed her up against the rich walnut-paneled walls.

Her hands slipped to his waist, holding him to her. "Don't regret this," she said softly.

As if he could. He took her mouth with his, leaving not one inch unexplored. He caged her face in his hands, tipped her head farther back so that he could go deeper.

He vowed to brand her all over as his. Her hair wrapped around his fingers, tying them together in one more way. He lifted his head. Her eyes were closed, her face flushed, her lips wet and swollen from his kisses.

He lowered his mouth to the slim length of her neck, nibbling at her smooth flesh until he encountered her blouse.

"Bare yourself for me. Show me you want this."

Her eyes opened. "I always want you."

Her hands came between them, slowly unbuttoning her silky blouse. He followed her hands, tasting each bit of flesh as she revealed it. He lingered at her belly button and then started back up her body, stopping between her breasts, which were still covered by the ends of her shirt.

"Offer me your breasts."

She shivered; he felt the tremble that swept over her body. Her hands tightened on the edges of her blouse until her knuckles were almost white. Then carefully she pulled back the edges, revealing first the incredibly soft white skin of her breasts and then her berry-hard nipples.

The elevator bell rang, signaling their arrival at his penthouse. He lifted her in his arms. "Wrap your legs around me."

She did as he commanded and he carried her quickly to his front door and keyed it open. Once inside he went to the floor-to-ceiling windows overlooking the city of Vegas. His city and his woman. He had them both in his arms.

He took her nipple in his mouth, suckling her strongly, trying to quench a thirst that had been a part of him for so long he wasn't sure when it had started. Only that he was still thirsty for her.

Her hands roamed over his back. He wanted her hands on his skin. He set her down and ripped his shirt from his body, tossing it aside. Shelby pushed her blouse off as well. When she reached for her skirt, he stopped her.

"Just take your panties off."

She nodded, reaching under her skirt to remove them. He took a condom from his pocket and quickly sheathed himself. Then he removed the ring, holding it in his fist.

He turned Shelby in his arms, bent her forward, supporting her with his arm around her waist. "This is my life, my kingdom. It means nothing to me without you by my side."

He rubbed his erection against her hot core and she moaned, undulating against him. He skimmed his fisted hand down her body, rubbing his knuckles over her hardened nipples as he bit lightly at her nape.

He slid his hand farther down her body, brushing over the tight curls at the apex of her thighs. He felt her wetness on his fingers, on the tops of her thighs. He loved how hot she got for him.

He slipped two fingers between her legs, teasing her opening. Pushing his thigh between hers, he forced her legs open wider. He held himself poised at the entrance of her body.

"Hayden…"

"Yes?" he asked, teasing her by rubbing in small circles around her core, dipping his fingers in briefly and then pulling them out.

"What are you waiting for?"

"For you to be wearing my ring," he said, bringing his hand up her body and opening his fist.

She caught her breath. "You kept it?"

"I had to," he admitted. He took her hand and pushed the ring onto her finger. Then he brought her hand to his mouth and kissed her. The scent of her arousal was on his fingers and inflamed the lust already straining the limits of his control.

He twined their fingers together and pressed their joined hands against the plate-glass window. "I'm not letting you go."

"Good," she said.

With his free hand he positioned himself at the entrance to her body and anchoring her with his arm around her waist, he plunged deep inside her. Her body tightened around his as he continued to thrust, driving her rapidly toward first one climax and then slowly building her to another.

This time he tumbled over the edge with her. He bit

her lightly on the back of the neck as his orgasm rushed through his body, draining him of his strength. They both collapsed against the window.

Finally Hayden straightened, lifting her in his arms and carrying her down the hall to his bedroom. He'd just claimed her in front of the world—his world, Vegas—and she would be his for all time.

Shelby called her mom—something she hadn't done the last time she and Hayden had planned to marry. Her mother was so happy for her and was driving to Vegas to spend a few weeks with Shelby. Next she called Paige, who promised to fly back for the wedding.

Shelby flew to D.C. for her meetings but missed Hayden horribly. More than she'd thought she would. They talked every night about everything and nothing. And for the first time in a long time, Shelby felt as if she was flying home, to her real home, when she returned to Vegas.

Hayden had suggested they exchange vows in the gazebo in the middle of the maze where they'd made love. She'd agreed.

Everything was going very smoothly—too smoothly. She knew she had to say something to Hayden before his father did. Alan was everywhere, always watching her with that gaze that said she wasn't good enough for his son. She knew it. He knew it. Only Hayden didn't seem to sense the undercurrents.

But she suspected he did. Suspected he was putting all of that down to the past. But Shelby knew that it was more.

And finally, after weeks of anticipation, tonight was her last chance to say something. Her last chance to come clean before the wedding tomorrow. It was the rehearsal dinner, being thrown at the Golden Dream by Deacon and Kylie.

Earlier today Hayden had taken her riding on his Harley out in the desert. She'd planned to tell him then but had chickened out. The day had been perfect, a quiet sharing of their thoughts, the kind of experience that made her realize how much she loved him. How much she didn't want to hurt him.

Now they were back at the penthouse. Hayden was on the phone talking with his security people. They'd found the man who'd attacked Roxy, and Hayden's lawyers were making sure the man went to jail forever. Shelby was dressing—or trying to, at least. Nothing she put on looked right. She'd changed clothes fifteen times.

Finally she just stood in front of the full-length mirror and stared at herself in frustration. Tears burned the back of her eyes and she just couldn't take the internal pressure anymore. She had to say something.

"Baby? What's wrong?" Hayden asked as he crossed the room to her.

He wrapped his arms around her, pulling her back into the shelter of his body. As she stood there, surrounded by him, her fears seemed ridiculous. Surrounded by him she felt as if there was no way he'd ever let her go. Surrounded by him she felt like the lowest person alive. She never should have let this go on so long.

He tipped her head back and lowered his mouth to

hers. He never said he loved her. But in that kiss she felt his emotions. They flooded her and wrapped around her wounded heart, assuring her that everything would be okay.

"I thought you were going to wear that sexy red dress," he said when he lifted his head. He skimmed his hands down the curves of her body. "But I like this dress."

It was a black cocktail number with a plunging neckline. The dress had no back and was held up by a wide band of rhinestones at the neck. The skirt was full, ending just above her knees. She'd pulled her hair up and left a few tendrils curling at her neck and the sides of her face.

"The red one didn't look right," she said. "I'm not sure about this one, either. I want everything to be perfect tonight."

"It will be. Clothing doesn't matter."

"Not to you. You look perfect no matter what you wear."

And he did. Tonight he wore a custom-made tuxedo that he'd special ordered from his Savile Row tailor a few days ago. She was so outclassed and not just by the clothing.

"What are you afraid of?" he asked.

"Everything and everyone. When we walk into that party tonight, once again everyone will know that you picked someone beneath you."

"Shel, no one thinks that. I'm a gambler. Half of the moneyed people in Vegas won't talk to me. The others only talk to me when they're winning. I've been the target of more accusations than you can imagine."

She shook her head at him. "But you're still so…sophisticated. I can't help it, Hayden. I feel like I'm one step away from the trailer park. And that all those people can see it."

"Don't do this to yourself. Your life is a success that few find, regardless of where they started. I'm so proud of you, of what you've achieved."

She smiled up at him. "Thank you. But…there's something I have to tell you."

"You love me, right?"

She swallowed. "More than I thought I could love another person. It's so intense sometimes I have to pinch myself to make sure it's real."

"Don't do that, Shel. I'm here and I'm real."

She wrapped her arms around his, needing to take some of his strength and confidence with her before she told him the truth of their meeting again.

Taking a deep breath, she stepped away and put a few feet between them.

"There is something else I have to tell you."

He turned to face her. With his brooding eyes, she knew he sensed he wasn't going to like what she had to say. For a moment she considered never saying a word but she knew that Alan wouldn't let the truth lie undiscovered for much longer.

The doorbell rang. "Can this wait?" Hayden asked.

She nodded, happy for the reprieve. She watched him leave, already feeling the coldness in the room and in her heart.

Twelve

Hayden crossed the room, grateful for the distraction. Though he'd never admit it out loud, he'd been afraid that something would happen and his wedding to Shelby wouldn't go off without a hitch. Turned out his gut was right—again.

He cursed when he saw his dad standing on the threshold. "Not now, Dad. Really, I'm not in the mood for one of your lectures. And we have to get over to Deacon's."

His father wore a suit by the same tailor as Hayden's. The cuff links that his grandfather had given him shone at his wrists. He was flawlessly dressed from head to toe. Hayden remembered what Shelby had said about clothing and understood what she meant for the very first time.

He'd never really thought about all he took for granted but now he understood that maybe he should have. There were differences between himself and Shelby he couldn't ever really comprehend.

"I'm not here to lecture. I have to tell you something," Alan said, crossing to the bar and pouring himself a drink.

This wasn't good. His dad gestured with the bottle and Hayden nodded. He had a feeling he was going to need the alcohol.

"Not you, too. What is it—confession day?" he asked, taking the glass from his father.

His dad clinked the rims together before tipping his back and draining it. "Who else is confessing?"

"My soon-to-be wife," Hayden said, draining his glass. He dropped it on the bar and reached for the bottle, refilling both of their glasses.

His father stopped him with a hand on his wrist. He seemed almost relieved. "Ah, well then, maybe I'm too late."

"Too late for what?" Hayden asked, knowing that he wasn't going to like the answer. But he hadn't gotten to where he was in business by ignoring the cold harsh facts that life sometimes dealt his way.

"To tell you that I bribed her to get her back to Vegas and take up with you again."

Hayden swallowed. "What did you offer her?"

"That's where I screwed up, son. I told her she could have whatever she asked for."

"Dammit, Dad."

Alan shook his head.

Hayden set his glass down on the bar and crossed to the partially opened doorway of his bedroom. There was no need to ask Shelby if his father's words were true. She was standing there in the shadows, tears running down her face.

She had her arms wrapped around her waist and he knew she was hurting, but he didn't give a damn. How the hell had he allowed himself to be duped by her again? Why the hell wasn't he enough for her? When the hell was he going to learn that money, not love, motivated Shelby Anne Paxton?

"Come on out. Let's hear what you were going to say," he said to her, pushing the door open.

"Not in front of your father," she said, her eyes begging him for a reprieve. But he wasn't feeling generous right now.

"Why not? You seem to have been conspiring with him all this time."

She grabbed a tissue from the box on the dresser and wiped her nose. "There was no conspiracy. Please believe me."

Alan stood in the doorway saying nothing. Hayden wanted his dad to leave. The old man wasn't helping. Hayden knew there was more to what Shelby was telling him than what his father knew. He was angry and he knew that part of it was because of his dad.

"You came back here because of me, remember?" Alan said.

Shelby flinched but didn't look away from either of

them. "You're right, Alan. And you did promise me something if I came back here."

Shelby's voice shook when she spoke. A change came over her and Hayden hardly recognized her.

"I'd hoped this would help undo the mistakes I'd made when you were young," Alan said.

"Looks like you bet on the wrong woman again," Hayden said softly.

He saw her flinch and knew that his words had cut her deep. He felt an answering wound on his heart. Deep inside, where he'd felt safe hiding the fact that he loved this woman.

"I deserved that," she said. "But I'm fighting for our future, Hayden. I'm going to have to demand that you don't make any more remarks like that."

"You're in no position to demand anything," Alan said.

"Don't help, Dad. You've done enough."

Shelby looked away from him and straight at his father. "You said I could name my price."

Money. He'd known that was what she wanted. But a part of him couldn't believe it. This was the woman who wouldn't take any money from him at the black-jack table. The woman who'd fought to get where she was. He knew that his anger was clouding his judgment, that he was missing something really important here. But he couldn't put his finger on it.

He even understood why money was so important to her. But why couldn't she see that he had so much more to offer her? He could be her security if only she'd let him. "Dammit, Dad, you should have left this alone."

Alan stood in the corner, watching like the wily old gambler he was. Shelby watched him as if she wasn't sure whose side he was on. Hayden wanted to warn her the old man was always on his own side.

"What are you waiting for, Shelby?" Hayden stalked to his desk and pulled out his checkbook. "Name your price."

"I don't want a check."

"It's good."

"I'm sure it is. But the only thing I want is you, Hayden. I came back to Vegas for one reason—to reclaim the man I never forgot."

"My father bribed you."

"He threatened to go to the magazines with the truth about how I got the money to start the boutique. Tell them that Paige and I would do anything for money. I couldn't let him do that. But I sold myself once and I never will again. After he left my office, I realized that I'd never stopped thinking about you and…well, it seemed like the perfect chance to come back and take that gamble I wouldn't the first time."

Hayden dropped his pen and checkbook and she saw in his eyes the flame of desire and the hope for the future. "What gamble is that?"

"Double or nothing. Without you by my side that's what I have. Nothing."

"Looks like I won again," Alan said, finally bowing out gracefully, as if he suddenly accepted the inevitable. "Now get busy and give me some grandkids to spoil."

* * *

Hayden was staring at her as if he didn't recognize her. She closed the gap between them, taking his hand in hers. She lifted it to her face and kissed him gently. She knew she'd given him the shock of a lifetime and couldn't bear the thought of losing this man again.

"I appealed to the gambler in you because I know that you like to take long-shot bets. But if that doesn't work, then I'll beg. And if that doesn't work, then I'll simply stay here and wear you down until you can see the truth."

"What truth is that?" he asked, his voice low and husky.

"That I'm not asking you to take this leap by yourself. I'm scared of your world, of not fitting in. I'm scared to stay with a man who doesn't love me. But I'm more afraid of living the rest of my days in that lonely state that my life had become without you."

He said nothing and she couldn't stand the intensity in his eyes. She took a few steps away, reaching behind her to steady herself on the edge of the couch.

"You're wrong, Shel," he said, his voice deep and husky, brushing over her senses like a warm desert breeze.

"Wrong about what?" she asked. She was afraid that it was too late for them and she didn't want to give up hope. Not yet.

"Me not loving you."

"Really, Hayden, you don't have to say it. I know you can never love a woman whom you can't trust. You won't even have a wedding ceremony where you wait for me at the front of the chapel."

He closed the distance between them in three long strides. Grabbing her shoulders and pulling her up toward him, he took her mouth in a fierce kiss that left her battered soul wanting more.

"You're right, I didn't trust you. But I've loved you for more years than either of us realized. And my anger at you and my dad…well, it was due to the fact that I didn't have the courage to go and find you."

"You didn't know where I was."

"I never tried to look. I do love you, Shelby. I meant what I said when I asked you to marry me—you make all of this worthwhile."

Hayden pulled her down onto the couch, but the subsequent pounding on the door pulled them apart. "Go away. We're not available right now," he called out.

"Oh, hell, yes you are. I'm not going back to Kylie and telling her the guests of honor are no-shows."

Hayden cursed but she saw the smile in his eyes. He rubbed away the tracks her tears had made on her face and kissed her gently. "Later, I'm going to make love to you. But for now, let's go celebrate our marriage."

Hayden nervously stood in front of the preacher at the outdoor gazebo in the gardens at the Chimera. The afternoon was perfect, with the sun shining brightly down on them. Deacon stood at his side and Hayden was glad to have his friend there. Scott Rivers and Max Williams were there as well, serving as ushers. The two bachelors couldn't believe he'd given up his single days so easily. Hayden didn't even attempt to explain that life without Shelby wasn't nearly the ride that life with her was.

Shelby's mother waved at him from her seat in the front row, Roxy beside her. The two women had bonded. Terri Paxton needed to mother someone and Roxy needed someone to take care of her as her wounds healed, both mentally and physically. Terri was a stunningly beautiful woman and she loved Shelby. Shelby and Hayden were trying to convince Terri to move back to Vegas, and she was thinking it over.

His dad sat on the opposite side of the aisle, arms crossed over his chest, looking like a man who'd gotten what he wanted. Hayden shook his head thinking about how his father had played him and Shelby. But he couldn't be angry, not anymore. Hayden was grateful his father had interfered for once. Otherwise, he'd still be missing Shelby.

The music started and Hayden turned to wait for his bride. He'd been reluctant to do this again, to wait for her at the end of the aisle with his friends in attendance, but ultimately it was a little gesture that had meant a lot to Shelby and to their life together.

Paige came up the aisle first and then came Shelby. She came to him on her own, with no family to give her away. He felt the depth of his love for her overwhelm him, and tears burned the back of his eyes. Never had he guessed that she would mean this much to him.

She reached his side and he took her small trembling hand in his. Though the preacher was saying words of welcome to the congregation, Hayden bent and kissed Shelby.

She smiled up at him. His heart kicked and his gut tightened. Being married to Shelby was like winning the grand prize.

Her High-Stakes Affair

by

Katherine Garbera

"**H**ey, sexy lady. Where do you want me today?"

Raine Montgomery bit the inside of her cheek and forced herself not to respond to Scott Rivers. Every morning it was the same line, or some variation of it. It should have sounded like a pick-up line but didn't. Instead, he made her want to believe she was a sexy lady—even though she'd had enough experience with gamblers to know they never told the truth.

"Can't decide?" he asked, slipping an arm around her waist.

She stepped away from him. "In your chair at the table."

"Honey, when are you going to loosen up with me?"

"When you stop flirting with every woman who walks by."

"Is it making you jealous?"

"No."

He laughed and walked away from her as the other players trickled in.

She'd gotten into the film business for one reason and one reason only—she'd dreamed of the day when she'd be called on the stage at the Academy Awards to accept her Oscars for best director and film of the year. She even had her speech rehearsed.

I'd like to thank the Academy for recognizing my accomplishments, and I'd like the rest of the world to know that Missy Talbot is a spoiled bitch and my dad isn't a loser.

Okay, so it was a little melodramatic, but she'd been in junior high at the time and it had seemed like the perfect solution to her dismal and dreary life in Atlantic City, New Jersey.

But her dream hadn't gotten her to the Oscar's. In fact, she wasn't even close to winning a People's Choice award, or any award at all. She doubted anyone was going to be giving her recognition for directing Celebrity Poker Challenge.

The show ran for four weeks. They had three celebrities and three champions from across the country to compete. In each week's episode, two games were played and at the end of the show two players were eliminated. At the end, the remaining two players played two high-stakes games to determine the Celebrity Poker Champ.

Each person on the show signed a waiver promising not to reveal the results of the show. Viewers had the chance to vote on who they thought was the best and win a myriad of prizes that had been donated by sponsors. The celebrities were playing for charities as were the champions.

She'd given all the players wide berth because her producer, Joel Tanner, didn't like her or any of the crew fraternizing with them. In fact, there was a clear no-fraternization clause in the contracts everyone on the set signed for both in front of the camera and behind the scenes. He wanted to make sure they didn't end up with a lawsuit because of the way the players were shown.

She rubbed the back of her neck and headed toward the director's booth. Some people called it the God booth because she wasn't on the set and her voice could be heard but she couldn't be seen. But Raine knew she was as far from God as any person could be.

Especially right now, since she was having impure thoughts about Scott. She entered the booth and put on her headphones. All of the players were miked and she heard their small talk.

The deep, sexy tones of Scott's voice came over her headphones and she paused to listen.

"Shot down again, eh, stud?"

Scott glanced over at Stevie Taylor, the notoriously debauched lead singer for the heavy metal rock band Viper, which had been on the cutting edge of music fifteen years ago. Stevie had the kind of talent and energy that had kept him in the mainstream, changing his style through the years to fit the younger audiences' tastes.

That being said, the man was an ass sometimes and Scott suspected Stevie was still pissed about losing to him at the PGA/Celebrity golf tournament last month in Hawaii. Or maybe it was the fact that Scott had unwittingly been the object of Stevie's third wife's affection.

"Some women take more time than others," Scott said. "They aren't all impressed with long hair and fast cars."

"I guess that means you have to try harder?" Stevie said.

There was an edge to his voice that Scott chose to ignore. Every day was work for Scott. He'd grown up on a soundstage and had learned early on to act the way others found acceptable. With Stevie, he acted like a babe magnet, always on the prowl because that was what the legendary rock front-man understood. With Raine he acted…unfortunately he wasn't doing such a great job of it. She made him forget he was playing a role.

"Sure. Everything worth having takes some effort." And Raine was definitely worth the effort. He wondered how she felt about the no-fraternization clause they'd both signed. Scott was honest enough to admit that the gambler in him wanted to take a chance on her.

"You're working up a sweat and she's barely noticing you, Rivers. What would your fan club say?"

Scott didn't respond to the goad. He didn't have a fan club and Stevie knew it. His child stardom had translated into cult-classic films in his early twenties and two one-offs that had turned into blockbusters. He acted when he felt like it, preferring to spend most of his time working with the charitable trust he set up with his own money. "I'm not worried, Stevie."

"Some boys aren't meant to play in the big leagues," the other man said.

"Whatever. You know she can't really show that she's attracted to me."

"Because she isn't?" Stevie said with a snicker.

"Because we work together." A man like Stevie would never understand the distinction, but Scott knew that Raine would. That her job and her reputation would be important to her. He understood why.

"I wouldn't let that stop me."

He wasn't going to do this. Defend himself like some sort of teenage boy with his first woman. Scott was thirty-eight, long grown up; he wouldn't get drawn into this conversation.

"What, no glib remark?"

Stevie wasn't going to let this go. Scott had to find a way to shut him up.

"What would it take for you to drop this?"

"How about a little wager?"

"On a woman? Have you been living under a rock for the last twenty years?"

"There's no reason anyone other than the two of us has to know about it."

Famous last words. He glanced around the set. They were far enough away from anyone that they had the kind of privacy that was something of a luxury on a television or movie set.

"What'd you have in mind?"

"A simple bet…you get her in bed before the show wraps."

Scott felt a tingling at the back of his neck that he always got before he did something risky. Like sky surfing or kayaking down a class VI rapid. Something that all of his self-preservation instincts said not to do. But if it got Stevie off his back, then it might be worth it.

"You're on. What's the wager?"

"Fifty thousand."

"Okay."

* * * *

Look for Her High-Stakes Affair
on the shelves next month.

SILHOUETTE®
Desire™ *2 in 1*

ENGAGEMENT BETWEEN ENEMIES

by Kathie DeNosky

(The Illegitimate Heirs)

After a scandalous rumour erupted, honourable tycoon Caleb Walker made employee Alyssa Merrick an offer she couldn't refuse...

TYCOON TAKES REVENGE by Anna DePalo

Infamous playboy Noah Whittaker gives gossip columnist Kayla Jones a taste of her own medicine, but finds that love is far sweeter than revenge.

THE MAN MEANS BUSINESS by Annette Broadrick

Business was millionaire Dean Logan's only thought until his loyal assistant, Jodie Cameron, accompanied him on a passionate Hawaiian vacation and put marriage on the agenda!

DEVLIN AND THE DEEP BLUE SEA

by Merline Lovelace

(Code Name: Danger)

Helicopter pilot Elizabeth Moore thought sexy stranger Joe Devlin was a mystery to solve—and if she hadn't just been jilted, she might have made an effort to uncover *all* his secrets!

BABY, I'M YOURS by Catherine Mann

Three months after their whirlwind affair, Claire McDermott discovered she was carrying Vic Jansen's child and that she wanted more than just an honourable offer of marriage...

HER HIGH-STAKES AFFAIR by Katherine Garbera

An affair between them was strictly forbidden, but when passion struck Raine Montgomery and rich, sexy Scott Rivers under the bright lights of Las Vegas, it was on the cards!

On sale from 19th January 2007

Visit our website at www.silhouette.co.uk

0107/SH/LC157

SILHOUETTE®

Desire™

Dynasties:
THE ELLIOTTS

Mixing business with pleasure

January 2007
BILLIONAIRE PROPOSITION *Leanne Banks*
TAKING CARE OF BUSINESS *Brenda Jackson*

March 2007
CAUSE FOR SCANDAL *Anna DePalo*
THE FORBIDDEN TWIN *Susan Crosby*

May 2007
MR AND MISTRESS *Heidi Betts*
HEIRESS BEWARE *Charlene Sands*

July 2007
UNDER DEEPEST COVER *Kara Lennox*
MARRIAGE TERMS *Barbara Dunlop*

September 2007
THE INTERN AFFAIR *Roxanne St Claire*
FORBIDDEN MERGER *Emilie Rose*

November 2007
THE EXPECTANT EXECUTIVE *Kathie DeNosky*
BEYOND THE BOARDROOM *Maureen Child*

www.silhouette.co.uk

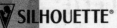

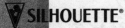

MILLS & BOON®
Live the emotion

Blaze™

PRIVATE RELATIONS *by Nancy Warren*

Do Not Disturb

PR director Kit Prescott is holding a contest to promote Hush, Manhattan's hottest hotel. The first winner is sexy, single – and her ex-fiancé, Peter Garston! How can Kit entertain the man who has never stopped starring in all her fantasies?

NIGHT MOVES *by Julie Kenner*

24 Hours :Blackout Bk 1

When lust and love are simmering beneath the surface, things can come to the boil… Shane Walker is in love with Ella Davenport. But she just wants to be friends. It looks hopeless – until a blackout gives him twenty-four hours to change her mind…

SUBMISSION *by Tori Carrington*

Dangerous Liaisons

Sexy detective Alan Chevalier is at the end of his tether: he's being taunted by the Quarter Killer, a dangerous murderer stalking the streets of New Orleans. Oh, and he's fallen for the twin sister of one of the killer's victims, too…

LETTING GO! *by Mara Fox*

On board a sexy singles cruise, Emma Daniels falls for a hot Latin lover, Andreas, and together they begin to explore their fantasies. But back on dry land, things start to get complicated, not least because Andreas turns out to be not quite the man Emma thought he was…

On sale 2nd February 2007

Available at WHSmith, Tesco, ASDA,
and all good bookshops
www.millsandboon.co.uk

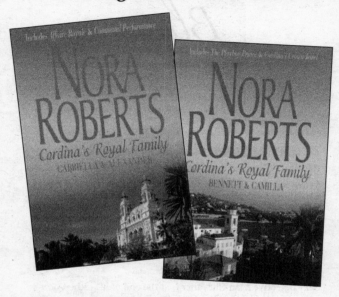

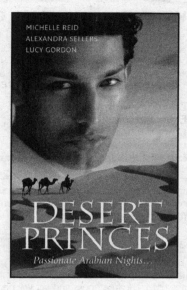

2 FREE

BOOKS AND A SURPRISE GIFT!

We would like to take this opportunity to thank you for reading this Silhouette® book by offering you the chance to take TWO more specially selected titles from the Desire™ series absolutely FREE! We're also making this offer to introduce you to the benefits of the Mills & Boon® Reader Service™—

- ★ FREE home delivery
- ★ FREE gifts and competitions
- ★ FREE monthly Newsletter
- ★ Exclusive Reader Service offers
- ★ Books available before they're in the shops

Accepting these FREE books and gift places you under no obligation to buy, you may cancel at any time, even after receiving your free shipment. Simply complete your details below and return the entire page to the address below. You don't even need a stamp!

YES! Please send me 2 free Desire volumes and a surprise gift. I understand that unless you hear from me, I will receive 3 superb new titles every month for just £4.99 each, postage and packing free. I am under no obligation to purchase any books and may cancel my subscription at any time. The free books and gift will be mine to keep in any case.

D7ZED

Ms/Mrs/Miss/Mr ....Initials ....

BLOCK CAPITALS PLEASE

Surname ....

Address ....

....

....Postcode...

Send this whole page to:
UK: FREEPOST CN81, Croydon, CR9 3WZ